Renee Lake

THE INFESTED. Copyright 2023 © Renee Lake. All rights reserved. No part of this book may be used or reproduced in any manner whatsoever without written permission except in the case of brief quotations embodied in critical articles and reviews. For more information visit www.hansenhousebooks.com.

Cover design by Elizabeth Jeannel

ISBN 978-1-956037-27-2 (hardcover)

ISBN 978-1-956037-28-9 (paperback)

ISBN 978-1-956037-26-5 (eBook)

First Edition

First Edition: October 2023

This hardcover edition first published in 2023

Published by Hansen House

www.hansenhousebooks.com

Hansen House

CONTENT TRIGGER WARNINGS

The Infested is a New Adult horror novel with adult themes, including but not limited to: eating disorders, anxiety, death, murder, light body horror, generational/family trauma, colonization and body image issues.

DEDICATION AND THANKS

To Lia, Tot, Jareth and Vincent. My four beautiful, amazing children, who have all inherited my love of spooky stuff. May you all be free to live your lives the way you want, and love who makes you happy. Extra thanks to Tot whose personal experience in the park inspired a scene in this book.

To my husband Chris, my Boo- who is always supportive and lets me ramble on about my current project/obsession/fictional boyfriend. Without him holding down the fort none of this would ever get done. I love and appreciate you more than I can say.

To my mom, Carmen, who has encouraged my writing since I was small and even when it's not her thing (like this creepy book) always beta reads for me.

To my "sister" Katie who always reads the roughest of rough drafts and tells me it's amazing every time and is always excited when I have something new to show her.

And lastly, to my bestie Lucy who doesn't understand the writing world and really doesn't care about New Adult and YA horror but still helped me with plot holes, problematic scenes and listened while I talked (way too much) about characters and events she didn't understand or have interest in, but was excited for me with every step.

This is for all of you.

Bright Blessings!

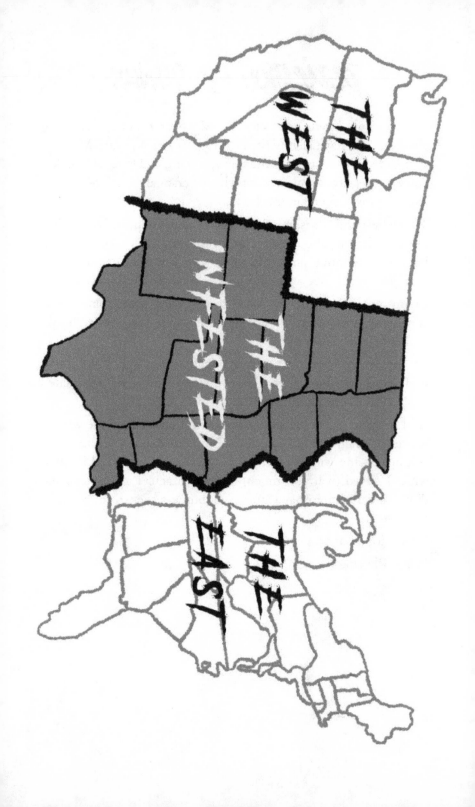

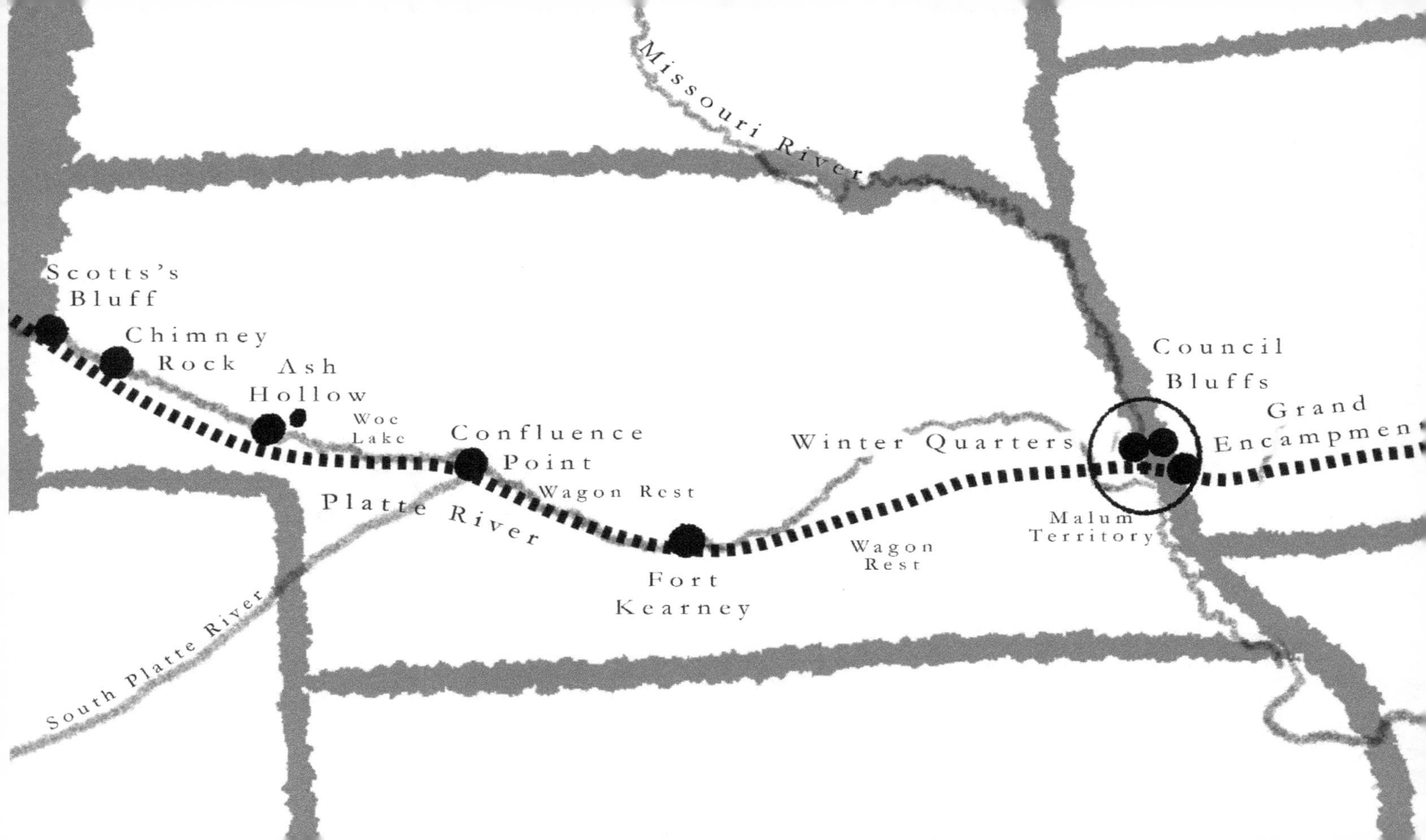

South Platte River

Scotts's
Bluff

Chimney
Rock

Ash
Hollow

Woe
Lake

Platte River

Confluence
Point

Wagon Rest

Fort
Kearney

Winter Quarters

Wagon
Rest

Malum
Territory

Council
Bluffs

Grand
Encampment

Missouri River

Chapter 1

May 1900

Day 1

Ash Hollow

The United States is Infested, and humans poisoned it.

They traversed the great divide between the East and West Coast and died along the way.

They killed each other, starved, died of diseases, buried their dead without proper ceremonies, and abandoned items they no longer wanted.

It shouldn't be a surprise that the land turned on them.

Demons are real. Spirits haunt the world. Monsters dwell in the shadows and forests. Ghosts float over the plains. Things feed on the dead, infest swamps, and scour deserts.

Trace a finger on a map of the United States to outline the barrier on either side of the Infested. Follow the lines of Montana and Wyoming, veering left to surround Utah and straight down to Arizona, finally connecting with Mexico.

Then again, from Lake Superior and Wisconsin's tip, following a jagged line that goes past Illinois, Tennessee, Mississippi, and straight down, ending in Mexico's Gulf.

This is in the invisible barrier between the West and East Coast, and all that lay between is the Infested. A dangerous land, full of monsters.

The East is overpopulated, busy, advanced, cultured, and full of politics, lavish foods, and sin.

The only people to come to the West from the East are the brave, the desperate, or the stupid.

One can try to cross through Canada or by boat and come up through Mexico—but it is illegal. Those countries fear America, and they fear that Americans will bring with them the madness that affects their lands. Getting caught by their government is a death sentence.

It is a three-month journey from Illinois to Wyoming, and even longer trying to pass through the salt flats to Utah or traveling to the green of Oregon or California's coastlines.

When people first decided to travel West and see what splendor lay on the other side of the U.S., they knew there would be issues like famine, disease, drought, extreme temperatures, and wild animals.

They didn't respect the land or each other, and many paid the price.

As each wagon train departed, the tales of what lay beyond Illinois became darker and the number of people making it to the West got slimmer.

More than 600,000 people decided to cross the trails West between 1811 and 1830, and only about half made it. The plains didn't turn sour overnight. It took years for the government to figure out whole trains had gone missing and even more time to find out why. Finally in 1835, the government from the East forbade any more wagon trains West. The West, cut off from many luxuries from the East, put time and money into retaking the trails and making the Infested safe enough for the shipment of goods.

Two caravans make the journey West to East. On odd years one from Utah to Illinois, and on even years from Oregon to Missouri, sometimes they come and go with no issues. Other times, they never come back. They bring back supplies and news, paid for by the gold and silver found predominantly in the West.

Almost no one lives in the Infested, and only a few families, like the Ash family, made it their home.

They had no neighbors, no church, and no stores near them. They didn't even know what it would be like to have people around to talk to other than themselves. The Wyoming border, where the West began and the Infested ended, was 150 miles away.

For Desdemona and her siblings, home was all they knew. The books in the parlor and office were the only windows to the outside world.

Home was a giant two-storied monstrosity in the middle of nowhere, turning sand brown against the elements, chipped blue paint slowly wearing away. Green prairie grass spotted the ground with tiny flowers all purple and white. Several buildings dotted the land, as well as animals.

The air tasted dry like despair. Desdemona stood behind the house, an acre away from the garden and feet away from the boundary fence. That fence marked an edge of their property. A warded magical barrier that kept the worst of the horrors outside.

She stared at her shoes, black boots with curled ends. She didn't want to look up, couldn't look up. As the oldest, even if only by twenty minutes, she had no choice. She raised her head.

Her siblings stood in a circle, surrounding a mound of dirt. They all appeared tired, haggard. They leaned on shovels and breathed heavily.

In their faces, she saw her own. The same grey skin, lavender eyes, and unruly curly black hair but in various lengths. She studied each of them. She wasn't ready to speak. Their chins were all round with the same dimple. They each had a pointed nose, though Ambrose's was crooked. They looked like exactly what they were—quintuplets.

If she stared at her siblings hard enough, could she forget what they were doing out here? They all had pouty lips, but their smiles were different. Helen had a chipped front tooth and Rowena, a gap between two of her bottom teeth. Ambrose's lip curled in the corner and Marian sported an underbite. Desdemona tried to smile at them, her slight overbite grabbing her lower lip as they frowned at her collectively.

She would see none of their smiles today.

"We should go inside," she told them and felt their communal sigh, saw the relief on their faces. She watched as they dropped their shovels to the ground.

They were done with this task.

"We need to air out her bedroom," Helen said, hands twitching at her sides.

"Burn the sheets and give it a good scrub." Ambrose's voice, so much deeper than the others.

"Tomorrow! We can do it all tomorrow!" Marian practically wailed it, tears flooding her eyes.

"It will be okay, Marian," Desi said.

Annoyance filled her. It was just like Marian to act like a child. They didn't have the luxury of falling apart.

"It never will be again. I wish…"

"Marian!" Ambrose exclaimed, hushing her.

Marian blushed, shame filling her cheeks. "Sorry. I mean, I hope things are happier tomorrow."

"Should we pack her things?" Rowena asked. She gathered the fallen shovels, bending slowly like an old woman.

"No, we should wait for father to get home," Desi said. "It's bad enough he wasn't here for her burial."

She sidestepped a small headstone made of grey rock. The back half of their property was littered with them—dead babies, siblings she never saw or only briefly knew existed, grandparents, a few aunts and uncles, and several travelers who their mother and Helen couldn't heal.

"We should try and get back to normal," Desi said. That's what they'd been taught. The Infested threw tragedy at you and you had to meet it.

"We just lost our mother!" Marian exclaimed.

"She's right," Helen said. "There is too much to do for us to all break down and start crying, and Mama wouldn't want us to anyway."

They were quiet as they finished their walk back to the house. Weaving in and out of corn stalks and wheat, passing all manner of vegetables and fruit trees.

"Do you think she suffered?" Marian asked.

They climbed onto the back porch and kicked their boots off, hoping to leave some of the dirt and grime outside. Rowena piled the shovels up on the back porch.

"I don't know. Once Mom realized she was sick, she locked herself in." Desdemona tried not to think about how they'd listened for days to her cries and moans. Helen and Rowena had pounded on the door, begging to be let in. Until finally, after a week, it went quiet. No more shrieks and screams, just silence. Desdemona and Ambrose broke down the door to find her curled up on the bed, fist jammed in her mouth. Dead.

They walked in through the mudroom, past the large kitchen and pantry—the dining room door was closed on the right, the bathroom shut on the left—until they reached an enormous front parlor with large windows covered by thick green curtains, paled at the edges from being bleached by the sun.

"Just be glad we didn't have guests while she was sick," Ambrose said, plopping down on one of the settees, golden brown and ragged from over- and unkind use.

"Ugh, guests would have been a nightmare," Rowena agreed.

Their home was one of the few that specked the divide between the East and West: a haven against the monsters.

"Guests?" Desi scoffed, leaning against a wall and slowly lowering herself down to the floor. She hugged her knees, feeling the hardwood cool beneath her. "We haven't had guests since before Father left."

Those who were foolish enough to travel along the trail could seek shelter in the few warded zones along the way, whether a fort, outpost, or homestead. Along the entirety of the trail, there were maybe ten places of safety.

Their farm, with its giant wood plaque reading, "Welcome to Ash Hollow," was one of them. It was fifty acres of land surrounded by death with a small river running through it.

As Desi tried to relax, she felt the panel behind her back. She wanted to forget about what it hid. Just another new responsibility.

Rowena and Marian squished together onto an oversized chair, holding each other tightly, while Helen threw herself onto the antique purple fainting couch. As they were all tall like their father, her feet hung off the end.

"Dad will be back soon, right?" Marian asked, tracing the spattering of her lilac freckles with a finger. They all had them, tiny purple specks in various patterns.

"He should be," Rowena said, "and he'll bring presents and comforts from the East, just like last time."

Desi and her siblings never doubted he would come home. It was just a matter of time, a waiting game. Even before they were born, their father joined the Caravan coming from Utah once every other year and traveled back East for supplies. He lead the Caravan once it made its way into the Infested. The members welcomed his input and leadership because he was one of the few men to successfully homestead within the Infested.

Desi figured more people could if they came in with reverence and if it wasn't illegal to do so. The government of the

West firmly regulated The Infested. There were laws about who could live there and any comings or goings. It kept the humans safe.

The Ash family had been there long before the law. Generations would live and die there. You had to have a certain amount of respect and fear in the Infested. There were rules you had to follow, rituals to perform and magic to cultivate.

Marian began to weep and Rowena frowned at her, but hugged her tighter.

"Marian, I know this is hard. It's hard for all of us and I promise when father gets back we will mourn her properly. We just can't right now," Desi said. She had pain in her chest over the loss of their mother. She just knew that duty had to come before their emotions.

"Mother would want us to continue on, as usual," Helen said. "Cleaning, chores, our studies."

Her voice was so much like their mother's—quiet and reserved. Her face was gaunt, making their glass-cutting cheekbones more prominent. She was probably starving herself again. Desi made a note to speak with her privately later.

"And we will, but I think we're allowed some time to grieve," Ambrose snapped.

Desi was surprised he agreed with Marian. The two of them were always bickering.

"Hey, hey. Enough." Desi glared at her siblings. "You're both right. And tonight, while you lay in your beds, cry, shriek, and rant to the world. Right now, we don't have time for it. Father will come home and life will go on, like normal."

Her anxiety rose in her like a wave. She hushed it with her mantra; *There's nothing you can do about any of this right now. Breathe.*

"What if I don't want life to go on as normal?" Rowena asked. "We can be sad all we want, but let's not pretend that things were perfect. Mama was amazing, but she was also cold, strict and cruel."

"Rowena, we all know what Mother was like," Desi said, trying to be kind.

Their mother hadn't always been the easiest woman. She was demanding and expected perfection. She was rarely physically affectionate, but she loved them. She protected them and she cared about their dreams and their happiness. It wasn't black and white. Their world, like their skin, had shades of grey.

"I just don't want to be here, doing what she did," Rowena huffed. "I don't want to wind up like her, is all."

They all looked at Rowena with the same questioning expression.

"What would you rather be doing?" Marian asked.

"Maybe when the Caravan drops Father off, I'll leave with it. Go to the West and do something with myself, instead of dry up and die out here."

"Why would you want to do that?" Helen asked.

But Desi couldn't blame Rowena for the thought, as out of the question as it was. They were nineteen now and she'd thought about it a few times herself. What would it be like to leave Ash Hollow? With their mother gone, what kind of future could they look forward to? But she knew this was an impossible dream, unless she went out into The Infested.

"Like we'd be accepted anywhere but here, especially me," Ambrose said, running a finger through his short black locks that barely fell around his ears.

"You're perfect, just the way you are," Desi told him.

He snorted and rolled his eyes.

"Life is perfect here!" Helen reminded them all. "We grow things, heal things—here, we are free."

"You sound like Mother," Rowena said. She crossed her arms over her chest. "All we know is what she told us, what Father tells us. I'd like to see for myself."

"I understand that's what you want. We will speak about it later," Desi said. She raised a hand to hush the protesting.

Desi would speak to her privately about how that wasn't realistic. She would have to tell them all the truth sooner or later.

"Don't you want to see the world?" Rowena asked them.

"Well, I would like to get married and have children," Marian admitted.

"Yuck. Why would you ever want to do that?" Helen cringed.

"Experiencing sex might be fun," Desi said.

"Sex? I've heard our parents often enough to know that is *not* something I ever want to do," Ambrose said, shuddering.

From the front gate, the sound of high tinkling stopped their conversation. Someone was calling, asking to be let inside the wards.

"Travelers? Now?" Helen asked, standing.

She went to the window and peeked outside. A packed dirt path led from their front porch to the stables, outer pasture, several other small work buildings, and a tiny guest house. The path also led to a large wood gate an acre away that served as an entrance to their home.

"There's a small covered wagon out there," Helen said.

"Just one? Strange," Marian commented.

"Business as usual." Desi pulled her skirt out from the waistband of her black leggings and it dropped dramatically to the floor, a deep sienna color. She had a white tunic tucked into the skirt and a black waist cincher. Her hair was braided off to one side and she tucked a fly-away hair as she went for the front door.

This was standard ware in The Infested, appropriate for greeting guests.

"Marian, into the guest house to make sure it's company ready," Desi instructed as she tied on a crisp pinafore. "Light the lamps. Make sure there is firewood. Ambrose, into the kitchen. They're probably going to want food and drink. It's almost supper time."

She opened the door and stepped into thick work boots. Rowena stood up to come with her. They might need help with their supplies or wagon, which was Rowena's job.

"Helen, gather up your healing supplies in case they have injuries and then plan to take their animals into the stables."

Desi closed the door behind her and Rowena and then grabbed the shotgun from the gun locker on the porch. Desi didn't like to use guns, but it was sometimes necessary in the Infested. The only ammunition her family used was rock salt pellets. They were made special; if fired at something with living flesh, it would sting but not kill.

Unfortunately, this also meant it wouldn't kill something from the Infested, but it *would* slow it down. She slung the gun over her shoulder and started to walk to the gate.

As she got closer, the tension between her shoulder blades increased. This was always the dangerous part. These could be simple travelers looking for warmth, food, and safety before moving on—or they could be a trick. Monsters trying to lure them out of the safety of the wards.

"There's a hole in their wagon's cover," Rowena said, "and no spare wheel on the back."

The small covered wagon had seen better days. Rowena was right. Six straining horses pulled it, very thin, eyes wide with fear.

Desi didn't speak; she had to concentrate.

This was her job. She was the only one of her siblings to inherit major magic. She focused on the wagon.

A woman, around the same age as Desi, sat in the driver's seat. A yellow veil covered her face and a matching top hat sat jauntily on top of blonde curls. A thin, tall, handsome man stood by the gate. He rang the bell again and, once more, a sweet and high tinkle rang through the air, into Desi's core, down to her soul, like an itch she couldn't scratch.

"Good evening!" Desi called out, coming as close to the gate as she could, peering through the fence.

They both looked shocked. The woman gasped, but her blue eyes smiled above her veil.

"Are you coming from East or West?" Rowena asked.

They didn't answer, like they weren't sure what to say.

"You're traveling from the West?" Desi guessed.

Had to be. For fifty years, western women covered their faces with colorful veils.

"Yes," the man said. He tipped his own black top hat and smiled. His face transformed, showcasing boyish good looks. Dark blonde hair slightly curled under his hat and his deep brown skin looked sun-baked. He couldn't have been much older than the woman.

Both their clothes looked worn and thin, like high-quality fancy wear that had seen much better days. Her blue and white poplin needed a wash, and several buttons and holes needed repair on his suit. Obviously, they dressed up like this was a fort, striving to make a good impression.

"You're alone?" Desi asked, eyes looking to the distance.

"We got cut off from the rest of our train," he said.

"I've seen it happen more than you think. Spirit fog?"

"Spirit fog," he agreed.

"Payment upfront," Desi instructed. The prices were written on a sign outside the fence. The amounts were non-negotiable and set by the government.

The man turned to his companion and they started talking. Every so often, her eyes flicked over to Desi and Rowena, and there was an unsettling emotion in them. One that made Desi warm and wary all at once.

Putting some coin into a bag, he threw it over the gate. Rowena caught it, counted it, and placed it in the pocket of her pinafore, nodding at her sister.

Releasing the gate wards, Desi removed the heavy locks and opened the gate, bracing her shoulder against the splintered wood and giving it a shove. She'd tell Rowena the gate would need replacing before the winter.

The couple drove their wagon in and a gust of cool air followed, tickling Desi's nose. The sun was steadily setting behind them and she frowned.

That wasn't a typical cool evening breeze—not for here and not for May.

Muttering the ward spell under her breath, she used both hands and put all her weight behind the gate to close it. She could hear something in the distance.

"Something followed you," she grunted.

She needed to get the gate closed.

"Here, let me help." The man jumped down, slamming his own body into the gate.

The temperature dropped and Desi's nose tickled again—a sign of trouble. Rowena came forward and added her own weight. She was grinning.

As they slammed the gate shut and Desi reset the ward, something unseen hit the fence. The gate and fence line shuddered, and the woman in the wagon screamed.

Desi slammed the locks shut as another shudder went through the whole system. She could feel each ripple through the wards, but they were strong and she wasn't concerned about them giving out. Desi doubted herself in many ways and worried about a thousand things, but the strength of the gate wards wasn't one of them.

"It's okay," she said. "You're not in danger."

"What is that?" he asked.

"You were led astray by spirit fog. Best guess, a Nebula." Shrugging, Desi watched as Helen came running from the house. "Helen and Rowena will take the wagon and animals. We'll see if we can repair any of it and install some ward bags so that you can, hopefully, get where you're going safely."

"Hopefully?" the woman asked, breathless.

"Best we can do. You knew the dangers when you decided to travel through the Infested." It sounded harsh, but that was the land they lived in, harsh and unforgiving. There was no way the wagon train they'd been with was legal. Any train worth its salt would have had a Bonum or two to help keep away anything dangerous. These two? Best they could hope for was getting back to Wyoming alive.

The man helped the woman get down from the wagon and handed the reins to Helen, who quickly mounted the seat. Rowena followed behind as Helen drove it away.

"I'm Samael Inkwell, and this is my sister Lavellen." He bowed.

"Pleased to meet you. That's where you'll be staying," Desi said, pointing towards the guest house. "Freshen up and relax, dinner in the main house at seven."

As they walked away, the Nebula tested the wards a third time. A low, sweet howl filled the air as it gave up, dissipating. Their new guests were lucky not to be dead; their pieces strewn all over the plains.

Chapter 2
March 1900
The Caravan
Malum Territory

The trail is rough this year. Harsher than in years past. I can't figure out why.

There's less game to hunt and what we do cannot be eaten. Most of the water is sour and discolored.

Are things getting worse out here in the Infested? Or have they always been this bad, but my youth and excitement led me to ignore it?

It's been twenty-one days since leaving Illinois, crossing the invisible barrier from safety to the wilds, and every day I am thankful my children and wife are not with me. Though I know Desi and Rowena grow restless at home.

The sky above us burns during the day—a sickening red-green, like the air is poisoned, but we can still breathe.

Marcus says it is my imagination that it tastes of sulfur. It is not.

This morning, we get up and put out the fires, all of us sleeping inside the circle of wagons for safety. Those poor souls on the last watch look tired and afraid, and I do not ask if they saw anything in the dark.

We eat dried beef and stale biscuits from the night before. Our cook, Lettie, makes a mean cup of coffee, but I can't wait to get home and have proper cream. Ambrose is the best cook I could ask for and I miss our cows.

It takes more than an hour to get going and we want to put in as many miles as we can. The first significant "safe" places lay a day's ride away: Winter Quarters. It is a fort built into the ground with rocks, herbs, and wards for protection. It may be cramped and damp, but a man can sleep there, trade with the caretakers, and get his bearings.

It will be good to see the caretakers—others like me who live in the Infested full-time. There are other safe places in Iowa, but they are no more than Wagon Rests. No one lives in Iowa.

Some of the Caravan people look at me with suspicion, those who don't know me and haven't traveled with me before. Others trust me but don't understand me. They don't know why I live in Nebraska, why I stay there with my wife and children.

All that matters is they listen to me. I am the expert here, not them, and that is why they ask me to come. Few others are as knowledgeable about the Infested as I.

I drive my oxen at as fast a pace as they can manage. They may tire or die before we reach home, but the less time this Caravan is in the Infested, the better.

The grass crunches underfoot. Much of it looks burned and dry. The large patches of rust-colored grass we found kills the livestock within minutes.

I bought such beautiful things for my kids, and I can't wait to get home and shower them with much-deserved presents. I even have several newspapers for Rowena, so she can see what goes on in the world outside.

The wagons used in the Caravan are of unique design, somewhere between a Conestoga and a Prairie Schooner. Made to be pulled by up to six oxen or horses, depending on what is carried within. In the Infested, no one walks, so you have to ride inside or sit and drive your animals by the rein. The ground can be as dangerous as the unnatural inhabitants.

Our wagons must carry goods to and from, and be stable, sturdy, and lightweight to travel the challenging trail.

I gaze over the sweating backs of my six beasts, chuckling to myself as I remember what Helen named them: General, Colonel, Captain, Lieutenant, Sergeant, and Major.

Major labors worse than the others. He is straining and too thin. I will put him out of his misery if he cannot get good food and water soon. At least those among the Caravan will eat well. But the loss of an ox will slow me down.

We've gone a few miles now when something stirs out of the corner of my eye. I stare straight ahead, refusing to look. There are some things you cannot unsee, things that will drive a man crazy. We lost two good men on the way to Illinois. One wandered away in the middle of the night called to by honeyed evil songs, and the other… I cannot even think about the horrors that await him, wherever that thing carried him off to.

The men and women of the Caravan chat quietly, but they talk. Some talk as they ride in the wagons or gossip on horseback. Others sing softly—prayers, hymns, lullabies; all meant to soothe and protect. The point is, we are not silent.

My eyes strain to look forward, trained on the land before me. As the most experienced, my wagon leads the way. A few men and women on horses ride next to me to ensure the path is marked. The horses who carry them whinny, ears flicking back and forth, eyes-rolling. The land is brown and red with hints of green, rolling along, mostly flat as far as my eyes can see. But I feel like I am being watched. There is a shadow in my peripheral vision, and the skin of my arms and the back of my neck tingle.

A hush falls over the train, a stressed silence, and I push my oxen to go just a little faster. We must make the Winter Quarters before night. Every instinct in my body knows this.

The rider on my left comes closer.

"We are being stalked," she whispers.

She does not look past me, keeps her eyes down on her saddle.

I nod. "Guns out, but don't look, don't engage."

The rider to my right must hear me because I hear the metal-and-rasp noise of his shotgun being drawn and the softening of hoofbeats as he falls back to tell the others. The bullets in our guns are special, a mixture of iron and salt. Every member of the Caravan had to be tested and licensed to carry a gun with real ammo and not just common rock salt or blessed water.

My weapon kills humans if I'm not careful.

There are nineteen other wagons in this train and ten additional riders on horseback. Sometimes caravans don't make it back. Sometimes horrible things happen within the Infested. I have never had more than a few tragedies, but I feel something more considerable, darker, on the horizon.

"Chloe, how do the lines feel?" I ask the rider.

Chloe closes her eyes, concentrating. "Murky and close. I can't really tell. It's been this way all trip."

We both know that isn't good. One of Chloe's gifts is the ability to sense the ley lines through the Infested. Ley lines are rivers of invisible magic. The cleaner and further away they are, the safer the Caravan is. Every Caravan has a ley line reader attached. It's been policy for years.

"How close?" Too close, and we will attract all manner of horrors.

"Not that close—not close enough to walk to—but closer than they should be," she says, sighing.

We ride in this state of hyper-awareness and fear until I can see the Winter Quarters in the distance. My muscles are strained and weary, and the tension is palpable.

I hear the collective sigh of the entire Caravan when the idea of safety comes into view, and just as suddenly as the presence came, it is gone, and I can look, there is nothing to my left, nothing but smatterings of trees and even more dead grass and soil. Shadows are lurking at the edges as the sun is starting to set. Slowly I hear the voices of the Caravan start up again.

I think about my wife and how she will love the fabric I chose. She loves to sew and create. I picked out silks in lavender and buttercup, taffeta in crimson and sky blue, poplin in various striped patterns, lace in eggshell, and a myriad of ribbons and beads as well.

The shop woman helped me. She was kind, but they don't always trust us Westerners back East. I know why a woman like this shopkeeper will never see the same things I have. She will wonder if the goods I purchase from her make it across the Infested—or if they will lay forgotten in a heap, aging and discoloring with the elements.

My mind strays back to my wife and love fills me. I wonder if she is starting to undertake the task we spoke of before I left.

We come to the Winter Quarters' entrance, a large area surrounded by spiked logs ten feet high with a gate. The logs are gray and worn, and I see something has left colossal claw marks on a large section of it.

"Harrison, what the hell is that?" Marcus asks me as he pulls his wagon alongside mine.

"I don't know. Something that tried to get in but couldn't, I suppose." I pull up to the gate and call out the phrase to access the traveler's code.

We wait in silence, then I call out again. Still, there is nothing.

"Harrison," one of the riders says to me, returning from circling the perimeter as per routine. "The wards in the wood have claw marks through them."

"See if you can get the gate open!" I call. I scan the ground from the train to the structure. I don't see anything that looks dangerous so I give an all clear call.

Men and women jump down from the back of several wagons and make their way to the large gate. If the wards still work, no one should be able to open it, not from this side.

They do.

It takes another ten minutes, but the thick wooden gate swings open and horror lies before us.

The caretakers' bodies are ripped to shreds, not even eaten, and scattered all over the ground. As I look at the gore, red and brown slashed across the dirt, I try to remember how many are housed here. I think it was ten. But now, they resemble so much meat and sinew, it is difficult to identify them as human.

I sniff the air. It doesn't smell like these are fresh kills, no scent of blood or body fluids, but how long have they been dead? I can't tell. I hear members of the Caravan crying and vomiting.

"Harrison, what do we do?" Marcus asks me. He is too pale, eyes too wide.

I need to decide.

"We go in and make camp. It is not safe to stay out here tonight, not with what stalked us earlier."

"What about..." The rider next to me trails off; she cannot finish her sentence.

"We burn what we can find—*outside* the walls—and see if we can reinforce any of the safeties."

People scramble to do my bidding. I don't know if they agree with me or not. I only know they are scared and will do as I say.

"What if whatever did this is hiding below?" Marcus questions, voice hushed.

"Take a few men down and clear it out. We need to sleep here this evening and it's getting dark."

I hate sending them. What if it's to their death? But it must be done or we cannot stay here—and we *cannot* stay out there, not tonight.

Within a few hours, the remains are burned. We find no evidence of anything residing below, in the sleeping quarters. The place is empty, without even animals or food, but we *do* find supplies for our animals and untainted water.

All the wards have been clawed through, and all the bags of protective herbs and stones are gone. All that is left is an echoing hollow and a gaping cavern underneath. It doesn't even feel haunted. It feels empty, leeched of life.

Once we establish the underground is safe and no hint of the dead is left behind, we bring the wagons and animals inside. It's packed tightly, but once the large gate closes, I see and feel the relief among the people. The horses and oxen are silent as we feed and care for them, but they do not seem afraid. This is a good sign.

We repaint the wards, but they do not lend as much protection without a Bonum to bless them. Chloe is our Bonum, our magic worker, but each Bonum's gifts are different and each Bonum connects with the magic of the Infested differently. Chloe keeps the Caravan safe but she cannot bless wards, not at this caliber of need. Setting up the Winter Quarters took a whole group of Bonum working together.

Some women put together new herb and stone bags and hang them. We start a few fires and warm ourselves, cooking and eating. No one plays or tells stories, but they hum our hymns and I watch them pray. They may feel safer, but no one can forget what we found when we came here nor the underlying thought; *What did this and where is it now?*

Finally, I tell people that it is time for sleep. I watch the unease seep back into them. Should they take their lanterns into the underground where there are soft beds and the dirt promises warmth and safety, but where they cannot see what may be coming for them? Or do they stay with the wagons, a little colder and slightly cramped, but where they can see the sky and anything that tries to breach the walls?

I still cannot believe the government is thinking of trying to reclaim the West. Most humans cannot survive out here.

I send Marcus below and announce that I shall join three men with the first watch. I will wake Marcus in four hours to relieve me with his group. More than half my people decide to bunker down below. Keeping my seat next to the fire, a warm cup of coffee in my hand, I watch the others climb back into the wagons, hoping to sleep.

Those who keep watch with me wander the inside perimeter. Guns are drawn and I worry they are too twitchy.

The night sky is large and clear, black with silver stars above me. I bet the land outside looks beautiful at night. It's too bad it is so dangerous. My Marian would love to stargaze.

It's then I hear the soft scratching from outside.

Chapter 3
May 1900
Day 1
Ash Hollow

"Will they be joining us for dinner?" Ambrose asked as Desi came inside, her bare feet smacking the floor.

"I think so, but they look exhausted. Marian is heating up water for them to bathe. If they don't, I'll have you take a plate over later."

"Well, it's going to be a simple supper. Grilled fish, green beans, and bread. I don't feel up to anything fancy."

"Anything fancy would need to be started this morning," Desi said, following him back into the kitchen. She leaned against the counter.

"True. Oh, the icebox needs renewing," he said, tying an apron around his waist and starting to shape the rolls.

Magic couldn't fix everything, but it did make some things easier, like keeping bugs away, keeping the icebox cold so milk didn't spoil, and making sure they had a variety of produce all year long.

Desi would have to do it all by herself now that Mother was gone. They each had gifts, but only Desi and Helen could use actual magic.

"I'll put it on my list for tomorrow," she said.

"You better eat tonight. You know you can't do magic without it. Power needs fuel," he quoted their mother.

"I promise, but let's make sure Helen eats too."

"I made her something special, don't worry. We all see it."

Desi frowned, thinking it was time for Helen to see a Bonum who specialized in mind healing. Desi tried to help, but there was a difference between talking to your sister and talking to a stranger who knew how to help. She'd speak to their father when he got home.

The front door closed again and Desi left Ambrose to his kitchen. She ran into Helen and Rowena in the hall.

"I think they're going to lose one of their horses," Helen said when she saw Desi, "but the others will be fine. A few days of rest and good grain will set them right."

"I can repair most of the damage to the wagon. Superficial, really. But I don't have a wagon wheel that size to give them," Rowena said. She sniffed the air. "Fish? Really?"

"Don't say that too loud. You'll make Ambrose angry," Desi scolded. "And yes, unless you'd rather we wasted precious other meat on travelers. Fish are easy to come by."

"You could always refuse to eat meat, like me!" Helen teased.

"Speaking of which, Ambrose made you something special. I expect you to eat all of it. What if they need healing?"

"Power needs fuel. I know," Helen grumbled, crossing her arms over her small chest. She left to go back to the stables.

"I had to take in her skirts again," Rowena whispered.

"And let mine out." Desi joked.

"Oh please. You're not fat."

"I am. At least, fatter than the rest of you. It's fine. I know why, and I'm okay with it."

Magic might need her to eat to have energy, but it did *not* burn fat. So, she ate twice as much to keep the wards working and sometimes gained weight. It didn't bother her. Her mother and aunts had been bigger women too. Desi was comfortable with her body.

"Your fat keeps us safe."

Desi snorted. "Don't you have something to do? Something to fix or sew?"

"I do have some mending to work on. I just don't…."

"…Want to go upstairs?" The sewing room was next door to their parent's bedroom.

Rowena nodded slowly.

"That's why I brought the mending basket downstairs," Desi said. "It's in the mudroom near the washing."

Rowena's shoulders sagged with relief. She kissed Desi's cheek and went off to work.

Desi went into the office and sat at the desk. She pulled out the household accounts and started to work. Their father and mother went to Wyoming every three months. They bought things they couldn't make or grow themselves and sold items you could only find in The Infested.

"They're so nice!" Marian gushed, coming and sitting on the edge of the desk, her blue skirt brushing over Desi's notebook.

"Who are?" Desi asked distractedly, pushing the offending fabric off her list.

"Who are? Really? Lavellen and Samael! And he's so handsome. They're washing up and then coming to supper! It will be nice to have conversations with someone else."

"We aren't interesting enough for you?" Desi put her pencil down.

"You know I didn't mean it that way."

"Just be careful. They're strangers. Don't get attached like you did to the last ones. He isn't staying here."

Marian blushed. "They didn't even ask about the skin color or the freckles!"

Desi closed the ledger. Apparently, she wasn't getting any work done. "Just means they've seen Bonum before. It's not that unusual."

The first Bonum was born in 1820 before people understood the Infested. Ordinary human women began giving birth to children who looked strange and could wield the magic of the Infested. Those first Bonum were killed, treated like monsters; babies drowned and smothered, children abandoned to the elements. But when it kept happening, the government decided they were a gift and began to use them.

Bonum were special. Having one in your family was seen as a boon. Bonum worked to provide the creature comforts the East took for granted, like electricity for lighting and refrigeration, protection, medicine, and other forms of what the East called "modern technology." Of the 400,000 people who lived in the West, eighteen percent of them were Bonum. The number grew more significant with every passing year.

"Their eyes have gold dust in them. Maybe they're like us," Marian contemplated.

"Maybe, but it's impolite to ask and you know it." Desi opened the pocket watch on the desk. Almost seven. "We should make sure the dining room is aired out and cleaned up before inviting people to eat with us."

Marian followed her out of the room and down the hall.

The dining room was narrow, with a long table and chairs with pink cushions. Desi lit the wall lanterns, brightening the room. Marian took a cloth from a basket on the floor and began polishing the table. Desi checked the cleanliness of the chairs.

They hadn't eaten in here since before their mother got sick, preferring to gather around the counter at breakfast and sit on the porch for lunch and dinner.

"Ummm, I think we have a problem." Rowena's voice came from the doorway.

"What kind of problem?" Desi asked, turning.

Her sister looked pale and afraid. "The kind where I'm worried the wards might not be working."

"Impossible. I just checked them."

"Come look."

"Marian, stay here," Desi commanded. "Make sure dinner gets served and don't act like there's anything wrong."

She followed Rowena out of the room and to the back porch. Helen and Ambrose were already there, watching something in the distance.

"I saw it from the stables," Helen whispered like she was afraid to be heard. "Thought I imagined it."

Desi looked in the direction she pointed. An old tree with a swing was between the garden and the animal enclosure, out near the river. Father built it for them when they were small.

Desi frowned, eyes narrowing as dusk settled, trying to make sense out of what she was seeing.

"Go inside," she told them.

"Really? You may need help." Ambrose said.

"With what? I am not engaging with whatever that is," she answered.

A figure was swinging under the tree—a black shape, resembling a woman from the waist up. Shadowy hair flowing behind her, red eyes gleaming with a broad white smile. Fear crept up her spine and under her hair.

Something had made it past the wards and was inside their fences.

"Go inside, all of you."

Ambrose slowly backed away. He grabbed Helen's arm. She was eyeing the creature fearfully. They went into the house.

"Rowena," Desi hissed.

"I am *not* leaving you out here."

Of course she wouldn't. Rowena was stubborn, like their mother.

"Can it see us?" Rowena asked, hands fisted at her sides.

"I think so. Stay very still."

As Desi watched the creature, the swing began to slow down. It was watching them. Desi could feel the hair on the back of her neck prickle as the creature's gaze focused on them. She felt like prey.

"Do you hear that?" Desi asked, suddenly.

"Hear what?" Rowena's eyes widened.

Nothing.

Desi could hear nothing. There should be hundreds of sounds. Their homestead was never quiet, never still, and it unnerved her. The Infested still had animals, birds, and insects that made evening noise. Their farm had chickens, pigs, cows, and horses. The nighttime song of Ash Hollow was not noiseless.

Desi concentrated on the land and the fences. The wards were still up and she could find no weak links, no broken spells. Their alarms weren't going off either.

The thing smiled wider, a bright white gleam of too many teeth in a face made from shadows. The red eyes closed and then opened, and Desi heard a sinister whispering as the wind picked up.

Sunset was almost upon them. Red and purple splashed across the sky as the blue darkened into night.

"Desi, I'm scared," Rowena said.

Always so impossibly brave until faced with something she couldn't explain and wasn't safe from.

"Me too," Desi whispered.

She felt like if they were too loud or moved too much, the thing would no longer be content with watching them. Her nose itched like crazy.

The swing stopped. The dark shape lifted an impossibly long arm and pointed at the guest house. It slithered out of the swing and stood up. It was tall, too tall, half the size of the tree. Dark tendrils absent of light seemed to make up the creature from the waist down. The creature began to fade, until all that remained were its red eyes.

Then it vanished.

"Where'd it go?" Rowena asked.

"I don't know, but it's already too dark for me to do anything about it. Get inside and stay there," Desi said. She pushed her sister towards the back door. She felt the desperate need to get inside.

The warmth of the house and the smell of the food were pleasant enough. Desi tried to forget what she'd just seen. But a sense of dread sloshed in her belly, killing her hunger.

"Should you check downstairs?" Rowena asked.

Desi gave her a stern look. "We don't talk about downstairs. You know that."

A frown filled Rowena's features. "That was Mom's rule. It doesn't have to be yours too."

As she and Rowena made their way into the dining room, Desi heard conversation and Marian's sweet laughter.

Their guests sat around the table. Samael wore a deep blue pinstriped suit and no hat which Desi could tell, like his previous outfit, had seen better days. Lavellen no longer wore her veil, and Desi was taken back by how beautiful she was and how similar she and Samael looked.

"Desi!" Marian exclaimed. "Samael was just telling us how nice it was to have hot water and a chance to rest on a real bed." She sat as close to the man as she could.

"I'm glad we were able to help." Desi smiled at them.

They all sat down and Ambrose brought the food in.

"It smells heavenly," Lavellen gushed. "Thank you so much. I don't know what we would have done if we hadn't seen your home on the map!"

"It's the least we can do for travelers," Helen said, picking at her food. Ambrose had made her oatmeal with honey and raisins in it. With Helen, the blander the food, the better. "Honestly, we don't get many guests."

Samael helped himself to large portions of everything while Lavellen grabbed a few green beans and a roll, nibbling on her food in a way that reminded Desi of Helen. For a few moments, there was silence as peace washed over all of them—Ambrose's small blessing.

"It's Desdemona, right?" Samael eventually asked.

"Yes."

"Is it just you and your siblings out here? Seems like a lonely place, just the five of you."

Small warning bells went off in her mind; about to lie, she opened her mouth.

"Oh no, our father lives here too," Marian said, "but right now, he's with the Caravan."

"Impressive," Lavellen said. "This trip has been harrowing enough. I can't imagine making it every few years."

"He also goes into Wyoming every few months. There's a fort there we stock up from."

Desi kicked Marian under the table. Did she need to gossip so much? Marian sucked in a breath and glared at her.

"Well, you are all much braver than me. It took years for Samael to convince me this was a good idea," Lavellen admitted.

"We've done all we could out West, sister. You know that. It was time for a change."

"What are you planning to do once you get east?" Rowena asked.

"I really want to apprentice to a dressmaker, and Samael is hoping to be an actor," Lavellen said. "That reminds me—do you have a sewing machine? I'd love to fix up some of our things before we head out."

"Of course. I can help you. I do all the sewing around here." Rowena puffed up in pride.

"How long do you usually house guests?" Samael asked.

Ambrose finally spoke up. "As long as it takes to make sure you have a decent chance of making it to the next safe zone. Are you heading for Illinois or Missouri?"

"Missouri," Samael answered.

"Fort Kearney will be your next stop," Rowena told them. "They'll have better supplies and you can buy a new wagon wheel."

As they emptied their plates and the food disappeared, Ambrose rose and began clearing the table.

"This was lovely," Lavellen said, standing up. "Thank you so much for your kindness."

Her body was graceful in her yellow dress. Desi caught herself staring at the other woman and forced herself to look away.

"I'll walk you back to the guest house," Marian quickly interjected, staring at Samael.

The smile he gave her was warm, and he held out his arm like a gentleman. "I'd be delighted."

Desi couldn't tell if he was humoring her or not. Either way, she wasn't happy about it.

"Marian," Rowena said, warning in her voice.

"I need to check the firewood and bring their laundry back with me. It just makes sense." Marian's excuse was hollow, but Desi nodded her head.

"Rowena, do you have any spare buttons?" Lavellen's smile lit up the room. "I'm not up for much work tonight, but sewing back on a few buttons and clasps are within my power."

Rowena smiled at the other woman, all too happy to have someone to talk to about such things. "Of course. Come up to my room. I have an entire box full."

Once their guests were gone, Desi felt as if she could breathe easier.

"That wasn't too bad." Helen stared down at her half-eaten bowl of oatmeal. "It's nice to have company."

"If I put it in the icebox, will you finish it for breakfast with some cream?" Ambrose asked gently, touching her shoulder.

"Yes, I promise." She beamed up at him.

"Desi, what was that thing outside?" Ambrose asked, scooping up Helen's bowl.

"I don't know, but it disappeared. Hopefully, it's not still on the property."

And if it was, it would soon find itself a prisoner, like the others. If she could catch it, that is.

Chapter 4
May 1900
Day 2
Ash Hollow

"There's nothing out here," Desi told Ambrose as they investigated the swing in the mid-morning light. "I don't feel magic or danger, and the wards haven't been tested. I don't know what we saw last night, but it's either too weak to be a threat or so powerful we'll all be dead before we are aware it's back."

"Cheerful thought," Ambrose said. He kicked a pile of weeds and stared around them. "We really should do something about this back pasture. We don't use it for anything."

"We use it if a larger train needs inside the fence."

Not that it happened often. Desi couldn't remember the last time the back fence was opened.

"I guess if Marian marries Samael, we could build them their own house." Ambrose snorted.

"Ridiculous, her and that idea."

First thing that morning, Marian had been up, bathed, done her chores in record time, and then dressed in her best and taken breakfast to the guest house. Then Samael had followed her into the front parlor and, for the past hour, they'd sat together on the settee while he read out loud and told her all about their home in Nevada.

"Maybe next time Father goes to Wyoming, he should take her. One of us should get married, at least."

"Ambrose, we were born and raised out here. Would you really do that to other children?" Desi asked.

"What else would we do with children? If we all die, this place will be overrun within days and our family's history would vanish."

"Then maybe you should get pregnant and have babies."

Ambrose frowned, wrinkling his nose with disgust. "No, I wouldn't like that. Not at all."

"I guess you're right, in a way. Better some guy from Wyoming than a traveler who's leaving in a few weeks."

They started walking back to the house. "You're giving them that long?"

"Two weeks is standard."

"And if they try to stay for longer?"

Desi bared her teeth at him.

"Ah, the angry face. We suddenly can't feed them, and everyone is cold and unfriendly. Got it. Like Dad says: if all else fails, just throw them out."

It didn't happen often, travelers trying to stay longer than they should, but when it did, they had plans in place, including direct and simple rudeness. Their mother hated doing it, but their home could not sustain a large group of people for very long.

The sun shone down on the property, skies so blue you could see for miles to the East; but to the West, Desi noticed a dark cloud.

"Stormcloud?" Ambrose asked, watching what held her interest.

"I hope so. It bothers me they ran into spirit fog this close to home."

"We've never had a Nebula test the wards before."

"I'm not worried, not yet... but Father... I didn't say it to the girls..."

"He should be back by now."

"Yes. By a week, at least."

"We can't lose them both, Desi. I don't know what we'd do." Ambrose dashed away the tears in his eyes with the back of his hand.

"We won't. Father knows how to deal with the Infested. It may just be... causing the Caravan to travel at a slower pace. If I have to, I'll send a message to him, but only if I have to."

They walked the path through the garden. Ambrose picked up an empty basket and started filling it with items for lunch and dinner; corn, onions, sage, and potatoes.

"You have to go outside of the fence to do that," he said. As he broke off sage leaves, the savory scent filled Desi's nostrils, almost comforting. "So only as a last resort."

"We need to make a plan just in case," she said. "You know that we're old enough to care for ourselves should the worst come to pass."

She needed a plan. Without one, her mind would spiral out of control and she wouldn't be able to take care of them.

"You and your plans. A plan doesn't fix things!" Ambrose snapped at her, pulling the basket to his chest.

"They may not fix everything all the time, but you don't complain when they *do* help."

"We'll lose Rowena and Marian if Dad doesn't come home."

At the mention of Rowena, Desi looked over to her shop, where the wagons went, and where she and Dad kept all the tools. Desi didn't hear anything from inside. Where was Rowena, anyway?

"Rowena maybe, but Marian wants to get married," she said. "She won't leave unless that's a for-sure thing."

"And we're back where we started." Ambrose mounted the back porch ahead of her. He stared down at her, lavender eyes hard. "Do you really think you could run this place without our parents?"

"I don't think I'll have a choice, but it would be great if you all helped."

With a furious expression, Ambrose disappeared into the kitchen to prepare lunch. Desi tried to drown out Marian's laughter and Samael's rich voice as she came further inside.

Going to the stairs, she snuck a peek at Marian and Samael, and shock flowed through her. They were sitting close enough together that their legs touched, heads bowed over a book, almost forehead to forehead.

"Marian," Desi called.

Marian started, guilty, eyes wide. "Yes?"

"There is still laundry to do today, yes?" Desi gave a pointed look out the window. If Marian waited too long, she'd lose the good light.

"Oh, yes! I'm sorry, Desi, I lost track of time. Excuse me, Samael." She stood up, a little shaky, and made her way toward the mudroom.

"It's incredibly rare to meet a woman who can read and enjoy literature," Samael said, leaning back and closing the book.

"We all can read and write. Most of us enjoy it."

"My sister is like that too. It's refreshing. Many girls I met at home couldn't be bothered to do much more than sign their name."

"Many men too, so my father says," she countered.

"Agreed. Education is so important. For being educated at home, your parents did a great job."

He sounded genuine, even though she wanted to lend condescension to his words. Desi was good at reading faces and he looked sincere. Before she could comment, he started speaking again in a rushed way.

"Is there anything I can do to help out? I feel rather lazy, sitting here. It's been a while since I had time to myself, time to do nothing. Driving the wagon is exhausting."

"Helen can always use help with the animals—she's out by the barn near the cow pasture—and Ambrose would probably welcome help in the kitchen."

Anything to get him away from Marian. It wasn't that she didn't like Samael. He was pleasant, smart, and well-mannered. But he would hurt Marian when he left and not even realize it.

"The kitchen sounds like a great idea," he said. "I'm not a bad cook, but animals and I? Well, aside from our horses, we don't get along."

Desi waited until he'd left, hoping Samael was more help than a bother to her brother.

Making her way to the wall near the front door, she bit her lip. Did the paneling look out of place? Kneeling, she ran fingers across the wood panels, a few seams shifted just a hair outside the norm. When had Mother been down there last? Desi had not gone down without her, so before she had gotten sick.

She pressed her fingers into a delicate pattern between the panels. They made a swooshing sound as they yawned open. She crawled through the small gap. It wasn't a tight fit, but uncomfortable. Once inside, she stood up. She lit a torch at the top of a narrow set of stairs and the panel behind her shut. She heard whispers from below. The torch at the top of the stairs set off a chain reaction lighting all the way to the basement, through the door, and into the inner rooms—more magic.

She descended into the deep, hands against the walls to reinforce the wards that kept those in the basement from breaking out. The magic tingled, like spiny bugs across her palms, letting her know it was a good thing she'd come down. The air smelled stale and feral, full of scents her siblings would never encounter if she did her job.

A black iron door with a large silver lock met her at the bottom of the stairs. Pulling out the key hanging around her neck, she unlocked the door, cold against her, burning her skin if she lingered. There was too much Bonum in her.

She entered, wary but unafraid. This did not scare her, but her guard was up. It had to be.

She walked past the bookcase that held her mother's books, stopping long enough to grab a large novel with a red feather as a bookmark, and paused at her mother's desk around a corner.

A jar full of moving shadows perched on the edge of the desk. Those inside were harmless, but creepy and needed watching. She opened the lid to murmur a soft apology and instructions.

The shadows swarmed out and up the stairs. Akin to farmhands, they would help around the homestead doing all the nonessentials chores her siblings hadn't the time to do, like weeding, fence repair, or herding. They had to be back in the jar before nightfall or the darkness would swallow them. Desi reminded herself to take the jar up the stairs when she left.

Nose tingling, she moved further into the room, waiting for the light to catch up with her.

"You've been gone a long time," a voice hissed from the dark.

"The mother died." Another voice, gravelly.

Laughter emanated from deeper within, and as the last torch-lit, Desi could see everything. The room held several different types of cages, each home to a different creature. Several were caught on their property and deemed too dangerous to let go. Others were given to them for safekeeping. One voluntarily requested sanctuary, even knowing it meant imprisonment.

These things did not need water, nor did they require sunlight. Some needed food but would not starve without it. Mainly they fed on things like fear, blood, and smoke.

As she walked to the back of the room, she checked each cage.

A large tank filled with green fluid greeted her first. A dark silhouette floated in it, as big as a dog. Fins and teeth drifted idly in the liquid. She couldn't see its eyes but knew the Malus Piscis watched her, more sentient than she'd like.

Three compact cages to her left held smaller animals that growled as she walked by, sending out tiny rivulets of magic meant to inspire fear and anger so they could feast on them and suck her dry.

"Behave, or I will put you all in the same cage to feed off each other," she warned. They sucked their magic back and fell silent.

Laughter from the next two cages, things that used to be people and were now half-shadow, half-monster. All teeth and eyes, immortal and insane. The leftovers of a dozen villagers who tried to live in the Infested and failed, their entire town consumed by a Malum and left to rot.

Further along, a woman was chained to the wall with glowing manacles. A harlequin, dark hair in pigtails, her eyes black holes, and mouth sewn with black x's. Skin pale white, in a short dress with pink cheeks. Sitting, she played her demonic instrument. The fingers of her right hand were all bone and they plucked out a sad tune from the tendons strung tight on her left arm. She paused, only briefly, to give Desi a tight smile.

From an iron-hanging cage came soft but beautiful birdsong. A bird, so lovely it hurt to look at, singing such a sweet song. Meant to lure you in, catch you off guard. Under the golden beak and velvet, jewel-toned feathers lay a killer.

"Hush. It doesn't work on me, and you know that."

"I have to try anyway," its gruff voice said. "It gets so boring down here."

"Shouldn't have come onto the property."

She kept walking. The next two cages were the last occupied, but several more lay empty, just in case.

In one was an older woman, still very beautiful, asleep in a bed. She never woke. The spell Mother put her under, heavy and permanent. Desi felt it was this last deep spell that allowed their mother to get sick.

"You've never been away so long before," said a soft voice from her left. Almost a hiss, like the speaker had a speech impediment or wasn't used to talking.

Desi sat in the chair near the bars of the cell that housed her best friend. "You heard the Tene Avem; Mom died."

"Ahem! I have a name. It's Medi!" the Tene Avem yelled. They ignored him.

"I thought that's what I felt flood through the house—death." The voice stepped into the light.

You couldn't really call her a girl, though she was female. Her long black hair was shadows and light, flowing from her grey skin, covering the room like a blanket. Spider webs and starlight hugged her lithe form, the outline of her breasts and hips against the ethereal fabric. Her name was Persephone.

"I'm sorry your mother died, Desdemona. I know what it feels like." The girl opened bright lavender eyes. No pupils, just glowing orbs in her face. Her black lips turned into a smile.

"I'm sorry too, Foni." Desi brought her knees up and rested her arms on them, still gripping the book.

"She was my aunt. I'll miss her."

Desi didn't acknowledge the statement and instead opened the book she'd grabbed to show Foni.

"Should we begin where we left off?"

Chapter 5
March 1900
The Caravan
Winter Quarters

The scratching continues. Soft, in the background, almost pattern-like. It makes the other watchers uneasy. They stop talking, gripping their guns.

"Harrison," Chloe whispers.

I am near the wall, not around the fire with them, one hand on the ladder to the walk at the top of the wall. I need to look down and see what's there.

"What is it?" she asks, hands ready for action. She is pale and thin, and she's lost weight since we left the East. Her light green hair is cut short and her deep brown eyes slightly glow against her silver skin.

"I don't know. I'm going to find out."

If we are to be killed, I want to know by what. I am thankful the ward pouches are remade. Chloe does what she can, but wards aren't her specialty. I think of my kids, of Desdemona. Maybe I should require more than one Bonum coming with every Caravan from now on. I've grown complacent, forgotten the one rule of the Infested: it is never safe. No matter how many times I make this trip in one piece.

I haul myself up the ladder, wood rough on my palms and knees creaking from the challenge. I may be getting too old to do this.

I should train one of the girls. Rowena would take my place nicely as Caravan leader, though Desdemona or Helen have more natural magic.

At the top, steeply pointed logs align the walk's rim—a defense should anything try to breach it. Each spike is dark, dipped in poison. It didn't help the caretakers.

As I pick my way towards the scratching, I look at the night sky, so beautiful, stars twinkling. I am gathering courage. I kneel, peeking between the logs for a view of the ground. There is nothing—just prairie grass and rocks. I don't see harm to the wood, either. I lean back, sitting, head against the logs.

Was it just my imagination?

The scratching starts again.

I do the same thing, over and over, following the sound and look. There's never anything there. Something is playing with us, playing with me, and I won't give it the satisfaction. I go back down the ladder.

"Did you see it?" Chloe asks, waiting for me.

"No, it might be nothing."

She looks skeptical.

"Or it could be playing with us."

Now she looks thoughtful. I know her. Like me, she is trying to think of all the different monsters it could be

"Any ideas?" Her eyes are wide and she's turning her head to look in every direction.

"I don't know. I want two people patrolling the wall, one down below and two at the gate."

She runs off to get the men up from around the fire, giving my orders. They all look in my direction and hop into action.

I don't answer her questions because it will just cause more fear, and that fear will spread. I don't want the people so terrified they can't react.

There are many awful things in the Infested, but only a few will play with you. Hunt you, yes. One minute, the trail will be clear; the next, a monster so awful your mind's eye will deny it, and you'll be dead. Very few make a game out of it.

The scratching comes and goes all night. The animals are restless. They can smell what we can't. Those who sleep in the wagons wake up, they hide in their canvas, and I hear prayers and whispers. Some people will not make this journey again and others like Chloe will. It's all she has. It has been her life and purpose for a decade. She will travel with the Caravan until she is too old or something drags her off.

Finally, around three in the morning, Marcus and a new team relieve us.

"I should stay awake," I tell him after explaining the long night behind me.

"We need you rested," he says. "Try and sleep. We leave at first dawn."

"No, not until the sun is fully up."

"We can't afford to lose time! We have to reach Fort Kearney as soon as we can."

"A few hours won't matter, Marcus." I put my hand on his arm to steady him.

"It's over two hundred miles away. We won't have a choice but to camp on the trail. It will take us at least fifteen days."

"We'll be careful. Have everyone create ward bags, as many as they can."

I sleep in my wagon, fitfully, half-listening to the people around me and the scratching that moves, stalking us until the sun begins to rise.

People eat and prepare for the next length of our journey. They hang ward bags from their wagons and draw symbols on themselves, the horses, and the oxen. The gates open as the sun rises high enough in the sky to warm the air and bring light to each shadow.

We leave a warning to anyone who comes after us, carved into every door and gate. Some poor soul may need to stay here, a lone traveler or a foolish unsanctioned train.

My wagon pulls out first. Riders on horseback nervously surround the rest of the Caravan, rifles and pistols drawn. Marcus brings up the rear with two armed riders behind him. Roger and Garrett have been with the Caravan a few seasons now. I trust them to keep an eye out.

Chloe rides up on my right, her horse breathing loudly, its eyes skittish. "No new markings on the wall. I don't know what was out there last night, but it left no trace."

"Then let's move, and quickly."

I set the pace, brisk but not so as to tire us. I want us to reach the next campsite well before dark. We need twenty miles between the Winter Quarters and us.

Most creatures in the Infested have territory. Hopefully, whatever killed the caretakers and spent the night tormenting us will follow this rule. I don't usually run the animals this hard, but I need to. They can't do it every day, but it is worth it.

Only the wheels on the ground and riders on horseback make noise. The quiet is eerie and I know people are afraid. I wish to get home to my family. Maybe it *is* time for me to retire.

My tailbone aches with each bump and rattle of the wagon, and they are worse the faster we travel. I padded the small bench next to the brake, but it's still not comfortable.

I glance behind me to watch the Winter Quarters disappear as the dust rises in the air. When Marcus gets back West, he will need to find new caretakers. We can't leave the building abandoned. Who knows what will move in. They'll need to send Bonum to secure the area.

Today is a better day. The sky is less green, and the red turns purple and blue around the edges. I don't taste sulfur. The grass is still dry and sick, but I see rolling hills of green in the distance.

I feel better as we ride, passing trail markers and stones painted white, marking old graves. Will-o'-wisps hover under tree clusters and I catch a glimpse of dancing bone maidens further off the trail. Blue ghosts float over the grass, flickering in and out of existence. Seeing these doesn't bother me. They all come close to the fences in Ash Hollow. They are some of the benign creatures that come with the monsters. Content to leave people alone, unless you harass them.

At least on the trip back, we haven't had weather issues. It's a seven-month round trip, plus our time in Illinois. The Infested is unpleasant during the winter months with rain and snow, but it's not as dangerous. It's a gamble for the Caravan to leave Ash Hollow in November, but most of the creatures seem to hibernate when the temperature drops.

I am alert, eyes in front, but my other senses are straining around me, picking out odd sounds and smells. The burning sun bears down on the top of my hat.

Our Caravan isn't the biggest group I've traveled with, but not the smallest either. It's a calculation. Each wagon is chosen with purpose, the number significant. Too many, and you can't protect them; too little, and the train is like a moving feast.

Some of these people have been doing this for years. For a few, this is their first time out and it might be their last, or it may strengthen their resolve to travel again.

Ten miles away from the Winter Quarters, people begin to talk. It starts low and murmuring, and then the prayer singing starts. Not loud, not enough to draw attention, but enough that I know they feel safer. They are all off tune, but it's beautiful.

They sing a song for safe travel, protection, and blessings— a melody known to every child who grows up in the West. I taught it to my own children. While Avery and I do not have faith the way most from the West do, I've seen enough to know the power in words, in thoughts, in hope. Avery and I teach our children to respect the Infested, to fear it, and to maintain the wards fiercely. The prayer songs and blessings mingle nicely with these teachings.

I hope things are going well at home. This spring is a critical point for our children.

General makes a noise and my attention turns to my oxen. They are tense, and I murmur low to them. I raised these animals straight from the wombs of their mothers. They know me, know my voice.

Something is bothering them.

I motioned to Chloe, who always rides close to me. "Do you see anything, sense anything?"

Gripping her pinto hard with her thighs, Chloe releases the reins. She swivels in her saddle, watching the end of the Caravan, back the way we came. Her horse knows the way forward. She looks in every direction, closes her eyes, takes a deep breath.

"I don't see anything," she says, "but something's out there."

"Something new?" There's always something out there.

"I… I can't tell." She grabs the reins again with one hand, the other still gripping her gun. "It's like something is hiding the ley lines from me. I can sense them, but it's like looking at them through a warped mirror. Something's wrong this year, Harrison."

All I can do is push us forward faster. I don't want to scare anyone or go so fast an animal gets hurt or a wagon breaks, but I increase our speed just enough to see the sweat on my oxen, a little foam at their mouths.

The trees condense as we pass a trail marker telling us five miles to the next campsite. Branches loom over the path, casting shadows that writhe with movement.

"Shadow Stalkers," Chloe calls to the rider closest to her. It will travel down the train, ending with the rider behind Marcus.

"They always infest here," I mutter. "The government needs to come out and do a control burn, cut away all the trees."

The people know not to go into the shadows. No one who enters comes back out.

"You don't live in the proper West, Harrison. The government tries; people don't want to."

A giant black oak tree looms to the left, dead and rotting, waiting for its roots to give so it can fall, decomposing into the earth, feeding it. I am not sure if this tree was here when we came by a few months ago.

"That attitude gets people killed," I comment.

She only nods in agreement.

As I pass the dead tree, I look up. The sky is blue, tinged in purple, feeling more like home. Taking a deep breath, the air is clean and fresh. I slow my animals, who look more at ease, still tense but not wanting to run away in terror.

A few bouts of laughter come from behind me and I smile. I think of Marian and her infectious laugh, the giggles that come from her over anything presumed funny. Thoughts of them are the main thing that keeps me sane.

Then I hear screaming.

Chloe's horse starts, but she swings around and charges towards the back of the train. More voices cry out and gunshots thunder. I stop my wagon as quickly as possible, which isn't easy, and tie the reins around the brake handle with shaking hands.

I hear others screaming, crying, yelling questions to the riders. Standing to teeter on the narrow bench, I grip the canvas and peer over the back of my wagon.

Marcus's wagon has passed the dead oak tree, but ventured little further. It stands out like a macabre statue marking the land. One of the riders behind him is gone, his horse too.

"Watch my boys!" I call to the wagon behind me, a father with his two grown sons. One jumps down from their wagon and comes to soothe my beasts as I sprint down the length of the train.

I stay out of the shadows, skipping and jumping like a twisted game of hopscotch. What may not attack a wagon or an animal would see me as a fine lunch.

I reach Chloe at the end of the train. Marcus is pale as a sheet, trembling on his wagon's lazy board.

"What happened? Where's Roger?" I don't know why I ask.

I know what happened to Roger.

"As my wagon cleared that tree, something grabbed him," Marcus whispers. "I didn't see it. I only heard it."

I turn to Chloe. "Did you see it? Did anyone see it?"

"Just a glimpse, but I don't know what it was."

"I saw it," says Garrett, the other rider who'd ridden behind Marcus. He looks angry, not scared. He'll make this trip again in two years. He's seasoned like Chloe, and they've both seen worse.

"What was it?" I ask.

"The air near the tree shimmered, and there was a wall of black...."

I cringe. I know what's coming next.

"A large taloned... not really a hand... but I guess a hand?" Garrett shrugs. "Reached out and snagged Roger and his horse."

I glance back at the tree. It's a clear day, and I can see dust and indents from the train. There is no darkness now.

"Then Roger started screaming, and I heard..."

"It eating," Marcus says.

"Shit," Chloe breathes. "A Malum."

"A Malum," I agree.

"Should we go back and look for him?" Marcus asks.

Chloe glares at him. "That tree is probably the boundary for its territory. I don't know what woke it up, but when we get home, we'll have to carve out a new trail around this whole area or get a dozen Bonums out here to put it back in the ground. But if you want to be its dessert go for it."

I can tell she's annoyed with Marcus. Marcus knows better than to ask. This isn't his first Caravan either.

"Now we know what happened to the caretakers," Chloe says.

I grunt in agreement.

"We need to go," I tell them. "The further away from here, the better."

I feel antsy. We're too close for comfort and I would rather not feed that thing again.

I return to my wagon. We don't have time to grieve. We need to get to the campsite before the people's fear gnaws away and puts us in more danger.

I glance around as we begin our trek again. If a Malum has awoken in the Infested after a decade, what else has?

Chapter 6
May 1900
Day 5
Ash Hollow

Desi stood peering out the slats of the gate, staring into the vastness of green and brown that comprised the landscape. Pressed into the wood, feeling tiny pieces digging into her skin, she wondered about the land beyond. What she wouldn't give to be able to freely go past the gates, even the few feet to where the giant oak trees were, the grass beneath them lazily swaying in the spring breeze. Any time she'd ever been in the Infested, her guard was always up. She had to watch where she walked and how her sound carried, and keep an eye on her surroundings—and always under the supervision of her mother or aunt.

What would it be like to run free with no fences or buildings? To just take off and go? Her hands gripped the slat and she wiggled her fingers on the other side. They only ventured outside the gate when they had to. There were no leisurely strolls through the Infested, no games of hide and seek or picnics sitting in the soft azure grass that smelled like laundry. She wanted it, though. She wanted to lay in that grass, stare up into the color-changing sky, be free from her responsibilities, and embrace her magic fully.

Desi sighed and shook her head, as though the motion could rid her of the thoughts. That way lay madness. She knew what happened to Bonum who indulged those fantasies, and it wasn't pretty.

"Mom said you shouldn't do this," Helen said, coming up from behind her.

Helen didn't touch the gate, but she stood with shoulder touching Desi's, also looking through the wood to the other side.

"Mom's dead."

"I know that. We all know that. There's a reason she warned us not to dwell on life outside Ash Hollow, and you know it." Helen sighed and crossed her arms over her chest, giving her sister a side-eye.

"I can feel you scanning me. I'm fine."

"You're not. You're taking on too much."

"If not me, then who?"

Helen grabbed her and they faced each other. She stared at Desi in the way only Helen could, an all-knowing look like Helen could see into your soul. It was calming and uncomfortable.

"Lean on us," Helen said. "That's what we're here for. You aren't doing this alone. And soon, Father will be home. Staying out here, wishing you could pass the gate, is a bad way to go and you know it."

Desi let out a breath, her shoulders sagging. "I can't help it. I know you all feel it, too, especially Rowena. I don't want to leave our home, but I want to know what it's like out there."

"Scary, and you've seen what happens when a Bonum leaves their sanctuary for the Infested."

"Rowena wants to leave."

"She wants to go to a big city, not wander the plains like a ghost and dig deep into the earth until the soil covers you and…."

Helen took a deep breath and closed her eyes. "We all feel it, see? Now come inside and do something constructive."

"Another of Mom's mantras." Desi tried to laugh but couldn't, instead, she linked arms with her sister and they headed back to the house.

"What do you think of our guests, truly?" Helen asked.

"I don't care for Samael, but his sister is delightful."

"It is nice to have company, especially people our age."

"They can't stay here much longer. It's against the rules."

"As long as they aren't here when Father comes home, it won't matter. They aren't our rules. We can decide when we're tired of their company."

Desi closed the door as they entered the main room. She heard laughter from the kitchen—Ambrose and Samael.

"It's good for him to have company he can relate to," Helen said.

"Agreed, and we know Ambrose isn't foolish enough to get attached."

Helen gave her sister a peck on the cheek. "I have chores to finish."

Desi put a hand on Helen's thin arm. Raising a hand, she traced the gauntness in her sister's cheek. "Please eat some lunch. Ambrose made a pot of those grains you like. Add a little honey and milk to them?"

"Promise not to go back out to the gate?"

"Promise."

"Then I will, as soon as I take the dining room rug out and clean it."

They parted ways and Desi headed into the kitchen only to freeze, unsure of how to react. Samael was perched on the counter and Ambrose stood between his knees. They were laughing and smiling at each other, but it was comfortable, almost intimate.

"Hey, Desi," Ambrose said upon noticing her. "You need something?"

Stiffly, Desi walked around them to the icebox. "Just getting some tea and heading to my room. How's it going in here?" Her heartbeat was too fast. What was going on in here?

"Made a new batch. See if you can tell what's new."

Desi took the pitcher from the icebox, poured a glass of the amber-colored liquid, and took a deep sniff. "Mint?"

"She's good," Samael said. "It took me a few tries. Ambrose really is great in the kitchen."

He hopped down from the counter.

Desi's mind raced. She needed to speak to Ambrose alone. "Samael, Helen said she didn't have time for lunch until she cleaned the dining room rug. You wouldn't mind helping her carry it outside, would you?"

Ambrose nodded, showing he understood and went to the stove where the grains simmered.

"Yeah, no problem," Samael said. "I can't see Helen carrying out that rug by herself."

"She can, but it would make the process faster. I appreciate it."

Samael tipped an invisible hat and left.

"Helen promised to eat?" Ambrose asked.

"Yes. Get the cream and honey out too. And put a little something special in it, please."

"She'll notice."

"Not if you're subtle." She watched Ambrose putter around the kitchen and drank her tea. "So... what did I walk in on?"

"Walk in on? What are you talking about?"

"You and Samael looked cozy."

Ambrose paused his honey search and stared at her in shock. "Nothing! He's just interesting and nice! I feel, I don't know, comfortable around him."

"Be careful, okay? Marian has a huge crush on him, and she'll be devastated if you and he become… affectionate." Finishing her tea, she put her glass in the sink.

"No! It's not like that. Desi, come on. You know me better than that." Ambrose's face colored pink along the edges.

Desi held up her hands in surrender. "Okay, okay. Just checking. Let me know if Helen doesn't keep her promise. I'm going upstairs."

Upstairs, Desi passed the room Marian and Rowena shared and heard Rowena giggling. That wasn't like her sister. The door was cracked, so Desi peeked in. Sitting crisscross on Rowena's bed were Rowena and Lavellen. Knees touching, they leaned close together as they sewed on buttons and repaired holes, soft voices full of conversation.

Jealousy rose in Desi's breast. Not that someone would find Rowena interesting nor envious that her sister made a friend. No, this jealousy was more wanton in nature. *She* wanted to touch Lavellen's knees, be close enough to smell her breath, and see the strands of her hair.

She took a deep breath and walked away from the door. Anxiety and desire sent her heart racing. Dark thoughts filled her mind, overanalyzing possible outcomes and situations that would put her within touching distance of the blonde woman. She darted to her room, shut the door, and sank back against the rough wood. The door handle caught her skin as she slid to the floor. She hated to admit how lonely she'd been for a while now. It caused her imagination to work over time. Especially at night, before bed.

In her mind, each scenario ended with Lavellen repulsed, disinterested, angry, and accusing her of being a monster. But Desi couldn't get the thought of touching her to go away. It felt like a compulsion.

There's nothing you can do about this right now. Create a plan and forget the nonsense. She repeated the mantra in her head.

A plan was required, something simple. Lavellen was a guest in her home. Desi could simply strike up a conversation with her and see if they developed the same rapport she'd found with Rowena. And if not, there were worse things than disappointment.

Like Mother dying. Her chest constricted with grief.

Wait, what was she doing? Rowena was obviously interested in Lavellen and Desi had more important matters to dwell on than attraction to some woman.

"It's not like you've never seen a pretty girl before. Get a grip," Desi muttered to herself. She went with her parents to Wyoming sometimes. She'd seen attractive men and women. She'd never been able to get close enough to talk to them, let alone be allowed to touch them.

She could hear Rowena and Lavellen talking and laughing through the wall. What could they be talking about? Buttons and which types of thread worked best on linen?

Desi heard Rowena make a slight gasping noise, and then there was silence. Her mind could only guess at what they were doing and she didn't really want to hear it. Maybe she was making it all up and they were just quietly working on their pieces.

She heard another gasp and the ruffling of clothes, and she shut her eyes. This was Rowena's moment, not hers. Her mind's eye became full of Lavellen and how her porcelain skin looked and felt under her dress. Digging her nails into her arm, she forced the thoughts from her mind. She didn't have time for this fantasy. Work needed to be done. What was going on in her mind?

Lavellen's voice, murmuring in the silence, was almost too loud. Just the gentle waves of her voice lapping over Desi, drawing her back in.

She took several calming, deep breaths and wished her mother were here. Their mother always knew how to drive the evil thoughts, the anxious downpour, away.

Then she heard footsteps out in the hall—a soft knocking at her door.

Desi heaved herself to her feet and opened it. Rowena stood on the other side, flushed and rocking from foot to foot.

"Are you busy? Can I come in?"

"What's wrong?" Desi ushered her inside. They sat on the bed together and Rowena gripped her hands.

"I've done something, and I'm not sure… I don't know what to do." Her eyes glowed happily, but she worried her bottom lip.

"Tell me," Desi encouraged gently. "It's okay. You can tell me anything."

"Lavellen came up this morning so we could sew together…."

"I know. It's kind of you to let her have some of your things."

"We sat there, just talking. She knows all about types of cloth and patterns and asked if she could teach me a few fancy stitches she learned in, you know… a proper town." Rowena gripped her hands tighter.

"That's great. You don't get to talk to people about that stuff much, especially since Mom died." Desi didn't want to hear anymore, but this was her sister. If something was making her happy *and* upset, she needed to listen, to help.

"She kept moving closer to me, telling me about dress shops and bakeries. Things we only read about in books. I'm so jealous! I want to see those things. Then, she just leaned forward and pressed her lips against mine! I was shocked. You know I've never kissed anyone, and she's a girl! But her lips were soft and her breath smelled like cloves. I let her kiss me, and she…." Rowena blushed.

"Yes? It's okay. Tell me."

"She put her tongue in my mouth and pushed me backward, touching my breasts and.... well, it all felt so good. I wanted her to touch me everywhere. Have you ever felt like that?" Rowena's cheeks flushed as she closed her eyes.

"No," Desi said, "but I've read about it."

She'd craved it, fantasized about it even, but when would she have experienced it? When would any of them have had the opportunity?

"Then she stopped and pulled away, told me she had things to do and would see me later." Rowena sighed sadly.

"Probably a good thing, right?"

"Why would that be a good thing?" Rowena asked irritably, eyes flashing open.

"Mother always said sex isn't something to do lightly. You've only known her a few days, and she's leaving."

Rowena opened her mouth and shut it. She looked like she was considering Desi's words. "I guess you're right. It's just out here— Well, I'm not likely to have the same chance at these experiences. If she wants to do it again, I will."

"That's your choice, and I respect it. Let me know if it's... nice." Desi choked out the word.

"Thanks, Desi. I don't know what we would do without you."

After she left, Desi pinched her upper arm until the pain made her other emotions recede.

She wanted her mom. She couldn't have her mother back, but she *could* go into her mother's room. The room needed cleaning. It was as close to her as she could get without crawling down into the ground with her. She could strip the bed and scrub everything. Make sure when her father came home, no trace of death or sickness remained.

Desi quietly opened her bedroom door. Tiptoeing down the hall, she opened the last door—her parents' bedroom. The room was dark. No one had been in to open the curtains. No one had been in there at all, not since they found her. It still smelled like her mother, the harsh laundry soap they used, and the little cheesecloth packs of cinnamon and rosemary to keep away moths and other bugs. The slight tinge of sick and death hid behind the herbs, and Desi wanted it gone. She would air out this room and make it shine, just like when Mom was alive.

As she started across the room to open the curtains, she caught a glimpse of movement on the bed not five feet from her—and froze.

Red eyes blinked at her from on top of the coverlet. From the light shining through the door to the hallway, she could see a swirling mass of black shadows on the bed.

She took a step back, those hellish glowing eyes tracking her every move.

Another step away from the bed and fear threatened to paralyze her. The temperature plummeted as the creature smiled—the same blinding white smile, vast and horrible with too many teeth.

Her fight or flight instincts slammed into her. She lashed out with magic and it *screamed*, a sound she heard only in her mind, a curdling echo that made her head pound. Desi scrambled away, almost slamming into the wall in her haste, heart in her throat. Her only thought for safety and light, even when she stood in the hallway, the door to her parents' bedroom closed firmly between her and those piercing eyes.

Chapter 7
May 1900
Day 7
Ash Hollow

"Hey, Desdemona! Wait up!"

Desi watched as Lavellen ran to catch up with her. Her tiny boots left delicate footprints in the dirt path. One hand gripped her sunshine-colored skirt so it didn't drag, another holding her straw bonnet to her head, wisps of yellow hair escaping.

"Is something wrong?" Desi asked as Lavellen skidded to a halt in front of her, gasping for air. Desi towered over the dainty woman. They all did, by at least a foot. Compared to Lavellen, Desi felt like a clodding giant.

"What? No, everything's fine. Marian said you were going to walk part of the fence and strengthen the wards, and I wanted to join you."

She was correct. Desi had been checking the wards every morning. She had to find out how that thing got in. No one had seen it again yet, so Desi was determined to figure out where it came from. But she didn't know why Lavellen would be interested.

"Why?"

"Well, to be honest, there's only so much sewing I can do, and I wanted to spend time with you. Is that wrong?"

"You could help with the garden or the animals," Desi suggested.

"Ugh, animals. Aside from our horses, I stay away from them. And I've played in the dirt enough this week, my fingernails are stained." She held up her hands to show off the broken nails and thin dirt lines under them.

"Okay, then." Desi still felt confused, but here was her chance to talk to someone else, to make a friend, a connection. "We're going past the well to the fence near the cemetery. Come on."

As the pair made their way over, Lavellen said, "I was sorry to hear about your mother."

"Thank you. Are... I mean, where are your parents?" The walk was familiar, the ground always the same. Desi could walk this path blindly. The garden loomed to their left, splashes of color and warmth, green and fresh and smelling of herbs, tangy and sweet.

"Our... father... died when we were born. We don't know what happened to our mother. One day, she was just gone. That was when Samael decided we should go East and start a new life."

Go East? Desi thought that meant Marian was wrong. They weren't Bonum. Bonum weren't allowed in the East. If a Bonum was caught in the East, they were jailed—or worse—and eventually sent back to the West. Bonum had no rights in the East, where they were considered no better than the malevolent creatures of the Infested.

"I'm sorry to hear that. I don't know what we would do if Mom and Dad hadn't always been around. It's..." Desi struggled to find the words, absentmindedly gripping the key around her neck, "hard to keep everything running smoothly when both of them are gone."

"I don't even really want to go East," Lavellen admitted. "But what was I going to do in Nevada without Samael? If he went without me, I'd never see him again. I wouldn't know if he was dead or alive. So, I told him I'd come. Look how well that turned out."

"You'll make it. Your timeline has just changed. The Caravan goes every other year and they seldom lose anyone. The Infested can be scary, but if you respect it and keep your guard up, you'll get the rest of the way."

"I think that was part of the problem. Samael is great, but I don't think he did as much research as he should have."

Desi glanced at her. "Didn't you do any yourself? You didn't talk to Caravan members or trail guides?"

Lavellen giggled. "No, which was stupid. I trusted Samael. I won't be doing that again."

They were halfway to the large, grey stone well. As small children, Desi and her siblings pretended it was a wishing well until Marian made a wish that came true in an awful way. It wasn't the well's doing, but that had been easier to blame.

"There are many books in the parlor on the Infested and Father keeps journals of the things he sees," Desi said. "We always let guests look through them. Father says that anyone who travels the Infested needs to be as educated as they can."

"Oh, that'd be wonderful! I wonder if I can get Samael to read them too—"

Lavellen tripped over a rock and Desi reached out to steady her, keeping a hand on her until her footing was solid. When Desi made to let go, Lavellen smiled up at her and held on, moving her fingers until they were holding hands.

The contact caused butterflies to fill Desi's stomach and she hoped her palms would stay dry. Lavellen's hand was soft and smooth, warm.

Lavellen's thumb brushed across sensitive skin and Desi flushed from head to toe. Wasn't Lavellen interested in Rowena? Was hand-holding merely a sign of friendship? Desi held hands with her siblings and sometimes her mother, but she'd read that it could be used for romantic affection.

"Tell me, Desi, what's the creepiest thing you've seen out there?"

Desi considered her words before answering. Did Lavellen want something genuinely awful? Or just a small fright? "There are these... fish... I guess. Sometimes we get a few of them if the ward across the river fades even a little. Nothing like a bigger section of river or a lake would."

"Fish demons!" Lavellen gasped.

"They're small and, in few numbers, easy to deal with. But when too many of them gather, they create one large fanged fish monster called Malus Piscis. It will poison up to a mile of water and attack anything that comes near it."

"And you've seen one?"

"Of course. They aren't that uncommon and easy enough to handle if you know what you're doing." Desi puffed out her chest with pride. Memories of hunting and capturing the ugly fish with her mother were easy to recall.

"Wow."

"Would you like to see something weird and uncanny?"

"Yes, but not something too dangerous!" Lavellen's soft pink tongue licked her lips and Desi's gaze fixed on it.

How would those lips and tongue taste? She shook off the decadent thought. After all, if she really wanted to know, she could ask Rowena. Bitterness filled her before she beat it back, tiny tendrils of anxiety filling her belly.

There was a dead stump of a tree cut down years before she was born. A little off the path, but worth it. Lavellen followed her to the knee-high stump.

"A tree stump?"

"Not everything is bad," Desi said. "A major rule if you travel through the Infested."

The stump bore hundreds of small holes where its pale brown bark flaked off. Desi tapped it with her foot and dragged Lavellen back a few feet. All at once, a hundred tiny bugs swarmed from the holes. Very small, each was a bright sapphire blue and scuttled along on ten legs. Lavellen squealed and gripped Desi's hand tighter.

"Don't worry," Desi murmured. "Watch."

The bugs never left the stump, but rather covered it until it shone a bright blue. Then the wave shivered and swept into the holes as the bugs retreated. The stump, however, didn't look nearly as rotten and sad.

"What?"

"Hyacims. It's why our garden flourishes and we have so many fruit and vegetable varieties. They bring life to the ground they inhabit, and they heal plants and soil of any kind." Desi smiled at the astonished look on Lavellen's face.

"Do they heal people too?"

"No. They're actually toxic, so I wouldn't advise touching or ingesting them."

"That's still incredible! Now show me this ward thing."

A small wooden fence framed the large plot of land to their right. Large rocks bore family names carved into their faces and near the center of the cluster, Desi spotted the mound of dirt where their mother lay.

The cemetery used to be calming to sit among the dead. It was a place without magic, just an empty, peaceful space that smelled of grass and the tang of rock. She could trace the names in the stone and cling to the knowledge that her family was more than just her parents, siblings, and Foni. She couldn't bear to walk among the dead now, not when her mother was freshly rotting feet down.

Grief sank merciless claws into her and she drew a pained breath.

"Desdemona? Are you alright?"

"Yes. We better hurry. I have other things to do." She pushed on.

"It's okay to be sad, you know. You don't have to be strong for them all the time."

Desi ignored her words, even as they hit home, and dropped Lavellen's hand. Lavellen's smile faltered. Desi didn't want to upset her, but she didn't want her advice, not about that.

Lavellen paused, pursing her lips.

"What?" Desi asked.

"Why don't you burn your dead? Aren't you afraid of something using them against you?"

"Bonum don't rise, and the wards protect from anything that might try and use the bodies unkindly," Desi said. "There's the fence."

She walked up to the twenty feet of fence that needed ward renewal.

"It looks like all the other fencing," Lavellen said. She put her hands on her hips and leaned closer, inspecting the wood and wire with narrowed eyes.

"To you, but look now."

Throwing caution to the wind, Desi grabbed her hand again, pulling her tight against her. Lavellen gasped, cheeks turning pink as they pressed chest to chest, thigh to thigh.

"Look," Desi commanded, tilting her head towards the fence.

"Oh my," Lavellen breathed.

This piece of fence trembled within the world, wavering in and out of focus, a pale grey while the fence around it glowed silver, solid and present.

"If the color fades and it disappears, the ward has totally failed," Desi explained.

"It's beautiful!" Lavellen's small hands wrapped around Desi's waist and squeezed. "Thank you."

Lavellen kissed her lightly on tiptoes, feathering her sweet little mouth across Desi's lips. Desi stood still, relishing in her first kiss. Lavellen's breath was spicy against her own.

Confused and aching for something she didn't understand, Desi pulled away. Lavellen wasn't Bonum. She couldn't touch the magic for too long, or something would notice her.

"This will only take a few minutes, then we can go back and maybe...."

What could she offer to keep Lavellen's attention? And what about Rowena? She couldn't hurt Rowena. Hadn't she just warned Ambrose away from Samael?

"Ambrose made some cake. It's his specialty. We could eat and have lemonade?" Were those really her words?

"I would love that!" Lavellen beamed and rocked on her heels.

Desi placed both her large hands on the fence and closed her eyes. The wards felt weaker than they should be. Something had been testing the fence, something big. She pushed power into them and, within minutes, the fence snapped solid, blinding her with bright silver light.

"Okay," Desi said. "Let's go."

Their cake was not to be had. Desi saw her siblings all coming up the path, intense and fearful expressions on their faces.

"How about a rain check? They need to speak with you, obviously," Lavellen said, disappointment in each word.

"I'm sorry. How about in the morning? Breakfast cake?"

"I have… plans… in the morning, but midmorning tea would be perfect." Lavellen winked at her and walked away.

Rowena spoke first when they convened. "Why was Lavellen out here with you?"

"Rowena, that's not important!" Marian exclaimed as they gathered in a half-circle.

"She said she was bored and wanted to watch me replenish the wards," Desi replied.

"Oh. Well then," Rowena said, pouting.

"I know you're besotted, but we need to talk," Ambrose said.

"I saw that shadow creature again, lurking near the shed," Helen breathed, hand on her chest. "Scared me to death."

"You did? I haven't seen it since it was in Mother's room," Desi said. After fleeing the room, she'd gathered her siblings up and told them what happened. They were all on high alert.

"It's cocky, I'll say that." Ambrose asked, "What are we going to do about it?"

"Kill it," Rowena said.

"We don't even know what it is!" Marian exclaimed.

"You could make a wish," Desi suggested.

Immediately, Marian's expression hardened.

Desi didn't suggest it lightly, but their mother had always said that in the presence of danger, you ought to use all your arsenal. While Desi and Helen had broader magic like their mother, Rowena, Ambrose and Marian's magic was more niche. They had gifts, singular things that they could do with magic and nothing else.

"I don't do that. *Ever*," Marian said. "You know the backlash is always worse than what the gift gives."

"Whatever we do, it needs to be fast," Helen said. "I don't think it can live in Ash Hollow without feeding. I've found two dead animals, and I think they were drained of their souls beforehand. Eventually, it will try to prey on people."

An uneasy silence hung in the air between them for a moment.

"Rowena, I'll need you to build a cage," Desi said.

"I can do that. My one specialty, coming up."

"Something special," Desi said. "This thing can phase through solid objects and affect them at the same time."

Her sister nodded.

"You'll need to find out what it is first," Ambrose said. "Check mom's books. Ask... umm... Well, just ask."

"This is going to be my last special job for the household," Rowena announced.

"What?" Ambrose asked, pinning her with a glare.

"I'm planning to go with the Caravan when Dad gets back. I've made up my mind, and I'm going to try my luck in Salt Lake unless Lavellen asks me to go with her."

"I cannot *believe* this is how you chose to tell us!" Marian screeched, eyes filling with tears.

"Traitor!" Ambrose growled.

"You don't mean that," Helen whispered.

Desi held up a hand for silence, reminiscent of their mom. She wasn't surprised, but she *was* ashamed. She had put off talking to her sister and there was something that Rowena needed to know about how their magic worked. She deserved to know, even if it wouldn't change her mind.

"Rowena," Desi started, "you can't be gone too long—"

"You have no say in that," Rowena argued. "I'm leaving and I am *not* coming back."

"But, Rowena, you should know—"

"Stop! I don't want to hear it!" Rowena shouted.

"I'm trying to warn you—"

"There's nothing to warn me about." Rowena crossed her arms over her chest, feet planted for battle.

"There is. Maybe you and I could talk later-"

"*No*. There's nothing you could say that will change my mind."

"Fine." Desi sighed. Rowena would have to learn the hard way. She'd always been stubborn. If she wouldn't listen, Desi wouldn't waste her breath.

"Desi!" Marian exclaimed. "How can you just accept this?"

"Don't assume you know how I feel."

"But…"

"Rowena, you obviously won't listen to me and I'm not going to fight with you on this," Desi said to her. "I would ask you something for me, before you leave."

"Fine," Rowena said.

"Make sure you've done as much as you can beforehand. Sewing, building, anything you can think of that will help out—and above all else, build me that cage." Her other siblings looked at her in shock, but Desi shrugged her shoulders.

Rowena had decided she wanted this path. She wouldn't listen to reason and their mother wasn't here to talk her out of it.

"I wouldn't leave you in the lurch," Rowena said before spinning away and storming off.

"But she is, in a way, isn't she?" Helen asked softly.

They nodded in unison.

Chapter 8
May 1900
Day 9
Ash Hollow

A scream echoed through the house, shrill and frightening.

Desi sat in the office, doing work so boring she had fallen asleep. Between the stress of her father being late, the drama with her siblings, and the shadow creature, she wasn't sleeping well.

The scream woke her, jerking her, heart beating a thousand times a minute.

Rushing from the room, head and eyes moving to find the noise source. She glanced at the panel leading downstairs, thankfully it was closed. She heard the scream again.

"Lavellen!" Rowena called from somewhere upstairs.

Desi couldn't see her because the shadow demon blocked her view.

It loomed over Lavellen's figure as she clung to the railing, trying to escape it. The monster flickered in and out of existence, like a hazy blink, the ink-like tendrils of its form flowing over the walls and staircase as if to snuff out the brightness of Lavellen's clothing and life force.

"What's going on?" Samael demanded as he and Marian raced in from the dining room. "*Lavellen!*"

Ambrose skidded to a halt, rushing in from the kitchen. "What in Spirit's name?"

"Keep calm, Lavellen," Rowena commanded. "Desi, do something!"

Lavellen gripped the staircase, hiding her head as she sobbed in terror. Her sobs ripped through the room as loudly as her screams.

Desi paused.

Aside from Lavellen, there was no other sound. The creature was silent as it floated, lending another level of eerie. For a moment, it felt like time stopped. Desi's mind scrambled. What should she do? Fear for Lavellen, anger at the shadow creature, and the heart-pounding need to protect those in her care all warred within her.

And then...

The thing began to laugh, a light sound coming from so dark a creature. It sounded crazed and yet joyful.

"Stop!" Desi yelled out, not sure what else to do.

She'd never encountered something so powerful before, at least not without her mother.

Hell-red and bright eyes focused on her, and Desi felt warm, not just like on a mild summer day, but as if she were being baked from the inside. Sweat beaded across her forehead. Her nose itched, the tingling sensation starting to burn.

"Desi, it'll boil us!" Marian openly cried as she clung to Samael, who didn't look like he would be standing up for very long.

It smiled, and Lavellen cried out again as it leaned over her with that shockingly white grin full of teeth. The room sweltered and the smell of decaying flowers permeated the air.

"Great, it's scary *and* it's smelly," Rowena grumbled from somewhere upstairs, but Desi could hear the panic in her voice.

"Do something!" Rowena yelled down at her.

Do what? Desi had no idea what would stop it, but she had to do something. With every second that ticked away, Lavellen's cries softened, and Desi worried the thing was leeching her life away.

Closing her eyes, Desi reached deep inside herself and pulled on the magic that tied her to the land, imagining a ball of light to toss at the creature. She could feel it blossom within her, cooling the unnatural heat. She raised her hands to collect it between her palms. Opening her eyes, she threw it.

Too late, it moved quickly and Lavellen fell back, tumbling down the stairs. It focused one last time on Desi and her heart stopped beating for a few seconds. Something about its face was so familiar—then she blinked, and it was gone.

"Helen!" Desi called as they all rushed to Lavellen's side.

Unconscious, with her cheek pressed against the floor and her limbs splayed, Lavellen looked like a broken doll. Desi couldn't see any blood, but the poor woman was too still and pale.

"Marian, make a wish to bring Helen here, now!" Ambrose yelled.

Marian bit her lip and her cheeks flushed. She looked like she wanted to refuse.

"I wish Helen would hurry up and get here." She sucked in a breath and let go of Samael.

He almost fell, steadying himself on the wall, and looked at her incredulously. She ran to the bathroom and Desi heard her retching. One of the wall sconces chose that moment to fall, crashing at Samael's feet, almost hitting him. He startled, jumping back, falling onto his butt, eyes wide but not seeing.

"Samael, get in a chair and stay out of the way," Desi snapped.

He didn't move.

"Lavellen, oh no!" Rowena knelt at the girl's side. "Dearest, no!"

She reached out and Desi moved to stop her. A hint of jealousy tugged at Desi. *Dearest?* Were they using pet names now?

Pale and trembling, Desi spoke in a warbling voice. "No, don't touch her until Helen gets here. You don't know how hurt she is."

Rowena stilled and settled on petting Lavellen's hair, cooing and talking in hushed tones. Lavellen didn't react.

Helen ran into the room moments later, out of breath with her medicine bag clutched in her arms. "Hey, what's going on? I had a feeling you needed me—" She stopped and stared at the scene, her expression hardening. Smooth and efficient, she swept over to Lavellen's side as she opened her bag.

Marian came back, breathing more comfortably, and wrapped an arm around Samael's waist to help him stand. She pulled Samael away to sit on the settee. She hugged him to her chest, fussing and consoling, rubbing her hands against his arms.

"Ambrose, tea. Quickly and as soothing as you can make it, please," Desi said, watching as Ambrose glared at Marian and Samael. When he didn't divert his attention from them, she snapped, "Ambrose!"

"Yes, yes. Tea, soothing. Coming."

Helen began running her hands over Lavellen, a soft song coming from between her lips and a pale silver glow from her fingers.

"Can't you just wish her better?" Samael asked, shuddering in Marian's arms.

Marian's face went from flushed purple to tinged in green. "No, Samael. Just no. It wouldn't... wouldn't be good. I'm sorry." She swallowed what Desi knew to be bile.

Marian got sick just thinking about her gift. Using it was worse. And the bigger the wish, the sicker it made her.

"Please?" Samael whispered. His haunted gaze never left his prone sister.

"Samael, enough," Desi said. "She can't."

It wasn't enough for her gift to sicken her. Just like a genie in a fairy story, Marian's gift twisted wishes. The bigger the wish, the more likely it would go horribly wrong. There was cause and effect with no rhyme or reason, and they'd learned this the hard way. A fallen sconce was tame. They'd gotten lucky this time.

"Why didn't you do something?" Rowena's accusation caught Desi off guard.

"Excuse me?"

"*You're* the powerful Bonum. Why didn't you do something?" Rowena hauled herself to her feet to be eye-level with Desi.

"I know I wasn't fast enough, Rowena. No need to rub it in my face." She'd tried, honestly. Her stomach turned as anxiety filled it, like furious moths burrowing in her skin. She'd be up all night, agonizing over her hesitation. She didn't need it from her sister, too.

"It just happened too fast," Marian jumped to her defense. "Back off, Rowena."

Samael laid his head on her shoulder, eyes tightly shut.

"Have you figured out what it is yet?" Rowena returned her attention to Desi. "The cage is almost done."

"No, but I will. Have I ever let you down before?"

Rowena didn't answer.

"Both of you hush," Helen said. "Let me work. Rowena, help me turn her over."

"Are you sure?"

"Rowena!"

Rowena helped turn Lavellen over, wincing at the bright bruise forming on Lavellen's cheek and how her nose was crooked and bleeding.

"Is she breathing?" Samael asked, refusing to look.

"Yes," Helen said. "I can detect nothing serious. A broken nose, a knock to the head, and some bruising. She shouldn't be unconscious."

"Are you sure?" Rowena asked, violet freckles more prominent as her gray skin paled to white.

"Of course, I am. Give me space to work and I'll see what I can find."

As Desi watched the unconscious Lavellen, she felt something inside her shift. As she stared at the girl, she recalled how they'd spent several mornings, long before Rowena awoke, having a quiet breakfast together. Lavellen's sweet prettiness was a stark contrast with the bland environment. Desi had always felt happy after spending time with Lavellen.

Desi took a step back as Rowena fussed and paced around the prone girl. Helen passed her hands over her in steady, familiar patterns.

Was this the same girl who had been laughing at her jokes only this morning? For some reason, it felt like Desi was looking at a stranger.

Desi shook her head like she was trying to get water from her ears. What had she been doing? Had she seriously thought Lavellen would choose her over Rowena? Desi would never hurt her sister. How had she even considered flirting with Lavellen? She concentrated and tried to find the feelings she'd been having ever since Lavellen and Samael showed up. They were gone.

Now it was like she was seeing someone different and those emotions were distant and cold. Who was this stranger on the ground who had wormed her way into their lives?

Gone were the daydreams about them growing old together. Rocking on the porch, sipping sweet tea, deliciously in love. Something was very wrong. She shivered; it felt unnatural.

"I can do nothing else," said Helen. "Help me get her to the guest house and into bed."

"Desi? Are you okay?" Ambrose came into the room, a steaming cup of tea in his hands.

Desi blinked a few times and frowned. There was something—it felt just out of reach... an explanation—but she couldn't find it.

"Desi?" Ambrose asked again.

"I'm fine," she said. "Help Samael."

Ambrose gently wrapped Samael's hands around the cup of tea and bid him drink. Desi narrowed her eyes at the dreamy look on Ambrose's face as he gazed at Samael.

"Drink this," he murmured, his voice soothing.

Desi had never seen her brother look so tenderly at someone. A chill went through her.

Something was wrong here.

Rowena picked up Lavellen, the other woman slight against her large frame. Helen, Samael, and Marian followed them out the front door toward the guest house.

"I should go with them," Ambrose commented.

"I think that's an awful idea," Desi said.

Ambrose glared at her.

"Watch yourself, brother. Now, sit here and keep watch until I come back."

She went to the secret panel and descended into the basement. She needed answers.

She was upset; of course, she was. Lavellen was hurt and her siblings were acting strangely, and she felt like her emotions were arguing with each other, and a shadow creature seemed to be hunting them. She had to prioritize. First she'd find out what the shadow creature was, and then she'd tackle the mystery surrounding their guests.

The torches lit. She palmed the key around her neck as she reached the door. Turning it in the lock, she took a steadying breath.

Those dreams were not reality. This was.

Sweet bird song and music met her upon entry. She needed to speak to Foni.

"Back so soon?" Medi asked as she passed his cage.

"Hush, you."

"What's wrong?" Foni asked from where she was curled up in the shadows, nothing but her bright eyes visible.

"There's a creature on the farm," Desi said, "inside the wards."

Laughter came, sweet and insane, from the Crassa Umbra—victims of the Malum.

"Impossible," Foni said. "Nothing short of a troupe of Malums could break the wards."

"It has. It's a shadow creature with glowing red eyes and a mouth full of teeth. I've never seen anything like it."

Foni remained silent, but the light of her eyes blinked out.

"Foni?"

"She's hiding from you," Medi said. "Doesn't want to tell you the truth."

A soft humming agreed with him as a sickening lullaby was tapped out by the Coryformia chained to the wall.

Foni *never* hid from her. When they were little girls, they'd played together, sharing secrets and laughter. She'd felt closer to Foni than the siblings she'd shared a womb with.

"Foni?"

Nothing.

"Do you remember when Aunt Serenity died?" Desi asked, and she didn't expect an answer. Of course Foni recalled the death of her mother. "When you hated Marian with every breath in your body? You never hid the hateful things you wanted to do to her, and I didn't judge you. I held you when you cried."

They'd been sixteen.

Still, her words were met with silence. Then laughter came from behind her and more sickeningly sweet music.

"And when you couldn't get past your hate and anger?" Desi continued. "When you started to turn and use your magic? When you'd sneak outside the wards and began to change? I hid it from Mom and Dad. *I* was the one who snuck you out to leave us when you couldn't control it anymore."

Finally, a sound. A sigh—or was it a half sob?

"I begged Mom and Dad to let you back when you came, keening, to the gate. You're my best friend, and I need help now. Foni? Do you know what it is? We need to capture it. The thing already hurt someone."

Desi gasped and took a step back as Foni appeared on the other side of the bars. Her long fingers curled around them as her shadow hair pushed against the barrier, unable to get past the iron and magic.

Up close, Foni was a beautiful nightmare, painful to look directly at. A Bonum who lost their way, who ran wild on the plains.

"You can't capture it," Foni said, "not if it's what I think it is."

"What do you think it is?"

"Desi, you need to let me go."

"What! You're talking crazy, Foni. You don't want to be let out."

"I need to leave here, and you need to let me. Please?"

"Foni, you surrendered yourself to us. You made Mother and I promise that no matter what, we were to keep you contained."

"I've changed my mind. It's not like I'm dangerous, and I can't stay here."

"Why? Is it because of the shadow creature? Foni, you're scaring me."

Foni sighed, long and deep, and slipped back into the corners. "I know, I'm sorry. Sometimes it gets to me, to be so confined."

"I promise, I'm still looking for a way to cure you. If I find it, I will."

From the moment Foni appeared at the gate, asking for asylum, Desi and her mother tried to find a way to reverse the wild in her. To suck out the excess magic so Foni could be a normal Bonum again. So far, nothing had worked.

It broke her mother's heart.

"I know," Foni said softly. "I know."

"Please tell me what you know."

"I think you should dig up your mother and see for yourself."

****

They waited until night. Samael kept a close watch on Lavellen, who had yet to wake. Ash Hollow was as quiet as it could get. With the animals asleep, the main sounds were the chirp of insects, the soft sigh of wind, and the whispering of the river.

"I don't know why we're doing this," Marian said, tapping her shovel against one foot.

"Because Foni told me to."

"Ah, since Foni said it, we must obey, eh?" Ambrose mocked.

"Stop that. She's family."

"Barely. My last memory of her was of her eyes the day before she ran away. Just bright purple glowing in her face. You and

Mother are the only ones to have contact with her since," Rowena pointed out, burying her shovel into the pile of dirt covering their mother's casket.

"She's our cousin."

"We are painfully aware of that," Marian said. She flinched whenever the subject was brought up.

"She's dangerous," Helen said, lifting her shovel to start digging.

"Mother said she wasn't," Ambrose commented.

"Mother wouldn't lie," Desi said. "Now dig. Let's see what we'll find."

"A rotting corpse, so don't mind the smell."

"Ambrose!" Helen scolded.

"Enough talk," Rowena commanded. "If we're going to do this, we're doing it. Now dig."

They dug in silence. Sweat cooled in the night air. Shovel after shovel moved the dirt until Marian's hit, a solid thunk as it connected with the wood coffin Rowena built.

They cleared off the rest of it before Helen dropped down into the grave and dusted off the lid. She placed a hand on the top and closed her eyes, saying a small prayer for the dead.

"Who's gonna open it?" Ambrose asked.

"I will." Desi dropped in next to Helen.

She sniffed, not smelling anything but dirt and Helen's perspiration. Maybe the coffin and cool dirt would make their mother's condition more tolerable. What could she have taken with her to the grave that would help them now? Had they missed something on her? In her dress?

"Why couldn't Foni just tell you what we're looking for?" Rowena asked.

"We were hasty burying her. Maybe she's got something in one of her pockets?" Helen suggested, almost reading Desi's mind.

"I hope so, or I broke a nail for nothing." Marian pouted.

"Marian, I'm the only one allowed to use bad humor," Amsbrose chided. "I thought you knew that."

"If we don't laugh, we'll cry," Marian said, shrugging.

Using the small crowbar, Desi began prying open the lid. With each creak and snap, trepidation filled her. She didn't want to look upon their dead mother again. Once was quite enough.

She wrenched the lid open, eyes tightly closed.

Marian screamed.

"I'll catch her!" Rowena called out.

Had Marian fainted? Still, Desi could not look.

Was it really that bad?

"Oh, Desi, oh no!" Helen inhaled.

She heard someone vomit.

Forcing her eyes open, she investigated the coffin, but what she saw rooted her with horror and shock.

"No... That... that can't be." Nausea rose in her stomach.

Their mother wasn't in her grave, but ten deep, horrid grooves were on the inside of the lid.

Chapter 9
April 1900
The Caravan

We are two days out from Fort Kearney and things are peaceful. Not every day is filled with horror and death in the Infested. There are lovely things too—prairies full of wildflowers, roaming buffalo, and various deer. White fluffy clouds dot an endless blue sky and the night sky can shimmer as bright as day with the stars.

Will-o'-Wisps dance far off from the caravan as we set up camp. The marked wagon rest is old and needs to be replaced, but it's as safe as it comes outside of a warded area. It lies near a stream that runs fresh and clear, without taint, with enough grass to graze the animals.

The wagons circle within the marked space, riders herd the animals inside, and I watch as people decide whether to camp on the ground and risk being nosed awake by an ox or sleep in their hard wagon bed.

It's late afternoon, and I pushed as hard as I was comfortable with to get here. I look forward to a rest before going on to the Fort.

Lettie starts a large fire and begins to cook. We caught some fresh, untainted game this morning and, using some of the precious vegetables and cornmeal, it looks to be the makings of a fine supper. We will restock at Fort Kearney, so I'm not worried that supplies are low.

Everyone is on edge. They know as well as I do that just because the Infested is quiet does not mean it is safe. The Infested has moods and cycles, like people and the weather.

Marcus gets out his fiddle and music starts, low and pleasant. He raises his eyebrows at me and I nod slowly. This is okay, but no louder. Music can attract specific attention. Some creatures in the Infested are attracted to noise or emotion. Others attack at random and some enjoy the hunt. Many don't care about humans at all and are safe to watch—from a distance.

Chloe rides with another man around the wagons to make sure all the ward bags are in place, touching each one and instilling it with a bit of her magic.

Several smaller fires are lit and the tense faces around me relax slightly.

Walking to mine and Marcus's wagons, I step between them so that I am within the wagon rest but can see the plains without anything in my way. I want to get a feel for the land, and it's impossible with so many people around. We make too enticing of a target. I can't imagine how any of the earlier pioneers made it West. With such large wagon trains, they would be easy prey.

I can't shake the feeling that something is wrong with this whole trip. I really want to get home to my kids and my Avery. Other, more political thoughts also weigh on my mind.

"Something up, Harrison?" Chloe asks.

She's on my left, staring out as I am. Watching the sunset. Splashes of crimson and mauve along the horizon.

I turn my attention to her. "I'm not happy about the news coming from the West."

"Agreed, but we're running out of space and the government wants to see if a few more homesteads could be successful." She shrugs.

"You know the few that are already out here are the exception, not the rule. We made this land awful when we tried to the first time, and no good can come of more humans in the Infested."

"Preaching to the choir," she says, but pauses and cocks her head.

"You feel it?" I ask.

"I feel off—itchy."

She has good instincts.

"Me too, and I'm not Bonum." I return my gaze to the horizon, enjoying the colors.

"Before the Malum, the trip was already rough, but things have been good the last week at least, easy even."

She doesn't say what we're both thinking: too easy.

On any other trip, I'd calm her with soft words and make her laugh with tales from my farm. A typical caravan year sees maybe one death and a scattering of Infested inhabitants, most harmless. This was not a typical caravan year.

"Things are stirring here," I say. "You need to tell the government to send out a team when you get home. We need new wagon rests, with proper wards, and a ley line study."

She snorts. "They won't. They'll cancel the caravans first. You can't have it both ways; more security, but fewer people."

"It's been years since they sent Bonums into the Infested, and they're due for it." A team of primarily Bonums would be safe in the Infested and they could establish new wagon rests, clear out the Malum, retake the Winter Quarters, and study why the Infested felt treacherous, even more so, as of late.

That's how I met my wife, my Avery. She and her sister were on a team that helped set up a new warded fort and clear out an extensive group of Shadow Stalkers. They also took samples of animals and wildlife back to the West for study, giving us a better advantage with future caravans.

"They won't do it, especially not with a Malum in this area."

"The Malum needs to be taken care of. It's in too prominent a place, too close to the trail."

"I don't think they'll listen to Marcus or me."

"I'll write up a report for you. They normally take my advice."

"You could come back with us."

"I've been gone from home long enough. I trust you and Marcus to take the caravan from Ash Hollow to Laramie without incident."

"Harrison, I'm serious. They won't listen. You haven't heard talk about the railroad they want to put through here. They are saying a fast train would be safe through the plains."

I turn to her. I had heard rumors, but the government can't be serious. Which I say to Chloe. She sighs and gives me a look that tells me I'm aggravating her. I grin.

"The East and West have been in talks for months. Plus, they want to install those new telephone lines the East is raving about." Chloe sounds disgruntled. "Not that we need any of that fancy tech. We have magic."

"Won't happen. After the first men go missing installing equipment, they will end the project. Or let's say they *do* manage with military and Bonum support to install the train tracks or wires for communication successfully... The first train that leaves the East and arrives full of ghosts, or the first time someone from the East hears nothing on the other end of the telephone but the wails of a Puer Planctu and in a trance goes walking past the barrier and is eaten... all that construction will just be forgotten to be reclaimed by the land."

"I agree but, Harrison, change is coming. I can feel it. All Bonum can. And what I feel isn't good."

The sky is darkening rapidly. During this time of year, it always does. In the winter and spring, night comes quickly like it's chasing off the sun so it can have more time to play. Hopefully there are stars and moonlight to brighten the gloom.

"When will you come to Laramie again?" Chloe asks. Laramie is the first large town when you cross the barrier into Wyoming.

"A few months, at least."

After a few more indulgent moments, we slip back inside the circle. I smell the stew Lettie's cooking and the fry of cornbread. People pass around weak ale and coffee. I grab two coffees and hand one to Chloe. Neither of us drink on the trail, not even the watery swill the Barren brothers always bring along.

"I'm going to be up for the first watch," Chloe tells me.

I won't. I will sleep now and be up for second watch. I'm better in the wee hours of the morning.

Sometimes Helen and I get up before the sun to ride out and tend to the animals. My Helen doesn't talk much, but her silence is some of the best and most soothing company.

Chloe walks away and I watch her talk to a few people. Two men grab large guns and surround a woman with a bucket—one last trip to get fresh water before everyone is in for the night.

I sit back against one of my wheels and doze until Lettie shoves a bowl under my nose. The rich brown stew steams my nostrils. My stomach growls.

She laughs and gives me a large piece of cornbread and a spoon. "You're the last to eat, Harrison."

Marcus no longer plays the fiddle, but someone else has taken up their lute. I hear the sweet tones of a nighttime prayer song. I settle back and eat my dinner. It tastes good, rich, and hearty. The cornbread is thick and dry, but honied. I chase it down with cold coffee and watch.

People meander, getting ready for bed. It's fully dark now. Chloe, gun slung along her back, walks with purpose towards her post. I don't see Marcus. He's asleep somewhere, I hope. He deserves a few hours off. We all do.

Finishing my supper, I cross my arms over my chest and don't close my eyes until the only people awake are those on watch.

Then I sleep.

Chloe wakes me. I can tell by moon and star placement it's after midnight. Her eyes are wide, but she doesn't look afraid. Yawning, I stand and stretch, noticing someone came and took away my dishes as I slept and covered me with a blanket.

"How goes the watch?" I ask.

"Some movement out there, but quiet. It feels off, though. I don't know how to explain it. I *do* know the lines around here are the brightest I've felt and are miles away, which is normal."

I stand and dust my hand on my pants, stretching out the kinks from my awkward sleeping position. Hearing her relief about normal ley lines squashes some of my unease.

"Get some sleep, Chloe; we'll be off in a few hours." I'll rustle everyone awake around five in the morning, as soon as the sun peeks out.

When I hand her my blanket, she gives me a tired smile and trades me for her shotgun. "You mind if I sleep in your wagon?"

"Go right ahead."

The first watch slinks into their beds and a group gathers around a fire, making coffee. Gentle whispers reach my ears as I walk over. They greet me with tired smiles and stress around their eyes. I divide them into two groups, each taking a different portion of the circle. I grab an oil lamp.

Marcus joins me and we wander to our post, neither in a great hurry. We step outside the circle of wagons, but no farther. Facing the stream, I see the lights of other lamps to my left and right, at least thirty feet away in either direction.

"Sometimes, I can't believe it's this pretty out here," Marcus says. He lights his pipe and leans back against a wagon, more alert than he lets on.

"You should come and stay out in Ash Hollow again. It's stunning."

He sniffs. "And subject myself to home cooking and being fussed over by Avery? Spirits forbid."

I've known Marcus since I was sixteen. He and I grew up in Laramie. Long before I'd met Avery, before the Infested became part of my everyday life.

"You could come and bring Eric with you." His son is the same age as my children.

"Thinking of him for one of your girls, eh?" Marcus studies my face and then nods. "I could arrange a meeting, yes. Which one?"

"Marian. She's itching to be married."

"I'll bring Eric out for Midwinter Festival. With his mother gone, it's a bad time of year for the boy." He pauses. It's still hard for him to talk about his wife. She died two years past. "If they like each other, I don't see why not."

We give each other huge grins, and then I hear the music.

"Harrison?" he asks with concern.

I place a finger to my lips, eyes straining to see beyond the stream. The stars are bright, but not enough. The music is lovely but sad, and it sounds off somehow; not like traditional instruments, something more otherworldly. Marcus hisses as six women come into view. They stay on the other side of the stream.

"Coryformia," I say out loud, though he knows what they are.

The women look identical, like twisted harlequins in black and white. Stark white faces stand out against tiny ruffled black and white dresses. Their pigtails sway with each step. Hollow cheeks frame empty smiles, mouths that look to be sewn on. Without eyes, Coryformia don't see like we do. Their music echoes off of surfaces, like bats.

Walking as if they are marionettes on strings, they arrange themselves in a group and continue to play.

"Go back into the circle and spread the word to the other watchers," I order softly. "If we don't act aggressively, they will leave us alone."

Coryformia are disturbing but not inherently dangerous unless provoked. I want to close my eyes and look away, but I can't. They are horrifyingly beautiful to behold, and my eyes are drawn to their musical instruments.

Several are strumming tendons from arms and legs, the sinew tight as their bone-tipped fingers pluck a harmony like a sick harp. I can see the rib cage of another, the bleached bones of her chest blinding in the night. No blood, no tissue. She uses two sticks to play herself like a xylophone. One uses the cavity of where her nose should be to elicit a flute-like sound. Another holds her scalp in hand, bells dangling from the pigtails, and she shakes it and smacks her hand into it. The disgusting tambourine finishes off their symphony with a dead ringing.

"Okay, what do we do?" Marcus is back, breathing heavily.

"Nothing. We just watch." I glance at the sky.

"Dawn isn't for another two hours."

"And they'll leave with the dark. You've seen Coryformia before, Marcus. You know how they work."

"Never a group this large. They make me sick to my stomach."

"Try to enjoy the music?" I suggest, and he makes a gagging sound.

Maybe I've lived in the Infested too long? Their music has an allure to it while at the same time a slight grate to the nerves.

"What are they?" Marcus asks.

He knows the answer; he's talking for his own distraction.

"Avery says they appeared on the plains after an entire wagon train of men, women, and children starved to death over winter. She says they are embodiments of grief and despair. But no one knows for sure."

Looking at Marcus, I recall all the times, as children, he asked me to frighten him around a campfire. It's different when the scary stories are only feet away.

Marcus draws in hard from his pipe. He is done talking. Now to wait for the sun to rise.

Chapter 10
May 1900
Day 12
Ash Hollow

Desi smiled in her sleep; the singing was soft and comforting. She rolled to her side, burrowing down in her blankets, warm. She didn't want to get up. There were siblings and duties to attend, and maybe Ambrose would make pancakes if she asked nicely.

Wait. Who was singing? Desi's eyes popped open and she froze. Inches from her sat the shadowy creature, staring down at her with its red eyes and song pouring from its shining mouth. If she moved, would it attack her?

The pit of her stomach dropped out as she noticed some changes to the creature. Where before was blackness in an endless void, now there were distinct cheekbones and a nose. Features of a face Desi knew too well—her mother. Desi took a deep, calming breath, trying not to make a sound. She didn't feel like she was in danger, not yet.

A creak and Desi's door swung open. The creature's song stopped as it vanished.

Lavellen stood in the doorway and Desi gasped, sitting up quickly. Her heart raced as she tried to get her breathing under control. What the hell had just happened? As her eyes focused on Lavellen, she felt emotion fill her chest. Why had she ever been suspicious of her? Desi admired Lavellen as she came into the room, lithe and delicate. A tingle went up the back of her neck, slightly painful, and Desi rubbed it, wondering if she'd slept poorly again. Her mind felt fuzzy.

"Lavellen, what are you doing? When did you wake up?" The other woman had been unconscious for three days, ever since her attack.

"No one was around when I woke up and… I'm afraid. I figured you were awake. I thought I heard singing," she whispered, coming farther into the bedroom.

"No, I was asleep." Desi didn't want to share with her what had actually woken her up.

"Oh, I'm sorry," Lavellen said.

"What time is it?"

"Not quite dawn."

This explained why Desi was still so tired.

"Can I sleep with you?" Lavellen asked.

Desi swallowed and nodded her head, lifting the blanket next to her. Lavellen smiled and rushed over, sliding in next to her. Her white cotton pajamas were soft against Desi's skin, adding extra heat. Desi wished she hadn't chosen to wear flannel to bed.

What else would she wear? She didn't have attractive nightclothes. Everything in her closet was practical. Desi closed her eyes tightly, wondering why it even mattered. Even if she *did* have something prettier than her flannel, she wouldn't wear it around a woman her sister was falling for. What kind of monster did that?

"Why not sleep with Rowena?" Desi asked.

Lavellen smelled like lemons and her blonde hair spread over Desi's pillows, begging to be touched. Desi formed fists with her hands to resist temptation. This wasn't like her.

Lavellen's eyes fluttered closed. "I feel safe with you." She snuggled against Desi.

Desi didn't know how to take that statement. She wanted to say so much, but the moths fluttering in her chest prevented her. What if Lavellen rejected her? What if she didn't, and Desi broke Rowena's heart? No, it would be better to remain silent. With Lavellen this close to her, it was like Desi couldn't think straight, couldn't remember something important. All her thoughts focused on the beautiful woman in her bed.

"Go back to sleep, Desi." Lavellen yawned and soon fell asleep, softly snoring.

Desi didn't think she would be able to get back to sleep. Between Lavellen and the growing dread in her stomach, she knew something terrible was going to happen.

She kept seeing that thing in her mind's eyes. It couldn't be her mother, could it? How could it be? Maybe something trying to look like her mother?

When she woke up a second time, Lavellen was gone and the sun's position in her room told her it was hours later.

Getting up, she washed in the bowl on her vanity. The cold water and rose-scented soap chilled her skin and alerted her senses. She felt her mind clearing so that she could finally think.

Desi bundled her hair at the nape of her neck and dressed in a long black skirt, pale blue tunic, and black waist cincher. She needed to speak to Lavellen. Something wasn't right. Desi pulled on a clean white pinafore, thick socks, and her curled toe boots. It was a working day, after all.

Once she got downstairs, she smelled breakfast. Entering the kitchen, she saw Ambrose at the stove, coffee brewing next to him.

"Did you read my mind?" she asked, pouring herself a cup and watching him flip a pancake.

"Nope, just know you. I also saw Lavellen is finally awake, and she'll need a good breakfast. Strawberry syrup and butter on the counter."

Desi added a little cream and sugar to her cup. "Am I the last one up?"

"Yeah, lazy. That's not like you." He handed her a plate.

With the first bite of soft buttery pancake and sweet syrup, Desi felt Ambrose's gift, the equivalent of a good hug and the words, "have a great day!"

"Nice addition," she said around her mouthful.

"Thought everyone could use a pleasant morning after the last few days." He loaded a plate, the red sticky syrup pooling over the brown cakes. "Take these to Rowena and Lavellen, would you? I have to start lunch prep."

"Helen and Marian ate already?"

"Helen had oats with cream and honey and is still with the animals. Marian is doing the washing." He frowned. "Samael is with her. Why anyone would want to watch someone wash clothes is beyond me."

"Don't be bitter. She likes him, and he likes her."

"He likes me, too!" Ambrose said, anger filling his features. "But she's always around, clinging to him like a moonstruck sap!"

"Ambrose!" Desi snapped. What was wrong with him?

"I'm sorry, Desi, I just feel so...so...." Then Ambrose did the last thing she expected. He started to cry.

Desi put the plate down and rushed to him. He put a hand up before she could touch him. She waited, giving him the space. He took several deep breaths and rubbed his eyes.

She hadn't seen him cry since before Dad told him he could wear boy's clothes all the time.

"Ambrose, what's happened?" Desi asked, concern knotting in her stomach.

"I slept with him."

Desi's mouth dropped open but she slammed it shut at the horrified expression on Ambrose's face. Her teeth knocked together as she processed his statement. Her brother had always been disgusted by the idea of sex. She had a thousand questions, but knew there was only one to ask.

"Are you okay?"

He let out a breath, a soft laugh upon his lips. "You're too good for us, Desi. I tell you that... that..." He shook his head and moved on, "and your first thought is, am I okay?"

"Well, are you?" Seeping anger tunneled under her skin. How *dare* Samael come into their lives and act like a cad.

"Yes, it was nice. He was... nice to me." Tears welled in his eyes again.

"Deep, slow breaths, Ambrose. I hear a 'but' at the end of that sentence." She placed a hand on his shoulder.

He did as she asked, and the rest came out in a rush. "But how could he do that... with me? And then act that way with Marian?"

"I don't know, Ambrose. But I am going to find out, and then they're both leaving." Desi spun away, outrage threatening to bubble out from her. Hands fisted at her side, fingernails digging into her palms.

"No, no!" Ambrose grabbed her arm and blocked her way. "No, Desi, please don't send them away. Just give me a moment to speak with him, find out what's happening."

She studied her brother's features, almost identical to hers, eyes swimming with an emotion she'd never seen them hold before.

"Fine," she said. "I won't send them away yet. I'll speak to Lavellen about his behavior. A warning for them both." She was slowly concluding there was something wrong with *both* of these siblings.

"Okay, compromise. Now, please take the pancakes out?" Ambrose dropped his hand from her arm.

She nodded, grabbed the plate, and swept from the room.

Her face must have reflected the emotions warring inside her, for when both Rowena and Lavellen looked up when she entered the dining room, the smiles on their faces died instantly.

"What's wrong, Desi?" Rowena asked, getting up and taking the plate.

"I need to talk to Lavellen."

"Do you need me to leave?" Rowena asked, her face a neutral mask, but Desi could hear the underlying message. She did not want to leave and there would be a fight about it later if Desi insisted. Rowena put the plate on the table and sat across from Lavellen.

"No, but what I'm about to say doesn't leave this room." Desi sat next to Rowena.

"Are you here to ask Samael and me to leave?" Lavellen asked, her face falling into a sensual pout.

"Of course not. Right, Desi?" Rowena reached across the table and linked pale grey fingers with sun-kissed ones.

Desi stared at their intertwined hands. Was this the same girl who had crawled into bed with her just a few hours before? As she stared at Lavellen, something finally became clear.

Her emotions were being manipulated, unnaturally.

Desi was ashamed how long it took her to figure it out. She took a deep breath and connected to the well of magic deep within her, letting it wash through her.

It took seconds and when she lifted her eyes to look at Lavellen, it was like a mist lifted. She saw Lavellen's beauty in a different light. Her light teasing, small gestures, and breathless conversation now were tinged with deep suspicion.

Lavellen noticed the change as Desi narrowed her eyes at her. She dropped Rowena's hand and sat back.

"It's your brother," Desi said. "You need to talk to him about his behavior, or I will insist you leave in the morning. You are both here as guests of Ash Hollow and our hospitality will not be taken advantage of."

Clamping down on the rise of magic in the middle of her chest, Desi tried to calm down. Part of her wanted Lavellen to be innocent in all of this, but a more significant part knew something was wrong. She hadn't noticed it before because the wards hadn't recognized Lavellen and Samael as dangerous—and maybe they weren't, but she had to make sure.

"Of course, Desi. What's happened?" Lavellen asked.

"I have been informed Samael has had—" how could she put this delicately? "—carnal relations with Ambrose while also engaging in courtship behavior with Marian."

"Desi!" Rowena gasped. "What an accusation. I'm sure that's not true."

"Are you calling Ambrose a liar?" Desi only had eyes for Lavellen.

The other woman's eyes were closed and a blush spread from neck to cheeks.

"Lavellen? Dear heart?" Rowena questioned.

"I am so sorry, Rowena, Desi. Yes, I will talk to him at once." Her eyes opened, burning with anger. "I did *not* think he would act like that here. I've seen him be affectionate with Marian and warned him away. Had I known he was also flirting with Ambrose, I would have said something earlier."

"What do you mean, act like that here?" Rowena's voice was like steel. She frowned at Lavellen.

"He doesn't mean any harm by it, not truly. Samael loves people, all people, and can sometimes be a bit... amorous with affections. We were not raised quite like other people."

95

"Oh spirits." Rowena put a hand to her chest. "I can't believe this."

Desi watched Lavellen in silence. Then she did something she should have done days ago, but she'd been too distracted by her feelings, by her grief: she covered Lavellen in her magic, throwing it out like a net. Lavellen cried out, stiffening as if cold water sprayed upon her. Her skin pimpled under the cold.

"Desi! What are you doing?" Rowena went to Lavellen's side, passing hands over her, trying to reassure her and warm her up.

It took only a few seconds and then Desi retracted her magic. "You're Bonum." Her nose twitched. Lavellen felt Bonum, but there was something else there too.

"What? Lavellen, why didn't you tell me?" Rowena sounded relieved. "That makes things so much easier."

Wrapping arms around herself, the woman shivered and glared at Desi. "We don't go around telling everyone. It hasn't made life easy for Samael and me."

"You knew what we were," Desi said. "Why keep it a secret?"

She felt betrayed and hurt. *This* was the woman she'd been fantasizing about?

"I didn't want any of you to think my affection wasn't genuine."

"Why would we think that?" Rowena asked, placing a hand on Lavellen's thigh.

Lavellen sighed as if a significant burden was released into the world, her entire body moving with the air. "Samael and I can sense the needs of others and adapt ourselves to meet those needs. We can inspire emotions in others as well."

Rowena jerked back her hand like Lavellen's white dress burned her. "It's not real?"

"Yes! Oh, Rowena, this is why I didn't say anything. It *is* genuine, and it couldn't be more real. Forgive me." Lavellen burst into tears.

96

Rowena stared at her for a minute, her face stony.

"You're the reason we've all been feeling so pulled to you?" Desi asked. "How can you sit there and tell Rowena it's real when you've been doing it to me too?"

"What?" Rowena turned to her. "Desi, how can you say that?"

Lavellen sniffled. "I didn't mean to with you. You just felt so... lonely." She reached out and took Rowena's hand. "I'm sorry. I do care about you deeply. Please believe me."

Reluctantly, Rowena drew Lavellen into her embrace and held her as she cried.

"You're buying this?" Desi asked.

Rowena glared at Desi. "If she says it's true, then I believe her. I'm not happy about it, but I believe her."

"I need to tell Ambrose and Marian," Desi said.

"Oh no, please don't!" Lavellen cried. "Samael will be embarrassed. I'll talk to him about it, make sure he fixes it with them."

"Fine, but they still deserve to know."

"I'll tell them, Desi," Rowena said, stroking Lavellen's hair. "Lavellen and I will talk to them together, alright?"

"Yes, please let me fix it!" Lavellen exclaimed. "We don't mean to hurt anyone, not ever."

Desi stood up, mulling over Lavellen's words. Desi would find out what other secrets the two siblings had, but not now. Desi felt better, not as confused. She could tell by the look on Rowena's face that her sister still had intense emotions for Lavellen.

"You have a fortnight," Desi said. "We've enjoyed your company, but you have two weeks longer to rest. We need to get on with our own lives."

Desi was furious. She didn't like being manipulated and really didn't like her siblings being treated like playthings.

Red-rimmed and puffy eyes looked up from Rowena's shoulder. "Alright, I understand—and don't worry. I will talk to Samael, I promise."

Desi left the dining room, out into the living room, and through the front door. Her feet took her quickly over the path and to the gate. Pressing her hands against the wood, she felt that hunger—to be out in the plains, to be wild and free—growing and burning in her chest.

She couldn't do this alone.

She didn't know how long she stood there before soft footfalls behind her. "Desi?"

"Helen, how do you always know?" she asked softly, without turning around.

"I can feel it in you. It echoes in me, trying to wake something up."

"We need Father here," Desi murmured. "He's overdue and I'm going to send him a message."

More silence followed before Helen spoke again. "You can't, Desi. You'd have to go beyond the wards."

"I have to."

Another pause, and then, "Alright. When?"

"Tomorrow."

Chapter 11
May 1900
Day 13
Ash Hollow

"I can't believe you're going out there!" Marian exclaimed as Desi hefted the pack onto her shoulder. Marian wrung her hands, standing in the dim light of morning.

"It shouldn't take more than a few hours," Desi said, "a day at the most."

"It's dangerous," Ambrose said from where he leaned against the wall, arms crossed. "Take one of us with you."

"And which of you would want to come with me?"

"I'll go," Rowena said. She sat next to Lavellen on the settee. They clung together, sides pressed tightly, hands intertwined.

Lavellen had not sought Desi out again after their previous conversation, which made Desi glad. She wouldn't hurt Rowena and she didn't believe her emotions for the other woman to be genuine or honest. Was she lonely? Yes. They were all lonely, and it wasn't a life conducive to companionship outside of their family.

"Would you really want to go, Rowena?" Helen asked.

"Yes, if Desi needs me." Rowena tucked a stray hair behind Lavellen's ear and murmured to her.

Lavellen looked truly scared—or was it calculating?

"I can go with you," Samael pushed against the wall and came over to her. "Let me make up for past transgressions by accompanying you."

Ambrose chuckled, dark and full of loathing. Marian's eyes flitted back and forth between Samael and Ambrose, lips pursed. Desi didn't know if Samael had told her what he'd done, but it was apparent she wasn't oblivious that something was going on.

"No, thank you," Desi said. Samael made her uncomfortable.

"You *are* planning to come back, right?" Helen asked. Perched on the bottom step, her thin form was almost hidden by the shadows. Desi could barely make out her wide eyes.

"What a thing to say!" Rowena exclaimed. "Of course, she is."

"Yes, Helen. I am planning to come back."

Marian burst into tears.

Helen watched Desi, too, knowing.

Lavellen stood up and went outside. Rowena looked after her, confused.

"I have to get this message to Dad. Things here are spiraling out of control and we need him home," Desi reminded them all. Their mom dying, Rowena wanting to leave, the Shadow creature, the drama Lavellen and Samael were causing—it was all too much. Desi needed help.

Desi tied her boots and fastened the waist-length coat. It felt snug, having been her mother's. It was infused with magic to protect. Desi had only been outside the gates a handful of times; Mother hadn't deemed it necessary for her to have her own coat.

She handed the bottle full of shadows to Helen. "You're in charge while I'm away."

This caused a minor uproar, her siblings all gasping like fish.

"I'm the eldest!" Rowena yelled, coming to her feet. "I should be in charge, after you."

"You're only older than me by ten minutes. She should leave *me* in charge. At least I'm not distracted." The arrogance in Ambrose's voice was palpable.

Desi pinched the bridge of her nose. She did not need this headache.

"*She's* distracted? Look who's talking." Marian glared at their brother and scooted closer to Samael, who smiled at her adoringly.

"Enough," Helen said, her quiet voice like a soothing balm. "You should all be ashamed of yourselves. There's more going on here than your petty squabbles."

Silence filled the room and Desi finished gathering what she needed, pack on her back with a shotgun slung over one shoulder.

"Are you sure you don't want any of us coming with you?" Ambrose asked.

"It will be safer if I do this alone."

"I'm coming with you."

They all froze as Lavellen swept in the front door. She wore deep brown trousers and boots, a charcoal-colored tunic, and a brown waist cincher. She'd pinned a wide brim leather hat to her head that sported a yellow butterfly brooch and her buttercup-colored veil. Gripping her own small satchel, she stood by Desi.

"Lavellen, what nonsense is this?" Samael exclaimed.

"I owe it to Desi to help out—and not only because of how you've behaved," Lavellen said. "We brought extra work to them during a time of hardship. I'm going, and that's the end of it."

"I don't want you with me," Desi said flatly. "I don't trust you."

"I know, but I'm coming anyway," Lavellen said. She had a stern look on her face that Desi had never seen before.

"Lavellen, dear heart...." Rowena came to her, putting her hands on either side of Lavellen's face. "Don't do this. It's dangerous out there. You may not come back to me."

Lavellen kissed her, causing Desi to roll her eyes. "I will. I'm tougher than I look."

Desi found that hard to believe, and she didn't want to take liability with her into the Infested. Though, Desi could be wrong. She wasn't sure any of them had seen who Lavellen and Samael truly were.

"Lavellen, I don't need your company, and I can't be responsible for you out there." She was worried enough about herself.

Lavellen broke away from Rowena and met her eyes. "I'm coming. And I promise if something does happen, you won't be responsible. Right, Samael?"

Her brother grudgingly agreed.

"Then let's go." Desi waited while Lavellen said goodbye to her brother and Rowena.

The walk to the gate was quiet as Desi steeled herself for the trip. She could do this. She'd been out of the gates with Mother several times, as well as trips with her aunt and Foni.

"Do we open the main gate?" Lavellen asked as they came to the fence.

"No. It's faster and easier to climb it." Desi gripped the wood and hauled herself up.

When she got to the top, she hefted herself over and dropped to the ground, breathless. On high alert, she focused on her surroundings and how different the ground felt. She always forgot. Forgot how clean and distinct the air smelled, how the earth felt rich beneath her feet. Magic bloomed within her.

"Wait, we're walking?" Lavellen asked, through the fence.

"What did you think we were going to do, hitch up a wagon? It's not far away and it's safe for Bonum to walk in the Infested. As long as we're careful, we should be okay. Now come on."

Steadying herself against the small high of being outside the wards, she waited for Lavellen to hop the fence. The wards around her home blocked the natural magic of the Infested. Beyond it, her magic felt more potent and more addicting without tampering down her senses.

"How is it possible it feels so much different out here?" Lavellen asked in awe.

"Didn't you notice it before?" Desi began to walk, keeping an eye out for trouble. She put out magic feelers as far as she could for danger while also trying to remain invisible and concentrate on how her nose felt.

"I've never stayed for a long period inside somewhere so heavily warded. It doesn't feel that different on the other side of the barrier."

No one understood how the barrier between the West and the Infested worked. No one created it; it popped into being on its own. People were afraid of what would happen if it disappeared or chose to change the borders.

"Now, how are we sending a message?" Lavellen asked.

"We have to find a Will-o'-Wisp."

"Where do we find a Will-o'-Wisp?"

"Try and keep your tone down. We don't want to risk being heard," Desi said, giving the other woman a side glance. Lavellen blanched. Pointing east, she continued, "there's a lake about two miles from here. Several wisps inhabit the area and are familiar with my family."

"Should I do anything to help us?"

"If you have any magic of your own, try and make your presence as invisible as you possibly can. I should be able to protect us, but I'd rather not have to. Slipping in and out of the Infested as quickly as possible would be the best outcome."

They trekked over the flatlands, past grass a fantastic purple color and trees bending sideways. The weather was pleasant and a cool breeze blew over them. Anxiety flooded Desi, her tense limbs readying for action.

About an hour after leaving Ash Hallow, Lavellen finally spoke. "Can we talk?"

"Yes, just not loudly. Mom and I found it eases tension during trips out."

"You seem mad at me. Why?"

Desi stopped and faced her. How could she not know?

"You made me think you cared about me. I believed what I felt about you was real, and it wasn't. I was on the verge of actions that would hurt my sister and I don't care to be manipulated."

She started off again, angrily. They really didn't have time to take a break.

"Oh." Lavellen's word was a slight, breathless sound. "I didn't mean for that to happen, Desi. I honestly enjoyed our time together and didn't realize my gift... was affecting you that much. I care about Rowena, too, in a way I haven't in a while. But how I was raised, well, it's different."

"I can see that by your brother." Just thinking about how Samael treated Ambrose and Marian made her furious. Eyes on the ground, she reached out a hand to Lavellen to stop her.

"Walk where I walk, please."

"Why?" Lavellen asked.

Patches of blood-colored dirt littered the area ahead of them, to which she gestured. "Don't touch the dirt, especially if you like your toes."

The color drained from Lavellen's face. "Couldn't we just go around?"

"Not without adding another thirty minutes to our trip," Desi said. The red dirt spread as far as the eye could see.

She bit her lip. She could do this—and she had to. She glanced at Lavellen, who was still pale with her lower lip trembling with fear.

"Tell me about your brother," Desi said to distract her.

In a disturbing game of follow-the-leader, Desi led the way, careful not to touch any of the dirt. The dying grass crunched beneath her boots.

"My brother has always been more like our mother," Lavellen said. "Sometimes too much. He isn't as careful with our gift, and I tend to indulge him."

She gripped Desi's shirt as she made the last leap behind her and lost her balance. Desi whipped around to grab her arm, but it was too late. Lavellen stepped wrong and fell back, her shoe touching a pile of dirt.

Desi yanked her forward, pushing her to the ground. She opened her pack, scrambling for something inside. "Quick, get your damn shoe off!"

Lavellen hiked her dress up and shrieked as she watched her boot start to dissolve like it was being eaten by acid. Her fingers ripped at the ties.

Desi found what she was looking for and took out a small vial of purple liquid, giving a silent thanks to Helen for thinking to pack it. She froze for a split second as Lavellen's shriek told her the dirt had reached the skin. Tears streaming down her face, Lavellen wailed and clawed at the boot now.

Desi opened the vial with her teeth and grabbed Lavellen's ankle. Pinning down the quaking girl, she ripped off the remains of the boot and hurled it as far away as she could.

"Spirits, Desi! Help me!"

"You have to shut up, Lavellen. I'm working as fast as I can." Desi spared half a second to glance around.

Who knew what had heard her cries—and they were too far from Ash Hollow to get back safely should something attack. Desi threw up a small ward. It should limit how far their sounds carried and warn her if anything came their way.

Lavellen was trying to kick her foot, thrashing and moaning. Gripping her ankle harder, Desi dripped some purple liquid on her foot, steam hissing from the affected area. It smelled like rotten flowers and death. Lavellen's eyes rolled back in her head, and she passed out.

Keeping Lavellen's foot pinned, Desi watched the purple liquid expand over her entire foot. She sat next to Lavellen and waited.

Once the purple absorbed into her skin, Desi got a better look at the damage. It wasn't as bad as it could be, but Lavellen's little toe was a gruesome sight to behold. The skin and muscle around the entire toe's bone were gone, dissolved by the dirt, and cauterized at the final joint.

Desi felt sick to her stomach, but this wasn't the worst injury she'd ever witnessed.

Getting up, she foraged. She didn't know as much about healing as Helen and her mom did, but enough to be safe on her own. This incident was one of the reasons she wanted to do this alone. Lavellen didn't know the land. She might be Bonum, but she couldn't feel things like Desi did. Bonum were special, born with their own gifts and, like her siblings, they didn't all have the same ability to control and use magic.

Lavellen began to whimper as Desi found what she needed. Two small plants lived in symbiotic harmony, one a thick and hard stick-like plant that looked dead and the other the bright green moss growing under it.

Kneeling next to Lavellen, Desi grabbed a canteen and brought it to Lavellen's lips.

"Sip slowly," she told her.

Sweat ran down her face. Her blue eyes focused on the sky above them. "It hurts," she moaned but sipped the water.

"I know. It won't hurt as bad in a minute. Don't look at your foot. Keep your eyes closed while I work."

Desi didn't wait for a response. She took some bandages from her bag and set to work, using the little wooden plant to brace Lavellen's toe. She knew the moment Lavellen looked; her whole body twisted and Desi glanced up in time to watch her throw up on the ground next to her.

"Don't move," Desi hissed.

"I'm sorry... I can't... can't help it. Spirits, it's awful, and it.... I can't stand the pain!"

Desi tightened her grip, knowing Lavellen would be bruised, but she needed to do this fast. Before their luck ran out and something caught wind of them, out in the open and unable to run.

Packing the moss around her toe, Desi wrapped the bandages around it all—wood, moss, and toe.

Slowly, Lavellen calmed down as the anesthetic in the moss set in, numbing sensation in the remaining flesh.

"Now," Desi said, "take some deep breaths and get up."

"I can't walk on that!"

"Trust me, you can. The stick I put against your bone will help and the moss will kill the pain for a while. We should be home by the time it wears off, and Helen will be able to help." Desi held out a hand and helped Lavellen to her feet.

"Help? Or fix?"

"Help. I'm sorry." Desi hugged her.

When she pulled away, Lavellen was still white as a sheet and looked ready to pass out or throw up again. They didn't have time for either.

"Now try to walk. If I have to take you all the way back, this trip just got a lot longer and more harrowing for me."

"No... I can do it."

Lavellen tested her weight on her foot. She winced but nodded, and they started off again.

"What was that dirt?"

"Sanglutum. Bad news for anyone. I've seen it take an entire cow in less than five minutes."

"Is it alive?"

"Kind of." Desi shot her a sidelong glance. "I know it's hard, but you have to pick up the pace. We have to reach the lake by noon."

Desi couldn't help Lavellen walk. She had to have her hands free, just in case.

They walked in silence until the lake came into view. Surrounded by willow trees, the small lake glimmered a deceptively peaceful blue. Making their way down the incline to reach the deep green sand that kissed the water, the sunlight died and everything darkened into an eerie blue-green twilight. A sound like soft, weeping music came from the waters.

"Where'd the sun go?" Lavellen whispered.

Desi noticed signs of strain on her face. The moss may have been wearing off sooner than it should have.

"It's just how the light is around Woe Lake. The Will-o'-Wisps can't abide the sunshine, so many of them live here. It's always like this."

"What's that sound?"

"The lake."

"The water's beautiful. Could you help me balance while I soak my foot in it?"

"No. If you put that foot in the water, you won't have one."

Lavellen gasped and glared at the offending water. As they walked along the beach, Desi peered into the shadows under the trees, trying to find a wisp.

"Will it dissolve my foot… like the dirt?" Lavellen asked.

"Not the water, no. I've never seen it myself, but something lives in this lake, and it's not friendly."

"How do you know if you've never seen it?"

"Because I've seen the skeletons it spits out when it's done."

"You could tell me these things with a little more tact, you know," Lavellen said, crossing her arms over her chest and frowning at Desi.

"Why should I sugar coat it? You chose to come with me, and you and your brother chose to make this trip. You should know how dangerous it is."

Seeing a blinking semi-translucent figure dancing a few feet away, Desi increased her pace but hesitated when she heard sniffles behind her. Maybe she had been a bit hard.

Sighing, Desi spoke again, "Tell me about your mother. You said your upbringing was unusual, and I know your dad wasn't around."

"My mom was very affectionate with everyone. She always had multiple boyfriends and girlfriends. But she was power-hungry and greedy, always wanting more. More money, more clothes, more… time. I think she loved us as much as she could, but it was hard sometimes."

"What do you mean, she needed more time?" They were close to the wisp now. A tiny ball bounced in the air, glowing brightly at its center.

"A Bonum with a gift for foresight told my mother she'd die young," Lavellen replied. "She left us to see about getting more magic to extend her lifespan."

"Die young? It takes a lot to kill a Bonum."

"I don't know. I only know Mother feared dying more than anything. Death can't be that scary, can it? I mean, most of your extended family is dead, right?"

"My grandmother died giving birth to my youngest aunt, who's still alive," Desi said. "We all live in the Infested. Before my mother and aunts grew into their magic and could help protect the homestead, it was inevitable that other members of my family died out here from disease or an attack. Besides, they weren't all Bonum, you know."

"Why didn't they live behind the barrier? They had to know it wouldn't be safe."

"My home was founded by a family from one of the original wagon trains. I think it was a point of pride. Do you know where your mother is?" Desi asked as she pointed out the wisp and wordlessly motioned for Lavellen to stay back.

"No. We think she must have died. That was more than a year ago now…. Is that a Will-o'-Wisp?"

"Yes. Now stay here. Don't talk. Don't move. Just let me do this so we can get home before night." Desi gave her pack and gun to Lavellen.

"It doesn't look how I thought it would," Lavellen said. "I've heard them described kind of like fairies."

What didn't she understand about keeping quiet?

"Fairies don't exist," Desi whispered. "Will-o'-Wisps do. Expecting anything in the Infested to be a beautiful, gift-giving mini-girl with wings is foolish. Now *hush*."

Desi walked calmly and carefully towards the wisp. When it caught sight of her, it flashed red and then back to its natural seafoam green.

"I come peacefully." Desi held out her hands, open palms.

It flashed a deep forest green and Desi breathed a sigh of relief.

"I need you to take a message."

Flash of red.

"I have payment."

Forest green.

Desi motioned for it to come closer. It did, the light enveloping her hand. There was a sharp bite in her right index finger, followed by stinging coldness. Then the light moved away and left a deep red set of teeth marks.

The wisp briefly glowed purple.

"My father, Harrison, is with the current caravan heading this way."

Forest green.

"He's late coming home, and we've had some issues. I need you to tell him we need him home as soon as possible."

Forest green.

"Ask him when he's going to be home and find out where along the trail he is when he gets the message, including the date."

Red.

"Yes, of course, more payment before I get the message back, but you have to come to Ash Hollow. I can't come back here."

Forest green.

"Thank you." Desi backed up slowly, hands still out. Reaching Lavellen, she took back her pack and gun as she said, "Now, quietly and quickly back the way we came."

Chapter 12
May 1900
Day 13
Woe Lake

Once away from the lake, Desi's heart stopped racing, but she wanted to throw up. She was shaky and tense. The sun's position told her it was already two in the afternoon, and nightfall would be at seven. They should still make it home before then, but it would be close.

"Can we stop to eat and take a moment?" Lavellen asked. "That felt stressful, and I don't know why."

"Because we were seconds away from death."

"Wait, what?" Lavellen exclaimed.

"Please, no more yelling, I beg you," Desi whispered, glancing around.

It was never wise to make a lot of noise in the Infested.

"Will-o'-Wisps drain your life force the longer you're around them and the more of them there are," she continued. "We were lucky that only one felt like being about. It's not that they mean to be dangerous; they just can't help it."

"And you paid it with blood?"

"What else would I pay with?"

"Point taken, but my original question stands. Can we stop?"

Desi looked around. She agreed with Lavellen. They needed food, water, and a few moments to catch their breath. But where? They couldn't stay out in the open, but other places that would offer shelter might be just as dangerous.

"Yes. I just have to find... Okay, follow me, quickly."

She went to the direct left and weaved in and out of tall grass, listening to Lavellen pant behind her. Lavellen's foot must be bothering her. Desi would have to do something about it.

A silver tree stood in the distance, a little far off the path, but the closest thing to a sanctuary they might find.

"Is that a silver maple tree?" Lavellen asked.

"Yes. Have you seen one before?"

"Not alive, but a friend of my mother bought a wreath made out of its branches and hung it, hoping it would protect her from death."

"It's got natural warding," Desi said, "and my mom says it developed the silver color when the first monsters appeared. I read there's an entire forest of them sheltering a native tribe down south."

When the trail and the plains became unsafe, most of the natives who lived within the Infested boundaries relocated West. They kept to themselves. Desi thought this was a wise choice as the other humans they'd come in contact with had ruined something precious.

Desi and Lavellen ducked into the shade the tree offered. Desi made sure nothing lay in wait before they sat down. Though she was hesitant to use any of her magical supplies yet, a nasty surprise under the tree would blow that plan to hell.

"What did you pack in your bag?" Desi asked.

"Some food, my sewing kit, socks, soap, water, and my first aid kit."

"Well, not useless then. I'd put a sock over that foot. It might make it feel better. I have some pain medicine. Eat whatever you brought so you can take it."

Lavellen took out her water, an apple, and one of Ambrose's cornbread muffins. She wolfed them down like she was famished, and she may have been. Pain fatigued all too easily.

"Why did you come to Ash Hollow? Why lie to us?" Desi asked, unable to hold back the questions any longer.

Lavellen hesitated. "I told you—Samael wanted us to go East, that much is true. We got attacked and saw you on the map. I don't know why we didn't tell you we were Bonum. I recognized you immediately. It wasn't smart, and I'm sorry."

"I'll accept your apology for now, but if you do anything else to hurt my family and endanger my home, I won't be kind again."

Lavellen seemed to accept that, and Desi started on her own meal of dried meat, carrots, and a mixture of dried oats and honey. She tried to relax, letting her muscles release the tension while staying alert.

Remembering the last time she and her mother made a short journey into the Infested, she said softly, "You know, the last time I was out here, it was for fruit."

"Fruit?" Lavellen laughed.

"Yes. Fall of last year. My father has a fondness for persimmon steamed pudding during the winter holidays." Desi smiled at the memory. "But persimmons are one of the few things we can't seem to grow. Luckily, there's a grove of trees about a mile and a half from the house."

"You went into the Infested, risked danger, so your dad could have dessert?" Lavellen finished her food and struggled to gently pull a cream-colored wool sock onto her foot.

"My mother loves... loved him so much. We all do. She wanted it to be a surprise." Emotion burned in the back of her throat. She missed her parents.

"It must be nice to have such a loving family." A dark emotion passed over Lavellen's features, which gave Desi pause.

Something darker lay inside this woman. Something that caused Desi's skin to crawl at times.

"It is... now here, take these." She handed her three tiny green pills. "They're made from the same moss I wrapped your toe in. Hopefully, they'll last longer. I don't have many. We've got to go."

They stepped out from the shade of the silver maple, and Desi swore.

In the distance, coming their way, was a storm cloud, deep grey and purple.

"A storm? That won't be fun to walk in. My sock and bandages will get soggy."

"A storm?" Desi laughed, a dry, sardonic laugh. Not at all pleasant to hear. "If only it were that simple." Fear uncurled in her stomach. She didn't know what to do. What would her mother do?

"Desi." Lavellen gripped her sleeve, knuckles white. "What is it?"

"A Nebula."

"Like the one hunting Samael and I?"

"Not like—one and the same. Nebulas are territorial. It would be very strange for there to be two different ones near Ash Hollow. Something about you must be interesting enough to keep it here." Desi's mind raced.

They would need to take shelter and ride out the storm. As one the nastier things in the Infested, Nebulas liked to hunt people, but they could only sustain corporeal form for so long.

"What do we do?" Lavellen asked.

"We need to hide."

"Where? There's nothing out here but grass and hills, a few trees. Should we go back to the lake?"

Desi considered her words and looked towards Lake Woe and the willow trees. "No. I don't think it would be enough shelter, and we'd risk pissing off the wisps and whatever lives in the water."

As they spoke, the clouds darkened and loomed closer, ominous and heavy.

"What will it do to us if it catches us?"

"I don't know, but Foni said it was awful." Desi cursed herself as the words left her mouth.

"Foni?"

"My cousin. I really can't talk about her."

"I didn't know you had a cousin." Lavellen pouted, eyebrows raised.

"And you should forget you did. Now come on." Desi started walking, moving as quickly as she could.

They might be able to get home before the Nebula got to them, especially if they changed their path to move around the storm. It might take longer, but it would be safer.

"Wait, this isn't the way we came."

"I know. If we loop around to the west, it'll take another hour but we won't be in its path. Nebulas don't move quickly. Like any weather, it can't change course as quickly as we can. We may luck out and confuse it."

"But how will we get to the gate?" Lavellen panted as she limped, trying to keep up with Desi's pace.

"We'll have to jump the fence farther in, but we'll be safe." At least she hoped so.

They trudged through tall brown grass and circumvented a few dubious puddles and an entire hill suspiciously out of place. Desi's legs burned from the exertion, but she refused to slow down.

Lavellen stumbled and Desi caught her arm. "You can't give up now, Lavellen."

"I'm tired, and my foot is starting to hurt again," Lavellen sobbed through gritted teeth, her eyes filled with tears. "I'm so sorry. I'm holding you up."

"I know you're tired, but I'm not going to leave you here. You have to help me. I can't carry you or do the work for you. I don't want to have to tell Samael and Rowena you died out here."

Desi helped her balance and waited while Lavellen drank some water and took another moss pill. All the while, she kept her eyes on the menacing clouds that still crept towards the lake.

"You didn't even want me to come," Lavellen said, a hiccup ending her words.

"I didn't, but I still won't leave you to die out here. Come on." Desi took her hand and yanked her into a quick pace.

Sweat dripped down into Desi's eyes, but she wiped it away. They moved behind trees and cautiously made their way over an acre strewn with yellow pebbles. Lavellen cried with each step. She sounded pitiful and weak, but she didn't stop again.

Desi had to respect her spirit. The girl was seriously hurt and trying to keep up. Desi felt some of the old warmth and emotion blossom in her chest, the same feeling she'd had when they'd first met. She squashed it down. There wasn't time for that, not now and not ever. Maybe after this, they could be friends. Desi liked the idea of having a friend outside of her siblings.

Once they were over halfway back home, they rested behind a large dead tree stump.

"Did your mother tell you bedtime stories?" she asked in a low voice, trying to distract Lavellen from the pain.

She warded the area, using dust made of iron and pollen to hide their scent and pushing her personal wards out to surround them both. She couldn't make them invisible, but she could camouflage them while they caught their breath and refueled. She couldn't do it while they were moving. If the Nebula changed directions, it would notice them eventually.

"Yes. Not often, but there were a couple," Lavellen said. She took small sips of water between each mouthful of berries.

"Which ones are your favorite?" Desi pulled out a roll and tore into it, trying to conserve her own water.

"I always liked the story of Rumpy Bumpy the Flying Hedgehog. Have you heard it?"

"I think so. It's a standard cautionary tale about strangers, isn't it?"

Lavellen's eyes lit up. "Yes! He takes strawberries from an evil fairy who wants to fatten him up for his fur. She lures him into her house and when he figures out she's evil, he steals a magic potion that lets him fly so he can escape." She finished her food and leaned back, eyes closed.

"I've always been partial to the Bone Maiden and the Harp," Desi admitted.

"That's a little dark, isn't it?" Lavellen yawned.

"You can't fall asleep. We're leaving in a few minutes." Desi peeked over the log to check on the Nebula.

She didn't like what she saw. The violent purple and black clouds reached the lake. It would realize they weren't there any time now and would come this way.

Her nose began to tingle, a warning.

"Come on. I'll tell you the tale the way my mom told it," Desi said. She stood, dusted off her skirt, and held her hand out.

Lavellen's hand felt soft and smooth in her own. Even a day in the Infested wouldn't change that she would never be rough like Desi, like Rowena, or any of them.

"I'm exhausted."

"Forty-five minutes. Maybe less, if you strain. You can see the fence line in the distance."

"Okay, but you promised me a story."

Tightening their packs, they set off again, slower than before. Desi couldn't keep up the earlier pace and knew Lavellen wouldn't make it all the way home if they tried.

Desi patted her shotgun. She didn't know how much help it would be against the Nebula. She'd never hit something with no real form before. In theory, the rock salt ammo should slow it down... maybe.

"One day," she said, "a Bone Maiden was dancing in a field when she came upon a harp. The harp was old, whitewashed, and made of bone. She felt connected with it and picked it up, taking it home. When they got back to the hollowed-out tree she slept in, the harp began to sing."

"That's not so bad," Lavellen said with labored breath. "I thought this tale was creepier."

"It had a beautiful voice and the Bone Maiden fell in love with it. However, it is known that Bone Maidens aren't supposed to feel emotion. They dance, and it's all they do until they fade from existence and, from their dust, another Bone Maiden grows."

The clouds were following them now. Whether the Nebula had tracked or spotted them, they didn't have much longer. If it caught them, it would surround them with a terrible storm, eventually drawing out their souls to help power the storm. Her mother said if you listened closely sometimes you could hear the screams of Nebula victims in the thunder.

"The Bone Maiden stopped dancing, preferring to stay in her bed and lounge the days away, listening to the harp sing and spin wonderful stories." Desi shivered as the temperature dropped, far too cold for the time of day and season.

"That sounds so romantic—" Lavellen stopped walking, holding her side.

"What's wrong?"

"I don't think I can go any farther. Everything hurts, and I'm having..." she gulped in air, "trouble breathing."

Desi wasn't surprised, pain and exertion could do that. "See that?" She pointed behind them at a swirling mist, seeping out ahead of the clouds.

"Spirit Fog."

"Spirit Fog," she agreed. "Once it reaches us, the Nebula will know where we are. There's a possibility my magic won't protect us and we'd become disorientated, just like your wagon train."

"There was never a train."

"*What?*"

"We set out on our own. We lied so you wouldn't know how foolish we were."

"Spirits, Lavellen… Come on!" Furious, Desi set an unforgiving pace, desperate to get home. "How could you both be so careless?"

"Samael never believed most of the stories. Trust me, I understand we could be corpses on the side of the trail if we hadn't seen Ash Hollow on the map."

"You started with a lie. Great way to make friends."

"Will you—" She broke off, her chest heaving with deep gasps, still forcing one foot in front of the other to keep up with Desi. "Will you finish the story?"

"…Fine. Eventually, the Bone Maiden's sisters noticed her absence and came to find her. They couldn't understand what she was doing. They took the harp from her and threw it into the center of a grove, crushing it beneath their feet as they danced."

The temperature plummeted as fog lapped at their feet. Desi's skin broke out in goosebumps. Only the sight of the fence warmed her with hope, a smile daring to pull on her lips.

"Grief filled the Bone Maiden," she continued, "so she waited until her sisters were gone and laid down next to the pieces of her beloved harp, swearing she could still hear its song faintly. Bone Maidens don't normally cry, but that day, she did. As she cried, her tears filled the grove, turning it into a lake, covering both of them. Her sisters came and still couldn't understand her decision, but they missed her, best they could. They danced around the lake for days until they each turned to dust and new Bone Maidens replaced them, ones who had no knowledge of what had passed before."

"Is that the end?"

"Well, my mom always added this: to this day, if you stumble upon the lake, you will hear a sad song, like a musical lamentation."

"Desi, wait. You can't be talking about… Are you seriously—"

"I'd love to discuss this with you," Desi interrupted, "but we've got to move. Fast, run!"

Holding hands, the girls burst into a run, Lavellen stumbling, her face pale and expression nauseated.

The fog was around their ankles now, the clouds catching up with unnatural speed. A howl rang out, the wind pushing against them as the Nebula tried to claim its prize.

"We aren't going to make it!" Lavellen screamed over the wind and inhuman shrieking.

The clouds blocked out the sun and shrouded the entire plain in unnatural darkness.

Desi didn't respond. When they reached the fence, she shoved Lavellen up and over it. The girl landed on the other side with a hard thud and didn't get up.

Fog up to her chest, Desi turned to face the Nebula. With an ease that screamed of practice, she gripped her gun tight against her shoulder and aimed into the clouds. Her nose burned, screaming at her about the danger.

She pulled the trigger. The gun lurched back into her shoulder with a thunderous blast that echoed across the plains. It felt like everything froze for a second, long enough for Desi to climb the fence and drop down to the ground on the other side, cradling the gun to her chest.

Desi rested on the ground in the dim glow of early evening. The Nebula clouds couldn't block the light now. Steading her breathing, she didn't take her eyes off the creature outside the ward, but she reached out to feel Lavellen, grateful when the girl's pulse thumped vigorously under her fingers.

Realizing it missed prey again, the scream of the Nebula shook the fence. The wards glowed a fierce silver. Her eyes remained glued to the swirling mass of clouds until the Nebula gave up and dissipated.

"See, Lavellen? We made it!" Desi laughed.

She rose on trembling, aching muscles. Her nose told her before her eyes that they were in the cow pasture. Several of the black and white animals stared at them. A few made noises telling Desi they were unhappy with the company, but seemed otherwise nonchalant about the commotion.

"Come on. Only a few more minutes until we're home," Desi said, returning her attention to Lavellen.

The girl was conscious, barely, but nodded. Desi put an arm around her waist and together, they hobbled the rest of the way home.

Desi gently lowered Lavellen onto the front porch, locked away her gun, and kicked off her grimy boots. "Stay here. I'll send everyone out to you."

"Will you ask Marian to draw me a bath in the guest house?"

"I think that can be arranged." Desi opened the front door and stopped dead in her tracks.

Standing there in the front room, smiling at her, was her mom.

Chapter 13
April 1900
The Caravan
Fort Kearney

We reach Fort Kearney in a flurry of excitement. The women spruce themselves up and the men shave. All of us want to look our best, a common practice of early pioneers that we still perform.

I can see the main fort and, to the east about a mile away, tiny buildings where other outposts and watchtowers are set up.

Fort Kearney is home to many families, many Bonum among them. The fort and its surrounding lands around it are enclosed by a heavily warded solid iron and salt wall, seven feet high and dotted with defense towers. Among its treasures are a public bath, a small market, a pub, and housing.

We are all tired from the journey, and I can't wait to get home to my wife and kids. I know Marcus and Chloe feel the same. The longing for your own bed is a powerful desire.

As we pull into the wagon rest in front of the large gate, a cheer goes up around me.

I get down from my seat, stretching. I creak and ache more than in previous years. Thoughts of retirement again fill my mind.

I will spend my days working the land and playing with grandchildren.

I walk to the iron gate and shout the travelers' call for safe passage. A pit sinks in my stomach as I remember the last time I had.

As I take another breath to call again, I hear the answer yelled from behind the iron bars.

Backing up, I raise a hand to the Caravan to wait. The gate swings slow and steady, and we are greeted by half a dozen people, all armed and wary.

"Verity?" I ask, and she steps out from behind the group.

She's the spitting image of Avery—tall with grey skin, long black hair, and bright blue eyes. She has run the fort for over a decade; but now, she looks unusually tired, haggard even. The men around her also look like they haven't slept well in days.

Despite her apparent exhaustion, she quickly closes the distance between us and throws her arms around me in a hug. "Harrison, I'm so glad to see you."

"I'm happy to see you too. Can we come in and camp, rest up?"

She lets go and calls over her shoulder, "You men, get those people in here!" She glances at the sky. It's a few hours to nightfall. "Quickly!" she adds.

I motion to one of the Harmon brothers to take my wagon in. The Harmons are thin, weather-worn redheads in their late twenties, but can drive a wagon well enough to lead everyone inside without causing a jam in the entryway.

Linking an arm with Verity, we walk through the gate together and onto the road that will lead to the heart of the Fort.

"Tell me, how are Avery and the kids?" Verity asks.

"They're good."

"Everything is in place?"

"Yes, don't worry. Avery has it all in hand. You should come for a visit."

As I look around, I notice something is wrong. There should be more people around, but the fort is silent. I don't see any children out playing nor adults bustling about with their end-of-day tasks. I feel like I'm missing something.

"And then have to make the trip back without a proper Caravan? I don't think so," Verity says. If she's seen how I scrutinize everything, she doesn't speak on it.

We pass through the main areas, making our way to her small two-bedroom home, a simple log cabin tucked away behind the Caravan office.

I always stay with Verity. She's family, after all—my wife's youngest sister.

"You could do it safely."

"Maybe, but why risk it? I'm happy here."

We mount the front porch and enter her darkened living room. She speaks a word I've heard often but cannot pronounce or understand, and light fills the room from oil lamps.

"I'm glad you're here, Harrison. I knew you'd be coming soon, but you're late this year." She sits in an oversized dark rocking chair and I settle into its mate. It feels good to rest on a comfortable cushion that fits my whole butt.

"We've had some trouble this year." I proceed to tell her about the Malum and Winter Quarters.

"That's why I'm glad you're here," she says when I'm finished. "We've had troubles of our own."

She seems worried and out of sorts. This isn't the Verity I'm used to. Verity is always the quickest to laugh out of the three of them. Not like my Avery—quick to anger, a passionate and fierce woman. Not like Serenity, who was quiet and studious.

"Troubles?" I ask.

"Did you notice how empty it was through the fort?"

I nod.

"Half our community is… dead."

"Dead?" I exclaim. "Is there sickness here? Are my people in danger?"

"There isn't a sickness, but they might be. They'd be in more danger if they were out there, in the dark."

"You got anything to drink around here?" I know this explanation won't be pleasant.

Verity leads me into her well-stocked kitchen, opens an icebox, and hands me an ale. The sour, hoppy brew is the first taste of alcohol I've had since we started out. I gulp it down quickly.

"What happened?"

Verity slumps against her counter. "About a month back, we took in a lone wagon. It was my mistake; I didn't notice they were tainted."

"Could happen to anyone," I murmur against the rim of the ale glass.

And it could. Avery and I have made that mistake once or twice.

"This was worse than I've ever seen before. Within a week, the whole family was dead. We burned the bodies and scattered them about a mile off."

While my family may have the luxury of burying our dead, most do not. It's safer to burn them so nothing can use the bodies for horrible purposes later.

"We do have some… Humanists at the fort right now," Verity said.

I want to spit on the ground, but I don't. Humanists are a splinter group from the East that preach in the West. They don't stay or survive long here. They believe if you burn a body, the soul won't reach the afterlife. They think you must have a flesh and blood body to gain entrance. It's foolish.

"Unbeknown to me," Verity said, "not all the bodies were burned. They rescued the children's bodies from the flame."

"Religion makes a mess of everything," I grumble, drinking deeply. I don't like where this story is heading.

"They took the two children and buried them outside of the wall."

I stand there, staring at her. "Please tell me when you found out. You dug them up and burned them."

"We tried." Verity buries her face in her hands.

"It was too late?"

"Are you hungry?" she asks.

"After you tell me. You're bad at avoidance."

"If I have something to do with my hands, this will be easier. You won't have time to eat later." She returns to the icebox and starts pulling out food: cold grits, tomatoes, bell peppers, milk, and butter.

"Cook and talk, Verity."

"When we reached the graves, they were empty." She moves to the stove, already hot. Despite the risks, she keeps the fire burning all day to be ready for cooking.

"An animal?" Please let it be an animal, I think, but I know it isn't.

"We hoped so, but we found out very quickly it wasn't."

She cuts the vegetables and adds them to a second pan. She's generous with the salt and pepper. Taking out a pot, she pours in the cold grits, adding extra butter and milk. The fort itself is quite large and has two smaller outposts, one for farming and another for tending to livestock. It's the closest to a city one gets in the Infested.

"Have they gone for the farm or the ranch?" I ask.

"No, and we've had communication every day. So far, they've seen no monsters and had no deaths."

"Then why not move people there temporarily? They aren't large, but the few families over there could make room while you figure this out."

"I won't risk them. Right now, they're safe. If we move people, they might be followed."

I understand and motion for her to continue.

"The children started to come every night, calling softly," she says. "I don't know what they've turned into, but I've never seen it before. People can't ignore their calling. They leave the safety of the walls and then the next night, their voices join them."

Pouring the grits into a bowl, she tops it with the veggies and hands it to me. It smells better than anything I've had in six months. Verity is almost as good a cook as Ambrose.

"And you can't do anything about it?" I ask between bites.

"We've tried earplugs, locking people in, and," she shows me the series of large keys she wears around her waist, "making sure I'm the only one with access to the gates. It doesn't make a difference."

"None of it has helped at all?" I eat quickly. A glance out the window tells me it's almost sundown.

"Holding onto the keys has helped. Locking everyone inside slows them down for a bit and it's harder to climb the walls than you'd think. But people keep dying. Luckily, not everyone is affected. Those with Bonum blood are immune. But we're all tired. No one is sleeping except those too young to walk."

"You've lost children?" I'm horrified.

"Not many. A few over the age of fifteen."

"What can we do? I *must* warn my people. We'd planned to rest up here for a week." I put the empty bowl and spoon in her sink. Normally I'd wash up, but we have more pressing matters. I need to speak to Chloe and Marcus.

"I'm hoping, now with more people, we can put an end to this."

I help her gather supplies and we leave her home.

"What's the plan?" I ask as we make our way to where the Caravan is resting with their wagons.

This fort symbolizes hope for those from the West and those of us who live in the Infested. It is possible to live here, safely and happily. We cannot let it fall. These things, whatever they are, prove that something has shifted in the Infested, and I worry for my kids and wife.

I need to get home. We are behind schedule. Avery would never forgive me if I let something happen to another of her sisters—not that Serenity is my fault. Avery blames herself for that.

"With my magic, I can protect a small group from the calling. Enough to take out those... whatever is out there. I hope," Verity says, her face is stern. I've never seen her so serious before.

"And everyone else?" I spot Marcus speaking to a few gatekeepers. He doesn't look happy.

"Those without Bonum blood will be rounded up in the underground food storage and guarded by those that do."

"And myself? I don't have Bonum blood."

"You'll be with me. You're the best shot here. I waited to attempt this until you got here."

"That can't be the only reason."

Verity stops and holds out a hand to me. "I need you to take me home and bury me next to Serenity. Or promise to burn me and scatter me to the winds."

"I promise. Let me talk to Marcus and Chloe. I know which of my people would be best to help and which ones need to go below."

"Meet me at the gate tower in an hour. They come at full darkness."

We part and I rush over to Marcus, motioning for Chloe to join us.

"What's wrong?" Chloe asks once she's within earshot.

I quickly explain.

"You don't think we could leave now and be safe?" she asks.

"No, and I don't relish spending another night without even the protection of a wagon rest or proper campsite." I can't say I didn't have the same thought.

"We have to help them," Marcus says. "These are our people too. I've known some of these families for years."

"You, Chloe, and the Harmon brothers will stay with me," I say firmly. "Send everyone else underground."

Night is falling. I know the Harmon boys won't have been drinking. They're too religious for that.

"What should we tell them? I don't want a mass panic on our hands," Marcus asks.

"The bare minimum. They're all tired and stressed enough as it is. Maybe have them down a few sleeping droughts and some whiskey. It probably won't stop the calling, but it might be helpful. Meet us at the gate tower."

Marcus nods and goes to get everyone settled. I send Chloe to talk to the Harmon brothers before I head over to my wagon. My shirt swallows the slight purple glow of the protection pendant Avery and Desi made for me as I tuck it away. I grab my rifle, choosing it over the shotgun from its protective case, and load up on ammo.

I'm glad I ate when Verity offered. I dread the long, sleepless night to come. A chill nips at my skin and I long for the protection of my moleskin coat.

I'm as ready as I can be.

I find Verity standing by the base of the gate tower with about thirty men with her. She wears a dual pistol holster and each man sports various weaponry. Exhaustion harrows their expressions, all of them.

I can almost *feel* the night falling faster.

"How do you want to do this?" I ask, counting up the ammo in my gun and pockets.

"I've made amulets for everyone," Verity says. "They should help against the allure of the creatures' call."

"'Should'? You don't know?" Chloe asks, coming up behind me with Marcus and the Harmon brothers.

"I haven't been able to test them yet," Verity replies. "I know they can't stop the call completely, but they will help you resist it. If at any point you still feel like jumping off the wall to join them, tell someone and we'll tie you to the gate."

"Chloe has Bonum blood."

"Then she wouldn't need the amulet anyway," Verity says.

Chloe relaxes, but her face remains stoic. "How do we kill them?"

"A straight headshot works best," one of Verity's men says. "Killed a few like that."

"You're sure they stay dead?" the oldest Harmon boy asks.

"Yeah," another man says. "In the morning, we go out and fire up the burn pit. Nothin' but ashes left."

"Stinks to high heaven," another says.

"How do you want us divided up?" Marcus asks.

"They come from all sides," Verity says. "I want two people at each tower and four stationed at each gate. They focus on the main gates, but people will try and leave any way they can. I have all the keys right now and everything is locked."

She speaks fast, eyes flicking to the moon as it rises in the sky. She pairs off her own men and sends them off—four to the back gate, four to the side exit, and two to each of the eight watchtowers. Those remaining assume position by the main entrance.

"Marcus and Chloe, take the left front gate tower," I tell them. "Harmons, you're in charge of patrolling the ground. I'll go with Verity."

She and I make our way to the right gate tower. As we mount the stairs, I hear the call. It's soft, a breathy moan in the wind, almost swallowed by the darkness. Verity tenses next to me.

Up the stairs we go, getting to the platform that gives us a starlit view of miles of grass, sparse trees, and softly rolling hills.

"There." Verity points.

I squint and make out more than a dozen shambling creatures. "They don't move very fast."

"They don't need to. Their call puts the victims into a type of stupor."

Reaching out, I give her hand a squeeze as we both ready our weapons.

The noise swells in volume the closer they get. It is the sound of the air through damaged vocal cords, but sweeter. My heart clenches in my chest as I feel the draw.

They want me to put my weapon down, to breach the gate and join them.

My belly stirs with intense nausea, and now I regret my meal. My personal pendent and the one Verity gave me flair to life.

The call wants me to think they are safe, wants me to believe I will find peace out there in the dark, but I know it's a lie. The only thing waiting for me is death.

"You okay, Harrison? I need to send you back to Avery in one piece." Verity is smiling. Her eyes show no mirth, but she's a singular person. She may be enjoying this.

"Let's do this."

Gunfire thunders further along the wall as the creatures amble within range. Their eyes glow a sickly green. Skin sloughs off with each step, rips off with each shot that hits, and open mouths release a poisonous song. The wind sweeps in a stench I can only describe as rotten swamp water.

I let Verity get those from farther away and aim at the ones coming close to the gate. My hands shake. It's been a while since I fought a battle of any kind, and that's what this feels like.

I miss my first shot. I need to focus. I am excellent with this rifle, and fear is something I cannot afford.

Swearing, I fire again and take off the head of one creature. The body pauses, almost like it's deciding if it can still go on without a head.

Then it crumples.

The night fills with bright pops of light and sulfur-smelling smoke, the side effect of bullets made with iron and salt. In the East, they don't have these bullets. They live without fear from the Infested.

A cry comes from my left. Verity pauses her reload and cocks her head to the side. More yelling comes from the side emergency exit.

"Harrison, go see what's going on!" Verity exclaims.

Running down the stairs, my knees hurt. When I hit the ground, I bellow, "Marcus!" towards the nearby watchtower, drawing the attention of some of Verity's men by the main gate. I may need back up.

Marcus pops his head around and sees me on the ground beneath him. I watch him say something to Chloe. Not taking her eye from her target, she nods.

"One of you, go help Chloe," I tell some of Verity's men. There's a pause as they all glance at each other, and then one of them tears up the watchtower steps with his gun at the ready. He passes Marcus on the stairs.

The moment Marcus's boots hit the ground, I beckon for him to follow and start sprinting towards the sounds of the yelling.

"How you holding up?" I ask as we run.

Marcus is already breathless. "Okay…. But man, Harrison, this may be my last year."

"I was just thinking that."

We round a corner and see a group of people trying to mob the guard at the gate. Some are from our Caravan, others are local. About eight people are pushing, trying to get to the gate. They are in a trance, and another four people are pulling them back towards the underground bunker's entrance.

Noticing our arrival, one of the guards calls, "Help me!"

Those trying to get out are becoming violent, screaming and hitting—not only the guards but each other, anything that gets in their way.

"Just stand down!" Marcus calls to them. "They can't get out. Verity has the keys."

The guard nods and dodges a fist. He circles back to stand next to us.

"Tell those people to get back," I tell him first. "Marcus, check the back gate. We can handle this."

I watch the people hit the iron gate as they search for weakness.

I can't save them without hurting them. Hopefully, Verity and the others can kill enough to silence the song. Would shooting them be better than whatever waits for them outside?

Before I can decide, one of the fort's citizens clambers onto the shoulders of the others, finds a handhold higher up on the gate, and climbs right on over the top, dropping to the other side.

Chapter 14
May 1900
Day 14
Ash Hollow

"Mom?" Desi asked.

Her siblings all sat around the room, staring at the woman in shock.

"Desdemona!" Avery said. "I was worried about you. You were gone far too long for such a simple errand."

The silent question in her eyes; *What happened?*

Desi blinked several times. This could not be her mother. It had to be an illusion. If it was an illusion, it was perfect. Every detail of Avery Ash was there. She was petite and lovely, a small woman with grey skin and black hair down to her waist, her voice strong and her smile crooked. Her eyes matched the same blue as the freckles across her nose.

"We ran into a Nebula," Desi said.

She answered because when Mom asked you a question, whether vocal or not, it was just what you did.

"Where's Lavellen?" Samael asked from where he stood awkwardly in the corner.

"On the porch. She's hurt," Desi said, emotionless.

What was she seeing? Was she going crazy?

"Oh no!" Rowena scrambled up from her spot on the floor and made to dart out, but Desi grabbed her arm.

"Let Samael go."

"Desi, Lavellen is hurt! Helen, we need to…." Rowena trailed off as Desi increased pressure. She glared at her. "Hey, you're hurting me!"

"Helen and Rowena will be out in a minute. Samael…" Avery waved a hand towards the front door, dismissing him.

He ran out of the living room, the door slammed behind him.

"A Nebula, Desdemona?" Avery sounded disapproving. "That's far beyond what I've trained you for."

"I wasn't expecting it, and I managed just fine. But Mom… how can you… I mean… You shouldn't be here." It couldn't really be their mother, could it?

Helen sidled up to Desi and whispered in her ear, "She showed up in the kitchen a few hours ago. Refused to answer any of our questions until you got home."

Her mother waved off her question. "Simple, really. Whatever I contracted caused my body to look dead when I wasn't. I've seen more disturbing diseases in the Infested."

She looked at Marian, who shriveled under her gaze. It was cruel to reference what happened to Foni's mom. Marian hadn't known making a wish in a fit of anger could kill someone. It was a hard lesson learned.

"What about the shadow monster? It looked like you," Desi accused.

Her nose itched. If this really was their mother, the question wouldn't bother her. Her mother would rally to protect them.

"What shadow monster?" their mother demanded. "Did something breach the wards? Desi, grab my bag!"

Desi inhaled, ease inching its way across her shoulders.

"No, Mom, wait!" Ambrose blocked her from leaving the room.

"Ambrose, you know the rules. Safety of the family first."

"Mom, there's no shadow monster, not anymore. Desi took care of it," Rowena said. They were all standing now, surrounding their mother.

Desi shot her sister a look. She hadn't taken care of the monster, and she didn't know what it was or where it went. Why did Rowena lie?

"Oh. Well, Desi, I'm so proud of you for taking care of everything while I was gone. I'll make sure your father knows how capable you've become." Avery seemed to calm down and smiled at them, hands on her hips in a stance Desi knew meant she truly was proud. But, Desi assumed, upon seeing her children's faces, the smile didn't last long.

"Why do you all look so distraught?" Avery asked. "Aren't you glad I'm not dead?"

"We're just shocked," Rowena muttered.

"You don't remember anything?" Helen asked. Her hands twitched at her sides. She and Desi made wary eye contact. Desi still felt like something wasn't right.

"Nothing after I got sick, and everything else is a blank. Suddenly I was standing in the kitchen, and Ambrose was screaming." Avery took a deep breath and closed her eyes.

"That must have been so scary!" Marian had tears in her eyes.

Their mother patted Marian's shoulder. "Rowena told me you all buried me. I'm so sorry you had to go through that, but it must have been a disease I picked up from my last time out in the Infested. I may have stepped on a Somnus Mortis cricket."

This made the most sense of anything else she'd said. Desi had never seen one or known anyone who had contacted the bug, but she'd read about them. They could cause a death-like slumber. In the back of her mind, small warning bells were still going off.

"I've never seen one around the farm…." Helen started to say.

"Don't you all have something to do with yourselves? It's late," Avery dismissed her children, abruptly.

"Mom…" Desi started, but her mother gave her a look that clearly meant: later.

"I better see to Lavellen," Helen said, sounding resigned, as she left the room.

"Please do. I want them out of here soon!" their mother called after her.

"I should go too," Rowena said.

"I think not."

"Mama?"

"It's after dark and if I know you, then I know you've left things unfinished. Either with the sewing or in your workshop. Go on." It was like their mother had never died. She slipped so quickly back into her place.

Rowena sulked off.

"Marian, enough crying," Avery said. "You don't need to tend our guests either."

Marian stopped in her tracks, halfway to the front door.

"But Mom, Samael…"

"What about him? Surely he can take care of his own sister." Avery turned her attention to Ambrose. "I believe you were proofing dough when I came in. You should finish dealing with it."

They all looked at Desi before leaving the room, and Desi knew her mother noticed. She nodded to them to go.

Avery grabbed Desi's hand before she could leave. "You and I have something important to do."

Of course, they did.

Her mother opened the panel and together, they slipped into the dark.

"Tell me what I missed," Avery asked as she activated the torches and gave a jolt of magic to the wards as the panel slid shut.

Desi hesitated. She wanted to tell her, but should she? Her mother's eyes narrowed and she took in a deep breath before resting a hand on Desi's shoulder.

"It's good you are cautious, just like I taught you. But come now, Desi, do you think the wards would let me into the basement if it wasn't me?"

This was an excellent point. Desi wanted to believe her mother was back, so badly. And mother was right; the wards in the basement would be going crazy if she were a danger to the family or house.

"Marian thinks she's in love with Samael, *Ambrose* thinks he's in love with Samael, Rowena thinks she's in love with Lavellen, Helen won't eat, a Nebula is stalking the property, and Father is late." The words came tumbling out. Desi hadn't realized how much she needed to talk to someone.

"My dear, that's quite a lot. Don't worry now. You've done a fine job and now, I can help."

They descended the stairs.

"Do you want the key back?" Desi asked as she reached for it, not wanting its weight to leave her.

Her mother studied her face, lips set in a firm, thin line. "No, it's yours now. Let's go in."

Desi unlocked the door and they entered.

"I want those two gone as quickly as possible. Something about them disturbs me," Avery said. She paused at her desk. "The jar?"

"With Helen. They're nice enough, but I agree. What are we going to do about Rowena, Marian, and Ambrose? Rowena and Marian want to leave with them."

"Calm, Desi," Avery said. She put both hands on her daughter's shoulders. "Breathe... in and out... that's a good girl."

Desi drew air deep in her lungs. Everything was fine, and if it wasn't, they could fix it.

"Now, don't worry. I will take care of it. I'll send Marian with your father into Wyoming to meet a nice boy and see if he can train Rowena to go out on the Caravan next year. That will appease both." Her mom bent down and rummaged through her desk.

"What are you looking for?"

"Something I found just before I got sick," she replied. Straightening, she pulled out two tiny vials, one a deep purple and the other a swirling silver.

"You found potions?"

"No, I found the ingredients for potions." Avery pocketed the silver and patted it as if she were making sure it was safe.

"You didn't say anything to me about a potion."

"I didn't have time. Something I encountered during my trip into the Infested probably made me sick."

They delved farther into the room. The usual sounds of rustling, sighing, music, and humming came to an abrupt halt as her mother stepped into the light of a torch.

Desi glared at the bird, daring it to make a comment. Nothing came from its jeweled beak. Most of them were afraid of her mother, always had been.

"Aunt Avery?" Foni's voice drifted from her cell. The shadowy tendrils of her hair wrapped around the bars with a hiss.

Desi hurried to the bars. "Don't be afraid. It's Mom. It's okay."

Foni reached out like she wanted to grab Desi's hand and then recoiled. They couldn't touch. Not in her current state.

Avery approached the bars and held out the purple vial. "Persephone, drink this, and then help us."

Hesitantly, Foni took the bottle with a grimace. "It hurts to hold."

"I know. Now drink it," Avery commanded.

Again, Foni hesitated. "Aunt, you shouldn't be here, and you know it."

"What I know is I've been given a second chance and won't squander the time I have left. What would your mother say?"

"She'd tell me to do as you say," Foni said.

There was a pause between them as Avery waited. She was a woman of few words.

Nodding, Foni popped the seal and drank it back like a shot of whiskey. She began to gag, hands flying to her throat. Her color darkened from pale grey to a deep purple as she choked on the liquid.

"Mother!" Desi exclaimed, reaching for the lock.

"Stop." Avery grabbed her arm. "Wait."

Desi trembled in fear and anger but did as her mother asked.

Foni fell to the ground and stopped moving.

Then it was as if light filled her cell, and Desi heard Foni take a deep breath.

The shadows of her hair retreated. It still didn't look like the black curls she once had, the locks still moving with invisible wind, but the movement was no longer quite so sinister.

Her clothing shrank, becoming a plain cotton dress and pinafore. Purple and grey, tattered around the edges and a size or two, too small. The same clothes she had worn the day she left.

She struggled to her knees and looked up, eyes glowing purple, lips no longer black. She gasped and then tentatively smiled, her teeth white and bright but no longer sharp.

"What... what did you do?" she asked, voice gravelly like she hadn't used it in forever, no longer the hiss and whisper of before.

"I did what I promised. Well, as much as I could," Avery said. She waved her hand and the cell unlocked. The door silently swung open.

Foni stood and stepped from the confinement. Avery released Desi, who ran to Foni and embraced her.

Foni felt cool to the touch and smelled like herbs. Desi wanted to cry from relief.

"Thank you, Aunt." Foni held a hand out to Avery. Avery smiled and took it, giving a quick squeeze before turning around.

"There will be time for this later. Come now."

Hand in hand, like they had when they were younger, they followed her back to the alcove that held her desk. Desi was happy and relieved that they were able to save her cousin, but she couldn't help but think it was convenient. Why hadn't her mother told her before she'd gotten sick? If there had been enough time to create a potion, then there had been enough time to have a conversation.

"Aunt, please, tell me—what am I now? I don't feel...."

"The same? Of course not. I can't give you back your old self, but I could contain the wild magic so that you aren't a danger to yourself or others."

"Why didn't you tell me you'd found a way to help her?" Desi asked.

"Simple; I didn't want you to tell your siblings, and I also didn't know if it would work. An excuse would be easier to tell you if she died rather than have you know a gamble didn't pay off."

Desi's mouth dropped open. "What? You didn't know if it would work?"

"Desi, it's okay," Foni said soothingly. "One of my mother's lessons was that magic always has a cost. I'm just glad to be here."

"Your mother learned that the hard way," Avery said, lips pursing.

It was hard to get over the death of a sister and even more problematic when she died because your daughter made a wish before she knew better. Desi could only imagine how her mother felt.

"We have to get rid of Lavellen and Samael," Avery said, pulling a book from the shelf.

Avery opened the sizeable black leather book and put it on the table. She briefly flipped through the brittle yellow pages. Her finger traced the words until she made a pleasant humming noise and stopped.

"Here." She turned the book towards Desi and Foni. "I think those two have brought something sinister to the property, and your siblings don't have enough magic to help. My sisters and I could perform this spell with our eyes closed, hands tied behind our backs."

Desi read the spell. It wasn't complicated, without many words or ingredients, but required a lot of magic. She'd never drawn on so much of the magic from the Infested before. There lay the risk—the magic burning through you, too much, too fast, to the point of losing control.

"I will need you two to study and practice before you're ready to help me, but we don't have more than a day."

Foni finished reading the spell and frowned. Foni had always been better at spell work than Desi.

"If this spell goes bad, I'll become as I was before," Foni warned, "and so will Desi."

"I trust you both can handle it. You're almost as powerful as your mother and Desi is more like me than she knows." Avery squeezed her daughter's shoulder. "I know you can do it."

Desi sat in her mother's chair and pulled the book into her lap. Foni perched on the table, peering over her shoulder.

"Foni," Avery continued, "I don't think it's a good idea for you to make an appearance quite yet. You girls stay down here and work. I'll come back for you in a few hours."

"Why not?" Desi asked. A laugh came from the deeper in the room and soft creeping music began to play. A chill went up her spine, but it was better than the silence.

"This is going to take your siblings some getting used to," Avery said. "Let's not shock them all at once."

"When will it be okay if I come up?" Foni asked.

"Tomorrow, after I've prepped everyone, especially Marian," Avery said. Without another word, she swept from the basement.

After she left, Foni spoke again. "Feel like she's not telling us something?"

"Doesn't it always feel like that? Your mom had a softer approach, but she acted the same way."

"I still think we should be careful."

"Agreed."

Another laugh came from the dark, followed quickly by the word, "Fools."

Desi's stomach flipped. She knew the bird was trying to cause unrest, but she couldn't help but slightly agree with it.

Chapter 15

May 1900
Day 16
Ash Hollow

"They can't leave yet, Mom. Lavellen still isn't healed from her ordeal in the Infested!" Rowena was yelling when Desi came down for breakfast. She paused at the bottom of the stairs, not wanting to have to deal with this particular fight. For two days, Rowena and her mother had been butting heads on this topic and it looked like it was finally coming to a head.

Desi was tired, running on only a few hours of sleep. She and Foni were confident they could perform the spell now, but their studies had taken time and energy on top of what she was also expected to be doing around the homestead. Plus, she hated keeping secrets from her siblings and it felt as if, recently, there were too many. Her anxiety swirled inside her, desperate to break free.

"I told you I want them gone," Avery said. "They've been here over two weeks, and no one stays here longer than that."

Desi sighed, rolled her shoulders, and walked into the parlor to find them squared off.

Rowena's face flushed with anger. "Then I will be going with them!"

"You won't. Think about it, Rowena. You don't really know them. This is your first romance, and I understand. Do you think your father was the first person I was ever in love with?" Avery smiled, a laugh escaping her lips.

"I want to see more of the world than this farm."

"And you will, I promise you. I'm not expecting to keep you here forever. This isn't your jail."

"Desi already said I could go."

Both women stared at her. Wonderful. This wasn't how Desi wanted to start the morning.

"You did?" Avery asked. She looked disappointed.

"Dad wasn't home," Desi said softly, "and you were dead. Not a lot I could do but say yes. Do I think it's a good idea for her to run away with someone we know is capable of emotional manipulation? No. ...Don't glare at me, Rowena. It's true, and we all know it."

"I thought you were on my side," Rowena said, crumpling onto the settee.

"I'm not against you. I just wish you'd really think about it. I tried to talk to you, but you wouldn't listen. I told you I had something important to tell you and you brushed me off. Like you've told me your whole life, I am not your mother." Desi didn't want to fight with her sister, but Rowena was too stubborn.

"There's nothing to think about," Avery said. "Enjoy Lavellen's company until she leaves. You won't be going anywhere."

"You can't keep me here," Rowena said.

Desi could tell she regretted it when the words were out of her mouth. Rowena quickly looked down at her stocking-clad feet.

A silence filled the room, cold and dark. Their mother looked as though a storm brewed behind her eyes. Avery waited for Rowena to apologize and take it back, and Desi wished she would. At the same time, she always wondered what the breaking point would be.

The seconds ticked by but Rowena stayed silent, staring at her toes.

"Do you really think so?" The ice to their mother's voice triggered a physical reaction, and Desi watched crystals form on the wall next to her. "You are, of course, free to leave. You're right; I cannot literally stop you."

Rowena crossed her arms over her chest and started to smile.

The argument, loud enough to be heard all over the house, had drawn in their siblings. Ambrose, Helen, and Marian slowly trickled in. Desi made eye contact with each of them, silently imploring them to be quiet.

"Once you cross from the Infested to either the East or the West, you will have, at most, a month before you lose all your powers."

Marian gasped.

"What?" Rowena asked. "That can't be true. Bonum children are born all over the West and use their magic without an issue."

"You're different," Avery explained. "A visit of a few days is fine, but any longer and the magic will seep from you. It won't return, even if you come back."

"Chloe lives in the West, and she's less powerful than we are," Rowena said.

"Rowena," Desi interrupted. She knew this tale and she wasn't sure if her siblings could handle it. "Mom, do you really think now is the time?"

"Desi, shut up!" Rowena yelled. "I have the right to know."

Desi was stunned, but she gave a tight-lipped smile and took a step back.

Avery sighed and closed her eyes. She addressed the room, "Have you ever wondered why there are five of you? How could I keep you safe in my womb and birth you all without complications? Quintuplets are rare, and never do they all survive, especially without a hospital nearby and powerful magic."

"The aunts," Marian said, like this was, of course, the only explanation needed.

Desi watched Helen's face. Her sister was silent and expressionless. Had she figured this out on her own?

"When I found out I was pregnant with you, I knew there was no way that you would all survive or that I would, even with my magic. I begged Serenity and Verity to help me," their mother continued. "But like you, Marian, Serenity's gift was double-edged. None of her magic came without a price. She made it so all five of you survived, while Verity kept me alive, but the price was that we are all now tied to this land, tied to the Infested. You are some of the few Bonum born in the Infested itself. You're special."

"This is why—" Marian swallowed a sob, "—why I wasn't punished for what happened."

"How could I punish a child for something my grown sister never fully got under control? I understood just as your aunt did. You need to forgive yourself, Marian." Avery walked over and embraced Marian, petting her head in a rare gesture of physical affection.

The room was filled with silence for a moment, and then Rowena stomped her foot with an exasperated snort.

"I can live without my magic. In the West... or the East... what need will I have to infuse material with magic?" Rowena huffed.

Avery's mouth turned cruel and Desi waited for the other shoe to drop. This wasn't new information to her, but for her siblings? It would hurt, and their mother wouldn't sugarcoat it.

"You think so? Tell me—the ability you have to face everything head-on or be fearless and confident in all you do. Do you think that is natural?" Avery faced all of her children, releasing Marian. "Do any of you think that simply because you cannot perform magic like Desdemona or Helen that you aren't gifted with more than the obvious? Marian and her deep caring and empathy, Ambrose with his quick wit and chameleon-like tendencies? Are you so vain you believe the color of your skin, your freckles... that these are all... *human* traits?"

Desi watched as the reality of her words sunk into each of them.

"Desi... did you know this?" Marian asked, sagging against the wall behind her, pale and drawn with the revelation.

"I did, but I didn't know you wouldn't get your magic back."

"But you didn't say anything. You told me I could leave!" Rowena yelled, eyes fierce.

"I did try, but you shut me down," Desi reminded her. "You wanted to leave, and I'm not your mother. If this is something you really want, then you should go."

"I'm stuck here, forever?" Rowena asked. A sheen glistened in her eyes.

"No, I always thought you would leave, Rowena," Avery said. "I don't expect all of you to remain here."

She sat beside Rowena and took one of her hands. Desi watched as their mother softened around the edges. Their mother had to be hard and cruel, the Infested did that to people, but she was also capable of love and affection. They were moments that Desi and her siblings treasured.

"You will find your own way," Avery said quietly. "There are many places within the Infested you can go. The Caravan always needs Bonum to go with them. You could move to Loup Fork, the Winter Quarters, Shawnee Mission, Scott's Bluff, or Confluence Point. None of them are large settlements, but they always need people to help keep the areas safe for travelers. Your aunt would love to have you at Fort Kearny as well."

"I hadn't... I hadn't even considered those," Rowena admitted.

"I know, and there are so many other places to explore if you're careful." Avery looked at Marian as she continued, "You could marry someone and stay here. The guest house wasn't always for guests, and there's an entire back pasture waiting for additional houses to be built."

"I want to go with Samael," Marian said.

"But does he want you to?" Desi asked. "Has he asked you?"

Marian's silence was answer enough. She glared at them all and ran off toward the kitchen.

"I'll make sure she's okay," Ambrose said and followed her on quick feet.

"Lavellen has asked me," Rowena said.

"Then you have a decision to make." Avery stood up. "There's work to be done today, yes? Off you go. Desi, you're with me."

Desi and her mother left Rowena, still sitting in shock, and Helen who stood in the shadows, observing.

As they swept into the dining room, Avery asked, "Are you and Persephone ready?" Before waiting for an answer, she handed Desi a cloth and a bottle of lemon-scented furniture polish.

"As ready as we can be," Desi said and followed her mother's lead, the two of them polishing the wood table and chairs. She found herself puzzled by her mother's actions.

"Tonight, we'll eat a good supper in here, all of us. I've asked Ambrose to make a special meal, something to celebrate." Avery checked the lanterns, examining their oil levels and wicks.

"Why?"

"I am having Persephone come up tonight."

"What about Lavellen and Samael?" The lemon scent burned Desi's nostrils but she had to admit, the shine to the table was lovely.

"They're invited, of course." Next, they each took a broom and started on the corners, sweeping and bending until the floor and walls were dust-free. It was nice to work side by side with her mother like this again.

"You hope Dad will be home soon?" Desi asked. She didn't know why, but she decided not to mention the message she'd sent.

"Ah, you've caught me. Yes, and when he does, each room of this house will sparkle." Avery grinned, looking years younger.

For a moment, the smile was a beautiful thing to behold, and then, just for a split second, it changed, and Desi saw the wide grin of the shadow creature. She gasped and took a step back, almost tripping over her broom.

Then the vision was gone, and Avery stood there staring at her.

"Something wrong?"

"No… No, sorry." Desi felt anxiety bloom and burst open in her chest. What had she just seen?

"Why don't you go into the kitchen and get a bucket? I'll grab the mops from the hallway and then we'll be done," Avery said. Desi was glad to have a reason to leave. She needed to get her heart rate and breathing back under control.

Desi made her way to the kitchen, grounding herself as she went. She whispered to herself five things she could see and another five she could smell. She ran her fingers over five different items and tried to pick out five different sounds. That's when she heard the shouting. Quickening her pace, she walked in on Ambrose and Marian.

"How could you do this, Ambrose? You knew I liked him!" Marian shrieked, her face red, eyes wide, tears streaming, hands fisted at her side.

"I'm sorry, Marian." Ambrose wasn't yelling. He looked sad, resigned. "I don't know why I did it. I like him too."

"What's going on here?" Desi asked, but she knew.

Marian glared at Ambrose. When Desi put an arm around her sister's shoulder, Marian quaked under her touch.

"Ambrose, he... he had sex with Samael!"

"Ambrose, why would you tell her that?" Desi asked.

"You knew?" Marian gasped as she pulled away, betrayal written all over her features.

"She kept going on and on about how they would get married and have kids. I couldn't listen to it anymore!" Ambrose threw down a washrag and took a deep breath, steadying himself against the counter.

"You're lying!" Marian screamed it.

"I am not. I wouldn't lie—not about this, not about him," Ambrose said.

"Stop it, both of you," Desi cut in. "This is Samael's fault. He and Lavellen are Bonum."

She should have done it earlier, but there hadn't been time with everything else going on. She let herself get distracted. Maybe if she'd told Ambrose and Marian the truth, they wouldn't be fighting now. She'd believed Lavellen and Rowena when they said they'd take care of it. Why did it feel like all she did was mess up?

"No, you're wrong," Marian said, wrapping her arms around herself.

"Who told you that?" Ambrose asked.

"Lavellen," Desi replied. "They can become what people want, in a partner, friend, anything.... They can manipulate the emotions of the people around them. Lavellen said she would talk to Samael about toning it down. Apparently, it's natural for them."

"Why didn't you tell us?" Ambrose asked, eyes large and hurt in his face.

"Rowena and Lavellen told me they would talk to you, and Lavellen said she would tell Samael to fix things. I didn't realize they hadn't."

"So none of it has been real?" Marian whispered.

"Marian…" Ambrose warned.

"Rowena seems to think Lavellen really cares for her. Maybe Samael truly loves one of you," Desi said softly, eyes focused on her sister like she were a hurt animal.

"But not me," Ambrose stated.

"I didn't say that."

"He loves me!" Marian cringed, holding herself tighter.

"But he didn't make love to you!" Ambrose's words were meant to hurt and Marian sobbed harder.

"Not helping Ambrose," Desi said.

"I can't help how I feel. If he may still love her, he may love me too!" Ambrose slapped the counter.

Marian whirled on him, her eyes bright and angry. "How could he love you when I'm right here!"

"Marian!" Desi grabbed her sisters' arm.

Marian had a history of wishing when she was upset and Desi worried history was about to repeat itself. She tried to put her hand over Marian's mouth, but it was too late.

"I wish Samael had never set eyes on you! I wish they'd never come here!"

"Marian!" Another yell echoed from the hallway as Avery strode into the room, furious.

Marian slapped her hands over her mouth as all the color drained out of her skin.

"What have you done?" Avery demanded.

"Get the bucket!" Desi yelled.

Ambrose scrambled for the cupboard, grabbing a deep blue bucket and quickly passing it to Desi.

Marian hit the floor on her knees, hard enough they cracked against the tiled floor. Desi shoved the bucket under her as she began to violently throw up. Food and bile poured from her mouth in violent waves.

"I'm sorry, Desi. I didn't mean to provoke her," Ambrose said, his lip curling as the smell of vomit permeated the room.

"I warned you not to say anything," Desi said as she rubbed circles into her sister's back. "You couldn't just keep your mouth shut."

"Desdemona, Ambrose and I will care for Marian," Avery said. "You need to see what havoc her wish caused. It's too big a wish to be granted exactly. Hopefully, the damage is containable."

She sat next to Marian, pulling her hair from her face.

"Relax into it, Marian. You know you can't fight it."

"I'm sorry, Marian," Ambrose muttered. Marian made a small hiccuping nose.

Before Desi left the room to find out what damage the wish did, she caught a glimpse of Marian's eyes. Blood leaked from the corners like tears.

It wasn't going to be good.

When Desi entered the parlor, Helen and Rowena rushed to her with a chorus of, "Desi!"

"Marian made a wish," Desi said without preamble. "Where are Samael and Lavellen?"

"A wish? Like a big wish?" Rowena asked. "Should I be worried about Lavellen?"

"You should worry about Marian," Helen scolded.

"Well, of course, but why would we need to find them if the wish wasn't about them?"

"Please don't argue. Just help me," Desi said. She needed a nap, and it wasn't even noon.

"They should be in the guest house. Come on." Rowena led the way. They slipped on their boots and raced out the front door.

"What happened?" Helen asked.

"Ambrose told her he slept with Samael?" Rowena questioned.

Desi simply nodded.

"Wait, Samael slept with Ambrose?" Helen asked. "Maybe Mother is right and they *do* need to leave."

"You're wrong. What did Marian even wish for?" Rowena asked. They crossed the packed dirt road between the main house and the small guest cottage. Desi didn't answer her.

With the cottage's peeling white shingles and the large beige door, it wasn't the prettiest house, but it had large windows with bright yellow curtains and a small flower bed outside. Desi never thought about who built it and lived in it until their mother mentioned it hadn't always been a guest house.

Opening the door, they stepped into a small living room. The cottage was a single story with two bedrooms, a bathroom, and a kitchen. It was nothing fancy, but it always seemed to have a softer, more feminine decor.

Desi's eyes scoured the interior the moment she entered. The main room walls were covered with wallpaper dotted with tiny yellow flowers and the fireplace mantle gleamed with white rock. Once upon a time, all the furniture matched in a pale blue shade but time, weather, and the sunlight faded it to more grey. She saw no sign of the siblings.

"Lavellen? Samael?" Rowena called, shutting the door behind them.

"We're here. What's wrong?" Lavellen came down the hall, overdressed, as usual. She'd gone all out with Rowena's sewing supplies, fixing all her old dresses and making a few new ones.

Her white hat cocked to one side on her golden curls, but she wore no veil attached today. She used a cane, deep brown and polished; that foot would never truly recover.

Rowena must have made the cane for her. There were tiny flowers carved into it and it glowed with hints of magic.

Desi's heart constricted in her chest at the sight of Lavellen's loveliness, and she reminded herself it was all fake and for show—and it was for Rowena.

Samael held her hand as she moved slowly, her injured foot wrapped tightly. He looked less put together, still handsome; he wore only black trousers and a white shirt, incorrectly buttoned.

"Is everything alright?" Samael asked.

"That's what we're checking on," Desi said. "Are you both well?"

They didn't look harmed, but Marian's wishes weren't always visible.

"Oh, dear heart, please sit down! You're doing so well with the cane!" Rowena gushed over Lavellen, taking her arm from Samael and leading her to the couch with much fussing.

"Yes. It doesn't hurt anymore. Now, please, Desi… what's happened?" Lavellen asked, sitting close to Rowena.

"Marian made a wish," Helen explained.

Both Samael and Lavellen blinked at them owlishly.

"Marian made a wish about you," Desi prompted, concerned by their confused expressions. "She found out about Ambrose and Samael."

"I'm sorry, but who is Ambrose?" Samael asked. "And what did I do with… them?"

"And who is Marian?" Lavellen asked.

Chapter 16
April 1900
The Caravan
Fort Kearney

As the man hits the ground on the other side of the wall, the monsters converge on him in seconds. He is beyond our help, and all we can do is stand and listen. The others have been dragged back underground now, and only a few of us still stand near the gate. The fear in the air is palpable. We stand together, still and silent in the night. There is anguish and grief on the faces of everyone who tried to save him.

I hear the poor bastard scream as the creatures attack him. It's a sickening sound of flesh hitting flesh. I can hear them beating the man to death. Obviously, they aren't eating him. They will need him tomorrow night. The singing is quieter. Have we killed that many?

I look up at the stars. It is hours to sunrise still. How have they endured this night after night?

I vow there will not be another night like this.

Marcus's voice reaches me before I fully realize he's returned. "There was a similar scene at the back gate."

"Lose anyone?" An idea forms in my mind. A drastic one. We need to hurry.

Marcus sounds weary. "Two managed to climb over. At least there aren't as many creatures at the back."

"I think I may have a solution," I tell Marcus.

"We need one. If we miss even one of these creatures, they'll be back tomorrow."

"Agreed." I am glad we are on the same page. We must kill all the rest, and I have a plan. I am not sure it will work or if Verity will be agreeable.

Marcus and I hurry back over to the front right watchtower, our footsteps and panting overshadowed by the echoes of gunfire.

Verity meets us at the watchtower's base. "What happened?"

"Breeches at the other gates," Marcus replies. "Three people lost. We were able to contain the others."

"Spirits. I guess it was too much to hope for no additional casualties," Verity says. She looks tired, and she must be running out of magic.

"We aren't killing them fast enough," I say. "More keep coming out of the darkness and we may run out of bullets before they run out of bodies. If we tell people to hold their fire unless they know they'll hit, more of our own will succumb to the call in the meantime."

"What do you suggest?"

"We need a better plan, something that can kill the rest of them all at once. Marcus, go check on Chloe," I tell him. I need to be alone with Verity.

As Marcus nods and jogs off, Verity and I climb the watchtower's stairs together. When we reach the top, I look out upon the plains, moonlight illuminating a gruesome fate.

"We don't have anything that can take them all out simultaneously. If we did, I'd have used it by now." Verity closes her eyes. I can tell she is thinking about what, if any, additional weapons they may have or where they may be storing more ammunition.

There are at least sixty of the creatures left, almost half of the bodies I see on the plains, but I can tell people are tiring. Gunfire no longer rumbles like thunder; each shot cracks out far too pronounced in the night, with far too much time in between. We will run out of ammo and gunmen before the creatures can be stopped.

"These can't all be people from the fort." I don't know why it took me so long to see it.

"It's not, but I don't know where the rest come from." Verity opens her eyes.

She won't like my next question, but I ask anyways, as casually as I can manage. "You have telum castitate here, don't you?"

This is not something I should know about, nor is it something she should have.

Verity doesn't look at me. "Harrison, you can't be serious."

"Avery told me she and Serenity made you some a long time ago. For an emergency. I think this qualifies."

Verity sighs and crosses her arms, flinching as another round of gunshots bang from Chloe's tower. "I do have some, but you know what will happen to me? To this Fort, if it gets back to the West that I had it, had it and used it, if other Bonum find out?"

"What other option do you have? It's your job to protect Fort Kearney and the people who call this place home."

"That aside, it's hard to make. If I use it now, and next year, it's something worse…."

I know she doesn't want to use it, but we know this is the best option. "Next year is a long time for the Infested. We need to think about the here and now."

Verity smiles as I quote Avery.

"Fine," she says. "I'll get the telum castitate, but who will take it out there?"

"I will." I don't care for the idea, it's dangerous, but there's no one else I can trust to do it and do it right.

"Harrison, you can't—"

"I can, and you can't, and we can't ask anyone else. I want you to go get it, meet me at the front gate in ten minutes, and then take everyone underground. I'll give you just enough time to get clear before I use it."

"Avery and the kids would never forgive me if you didn't come back to them," Verity says.

She gives me a hug before descending the stairs ahead of me. Slowly, I hear the gunfire stop, but the song outside the walls continues. It's not as loud as before, but it's there, this twisted, tormented noise upon the wind.

Chloe and Marcus await me at the front gate.

"What's going on, Harrison?" Chloe asks, gun held at the ready. "Those creatures are still outside."

"There are too many of them out there, and this isn't working," I tell her.

"I know, but what else can we do?" she asks. "For every one I hit, another seems to take its place. Do we even know where they're coming from?"

"Every grave for miles, if this is what I think it is," Marcus answers her.

"You've seen something like this before?" she asks.

"Not saw—read about," he says, "and this is small compared to that."

"What did they do then?"

I remember the tale. I hadn't put it together until now—the May Grave Massacre.

"They had triple the number of people, and it took a week, but eventually they killed all of the creatures before more could be made and burned the graveyard they came out of," I say, trying to recall the details. It had to be twenty years back. One of the stories cited when asked why we no longer bury our dead.

"It's why no one uses Fort Townsend anymore when they travel east from New Mexico." Marcus pulls a cigarette out of his coat pocket and lights it. The fruity smell of the tobacco lingers and I wish I hadn't quit.

I watch the smoke curl into the air, swirling around us, as I say, "It tainted the whole place. Half the people in that fort died. The only thing that lives there now are the ghosts."

"Well, we don't want that to happen to us," Marcus states.

"So, what's the plan then?" Chloe asks. She fidgets, ready for action.

"Verity is bringing me something, and then I'm going out." My words shock them. I can see it on their faces.

"No!" Marcus exclaims, cigarette dropping from his lips. He stomps it out and grabs my arm.

"You can't be serious." Chloe glares at me.

"It's the only way."

"What could she possibly have that needs you to go out into… that mess?" Her eyes are flashing with anger and confusion.

"I can't tell you. Just know it will fix this."

Marcus stares at me, and I know the moment he figures it out. His mouth gapes open and snaps shut. Marcus releases me.

"Harrison, I don't know. What would I tell Avery if you don't come back?"

"That I was able to save her other sister." It's the only reasonable answer.

I see Verity walking towards us. She's alone and has a tiny sack in one hand, gripping it so tightly that her knuckles whiten.

"I need you two to get below," I tell them, "especially you, Chloe."

"I'm not leaving you," Chloe argues.

"Chloe, c'mon. We have to go." Marcus's voice holds a tinge of panic.

I watch as he drags her off. They will be safe underground. Everyone will be.

Verity reaches my side. "Are you sure about this?"

When she offers the sack, I take it and something sloshes inside. It's heavier than I thought it would be.

"We have to save the fort. We already lost the Winter Quarters."

"Why does it have to be you?" She pulls the sizeable front gate key from her pocket and hands it to me.

"Would you trust someone else? And you can't use it. We've already talked about this." I check for my lighter and protective amulets. I stroke them.

"I don't know how much those will help you," Verity says as she walks with me to the front gate. The lock is a series of mechanics to unlatch a smaller human-sized door instead of opening the wide wagon width gates.

"Enough for me to get far enough out. Once it's done, you'll need a group of men to gather corpses and set them ablaze," I remind her.

"That's the easy part." Verity kisses me on the cheek.

"You can protect people from what's coming?" I ask.

"Yes. The telum castitate won't affect the people in the fort and under the ground. The wards will save us, but it will destroy everything else," Verity sounds sad.

She runs off. She must get below.

I feel bad for using this weapon. Not everything in the Infested is evil, after all. But this fort can't win a war of attrition.

The gate opens with ease and without sound, which helps. I stare out into the darkness and can't see anything, but that doesn't mean nothing is there. Stars twinkle above me, but a cloud blocks most of the moonlight.

The singing has quieted down now that the guns aren't firing. Are they still out there? Lying in wait for a new victim? Have they left, content with the three souls they were able to capture?

I slip out and close the gate firmly behind me. The wards will protect the fort. It was never about those creatures getting in; it was about the people getting out.

I walk slowly and as quietly as I can, my heart pounding and my throat tight. I am afraid. I would be an idiot if I wasn't.

I still see nothing and my knees creak with every step. The ground is hard beneath my boots. I pause as I hear rustling to my left. Holding my breath, I squint into the dark. I didn't take a torch or lantern because I didn't want to be seen, but this works against me as well.

I release a relieved sigh as I see that it's merely a small shrub, branches twitching in the faint breeze. I start to walk. I don't need to be far from the fort, but every step feels like it takes an eternity.

That's when I hear them, all around me, shadows deeper than the night, eyes glowing in the light. I freeze, wary of triggering a hunt too soon.

They watch me and then the singing starts—louder, harsher, and less beautiful at such a close distance.

I know they are closing in, surrounding me, but it doesn't matter. I take a few more slow and cautious steps. Finally I drop to my knees. The earth is cold and unforgiving underneath me.

I can smell them now, that rotten stench upon the wind, and I try hard not to gag. I am not a hero. I am just a man who knows what needs to be done. I hear footsteps, slow and steady at first, as I open the satchel.

Suddenly, footsteps pound the earth. One is almost upon me as I pull a large bottle from the bag. The liquid of the telum castitate swirls like a starry night.

The creature's hand burns with intense cold and feels too soft and squishy for something living.

As I turn to shove it away, it hisses and a sizzling sound comes from our contact. It jerks away and I feel the amulet heat against my skin. I doubt it can protect me from all of them.

The bottle has a thick stopper and I don't have time to remove it. I smash the bottle on the ground.

Another reaches me, not smart enough to understand why the first one let go. Fingers dig into my neck only for it to *shriek* in an uncanny and terrifying voice as it stumbles back. The amulet heats again, this time with less intensity. It is losing its power. I must hurry. Bile rises in the back of my throat and I swallow it down. I won't let my fear win.

Shimmering liquid pools in front of me and I bring out my lighter. Wind extinguishes the first flicker of flame. Terror curdles in my stomach as I make my cold fingers light it again.

Two grab me next, trying to pull me away. I hear the stone in the necklace crack and I drop the lighter into the liquid as they swarm.

I'm covered by them, pulling, grabbing, clawing me. I see the gnashing of teeth and light from dead eyes, and I pray. *Please, spirits, don't let me die here.*

Then light flashes—brilliant, bright blue light—and I close my eyes tight. The creatures scream.

Then there is nothing.

I am curled up on the ground in the fetal position. I don't open my eyes until I am sure the light is gone.

Finally, I open them, and it is painful. I blink spots from my eyes, but the world around me is dark. A simple, quiet night. I take a moment to breathe and just stare at the stars. The cloud moves and soft moonlight floods the area.

The air smells like burned hair, and I cough and look around me. The moonlight shows piles of black ash everywhere.

Standing, I brush ash off of me. That was too close a call.

The ground feels dead under my feet, and the Infested much too empty. I am not Bonum, but I've lived in the Infested too long to not pick up certain things.

The telum castitate has done its job, and it's not entirely a happy one. It has destroyed everything paranormal for a mile in every direction—everything inhuman, unnatural, whether harmful or not. It will take months for the magic to return to the land. It is why it's forbidden to use; but out here in the Infested, sometimes we must do the unthinkable to survive.

I make my way back to the gate, slowly, just in time to see it open, and Verity sprints out. She gasps when she sees me and throws her arms around me.

"It worked!" She sounds as exhausted as she looks, and I can't blame her.

"It did. Hopefully, there wasn't much else in the area at the time." I feel like I could eat a whole roast and sleep for a week.

We go back through the gate to see a group of people gathered, all excited and cheering. Chloe and Marcus are there. They both look relieved to see me.

"You can't tell them what we used," Verity says under her breath.

"I know."

If other Bonum found out Verity used the telum castitate, they would come for her. Avery told me that it's one of the only weapons that can kill a Bonum. They fear humans using it against them, and I can't say I blame them.

After all, it's our fault the world went crazy to begin with, our responsibility that demons haunt the Infested, that creatures roam and prey on us. It's our fault Bonum exists, to start with.

"You need food and rest, Harrison," Marcus says. He shakes my hand, grinning.

Verity barks orders to her men. They must burn any bodies within the radius of the telum castitate blast.

"What did you do?" Chloe asks me, but the suspicion in her eyes tells me she already has an idea.

"I would tell you if I could."

She gives me a long, hard stare and a tight-lipped smile, but doesn't ask again. I knew she wouldn't argue; Chloe knows me too well for that. All she says is, "You better think of a good lie."

People shake my hands and thank me as I walk through them. None of them are sure what I did, just that they are saved. I don't want or need their praise. We in the Infested must stick together.

I think of home. What I wouldn't give for a cup of Ambrose's coffee and to sit in the parlor while the children clamber around me, telling me about their day.

"Harrison." Verity finds me again, her smile positively luminous. "You *must* promise to stay at least a week."

"I think we'll need that much time just to rest up. We won't have a warded place to sleep again until Confluence Point, and it's over a hundred miles from here."

"I'll have my people make sure yours have everything they need. I can already tell most are making their way to the tavern. It will be a noisy night with the celebrations and grieving."

I look to where the Caravan members are huddled together. She is right. Many are starting to walk towards the center of town, to food, drink, and decent beds.

"Take Marcus and Chloe back to my house and rest. I'll make sure to have breakfast waiting in the morning. It's the least I can do to say thanks." Verity hugs me again and gives her people more instructions. She'll be in bed long after me. This is her fort, after all, not mine.

Marcus, Chloe, and I walk back to her house in silence. The fatigue and hunger roll off us. I debate making food, but decide against it. Chloe sprawls on the couch and soon, tiny snores drift from her mouth.

Marcus and I each take a guest room. Before sleep claims me, all I can think about is how those creatures smelled, like damp and rot, and how hungry they were. I will have nightmares for the rest of my life.

Chapter 17
May 1900
Day 16 – Evening
Ash Hollow

Desi and her siblings all sat around the dinner table. The atmosphere was thick. Marian cried into a white hanky while Ambrose sat stone-faced. This was not the dinner their mother had wanted.

They ate a creamy lentil soup full of vegetables paired with aromatic rye bread and cucumber salad. At least she felt safe. Ambrose had baked into the food a sense of safety and home, because he couldn't put in contentment or happiness.

"Dinner is so good, Ambrose," Rowena said, into the awkward silence.

"Thank you," Ambrose responded. Normally he would complete that by trying to explain every step of the cooking process, but not tonight.

Avery got up and came back with a bottle of wine. She opened it and poured everyone a glass of the deep purple liquid. Desi was surprised. Alcohol was a rare treat because they couldn't make it themselves. She took a large drink of hers, even though she didn't like wine. It burned going down, but settled her anxious tummy. She hadn't felt one hundred percent. Not since their mother got back.

Lavellen and Samael ate, but they kept sneaking glances at Marian and Ambrose then at each other. They understood their memories had been taken, and they seemed uncomfortable and upset by it.

Desi didn't blame them for their resentment. The unsettling notion that people, conversations, and emotions had been ripped away with no hope of returning—it would bother Desi as well. She hoped it would make them leave quickly.

Finally, Avery put down her spoon with a loud clank that caused everyone to jump. Sharp eyes focused on Marian. "Enough of this. You have mourned for something that couldn't and won't be. I raised you to be stronger than this."

"But Mother…" The whine in her voice irritated Desi.

"And Ambrose, you must accept part of this blame and move past it. Lavellen and Samael will be leaving soon." He didn't say anything but nodded without making eye contact.

"We can't leave," Samael protested. "The Nebula is still out there."

"You have had quite enough of our hospitality. You chose to drag your sister out into the Infested, and now you must continue your journey." Avery's words were the end of the discussion.

Rowena began to protest and Lavellen patted her arm, "No, your mother is right. We've caused enough pain here, apparently." She glared at her brother.

"Now, are we all quite done with the drama?" Avery asked.

"I think we are, Mother," Helen said. She pushed her soup around but didn't eat it.

"At least eat the salad, Helen," Desi pleaded. She would need to speak to her mother about Helen's eating issues. Helen nodded and pulled the salad bowl towards her. "It has nuts in it, just the way you like it."

"I have a surprise for you all," Avery said. She stood up and went to the closed dining room door.

Desi tensed, her stomach aching from the sensation. She didn't know how Foni would be accepted by her siblings. Her mother had decided to announce it at dinner. Desi didn't agree with the decision, but she didn't have much choice.

"A good surprise?" Rowena asked.

"Desi and I believe so."

All eyes focused on Desi, who just shrugged and gave a tight-lipped smile. Their mother opened the door and Foni stepped in.

At first, there was silence, louder than any scream. Then a gasp and the sound of chairs against the floor as Marian scooted away from the door and Ambrose stood up, fists clenched at his side.

"Calm everyone," Helen said, looking wary but not moving.

"Mother!" Rowena exclaimed. "What's going on? How can you let her in the house?"

"Samael, Lavellen, may I present my niece, Persephone," Avery said. "She's just returned from a… trip, and I'm sure we are all delighted to have her home."

She brought Foni into the room and sat her at a chair next to Desi. Foni looked nervous. She twirled a lock of her hair around her finger like she did as a child. Desi reached out and held her hand under the table, giving it a squeeze.

"What's going on here?" Ambrose asked. He didn't sit down.

"Foni has come home to us safely." Avery sat down and began to eat again.

"I'm happy to see you all," Foni said. "It's been a long time."

Marian flinched at the way Foni's voice sounded. It still didn't sound quite right.

"Foni… Are you… alright?" Helen asked.

"I'm as okay as I ever hope to be again."

Lavellen and Samael looked stunned by everyone's reaction. Samael reached out a hand, took Foni's smaller one, and kissed it as he said, "It's a pleasure to meet you."

"I can't believe this," Ambrose said. He snatched up his bowl and plate and stormed from the room. The dining room door slammed behind him. Footsteps stomped all the way down the hall into the kitchen.

Rowena stood and turned towards the door, as if making to follow him, but Avery commanded, "No, sit and finish dinner, all of you."

"So, Foni, is it?" Lavellen asked. Her cheeks flushed, a pretty smile upon her lips. "Where did you go? Did you travel to the West?"

"No, I was still in the Infested. I was visiting my other aunt," Foni answered. This was the lie they'd decided to tell anyone, not family, who asked. Desi's siblings may not have understood exactly what happened to their cousin, but they knew she'd been out in the Infested and that she'd come home changed. They knew she'd been in a cage in the basement and that she was dangerous. To have her now, upstairs, sitting and eating dinner like nothing had happened? Desi understood their reactions.

"That sounds wonderful. What a nice trip for you," Lavellen said, all politeness. Desi could tell she was confused by the hostility in the room.

Rowena and Marian eventually sat back down and resumed eating. Rowena watched Foni steadily while Marian looked anywhere but at their cousin.

The rest of dinner passed with little conversation. Samael and Lavellen soon scurried back to the guest house. Desi was relieved when dinner was over and their guests were gone. She'd never had such a tense meal in their home before. She just wanted to get up and run away from the entire situation. What kind of person did that make her?

Marian got up and began to clear off the table. Something so mundane around so much that wasn't. It was almost comforting.

"The rest of you have chores to do, yes?" Avery asked as began to help Marian.

Desi left as quickly as she could. Foni disappeared through the back door. Desi had a feeling she needed some time alone, so Desi went to the parlor.

"Desi?" Helen's soft voice called from behind her. Desi paused and perched on the arm of the love seat. Of course Helen would follow her. Desi so rarely actually got to be alone. Everyone always seemed to need something from her.

"Yes?"

"You knew she was coming up tonight, didn't you? For how long?" Helen's forehead was creased with concern.

"Only a few days," Desi admitted. "Mother found something to bring Foni back."

"Is she safe?" Helen asked.

Desi could see the memories of the day Foni came back to them, a dangerous creature. It had been a scary and awful day. She and Helen had been in the front, talking, and then like a dark angel, Foni appeared at the gate, wild and monstrous, begging to be let in.

"As she said, she's as well as she can ever be. Mother seems to think she will not harm herself or us."

"Or Marian?"

"She let that hate die a long time ago, Helen. You don't know what it's like downstairs. There's no room for grudge-holding in that darkness."

Helen studied Desi's face for a few moments before she smiled, gripped Desi's shoulder, and left.

Desi walked out the front door. She stood on the porch watching the sunset, feeling the breeze on her face and allowing the restlessness to take over for just a moment.

The intense sensation of needing to run, go, and not look back. To sprint across the plains and go anywhere but here. She wondered if her father received the Will-o-Wisp and when she'd hear back from him. He would worry and then come home to everything fine. It would be weird, but ultimately fine. At least that's what she was trying to tell herself. Had she jumped to conclusions in her worry? Would he be upset that she raised the flag of alarm too soon?

"Desi?" came Foni's voice from right beside her.

Desi blinked. How much time had she lost to the call of the wild? The sun was far lower than it had been when she walked out. When had Foni arrived and how long had they been standing together in silence?

"Sorry, Foni. What do you need? I thought you needed some alone time."

"I did, and then I wanted company. I'm complicated like that." She laughed, a sardonic sound.

Desi looked at her cousin. Foni was beautiful, lithe, and so much more and less than she used to be; but most of all, Foni had been free out in the Infested, running wild without expectations or duties to hold her back. Desi envied her.

"You don't want to go out there." Foni's words shocked Desi. How did she know?

"I've been out there. I know I don't." It was a lie. Part of her did—always would.

Instead of calling her out on the lie, Foni tilted her head to one side, stilling in a non-human way like she was listening to something no one else could hear. "We need to go inside. Someone has opened the panel, someone not allowed."

Fear and anger filled Desi. Was the panel open? Had one of her siblings gone down there without permission?

"Come on!" Desi barged inside and stopped suddenly, causing Foni to crash into her. Foni was correct; the panel was open a few inches. Someone was down there, snooping, sneaking.

"They can't get past the door, right?" Foni asked.

"No, only I have the key. Even Mom can't get in there now." Desi slipped through the opening, Foni behind her.

The torches weren't lit, so the trespasser either had little magic or didn't know how to use it to light the torches. Which of her siblings would stray into the basement? It was the number one house rule that no one was allowed downstairs without their mother's or aunt's permission.

Desi lit the torch and the panel shut behind her and Foni. She hurried down the stairs, but stopped suddenly when she realized who was at the bottom. Lavellen was crouched in front of the door, trying to peer through the lock.

"What in the Spirits are you doing here?" she asked.

Lavellen jumped up and spun around. She looked guilty and frustrated. She leaned on her walking stick, breathing quickly.

"You shouldn't be here. How did you even know this place exists?" Desi asked, trying to reign in her temper. Hadn't she gone back to the guest house? How long had she been down there, and better yet, how did she know about it?

"I wanted to see the monsters behind the door. That's all, I swear!" Lavellen exclaimed, hands fluttering at her side.

"Didn't you get enough of that when we went to Woe Lake?" Desi asked, incredulous. "Did you forget that we almost *died* to monsters?"

"I… I know, but it just made me more curious about what else there is! What else don't I know about? I'm just so interested," Lavellen tried to make her case. Her eyes were wide, too large for her face.

"She's lying," Foni hissed.

"I am not! I'm sorry, Desi. I just wanted to see the evil fish."

"Again, how did you get down here?" Desi asked, hands on her hips. "How did you know this was even here?"

"Rowena told me. Please don't be mad. I think she was bragging, really. And honestly, once she told me where the panel was, it wasn't hard to get in." She looked at the ground and muttered, "I wasn't expecting the giant iron door, though."

"That's because Rowena has never been down here. No one is allowed down here except Mom, Foni, and I." Desi narrowed her eyes. Lavellen looked shifty. She was hiding something, but what?

"Oh, please don't tell your mother," Lavellen begged. "She is truly frightening."

"You need to talk to Rowena," Foni said, her mouth curling into a snarl. "This is completely unacceptable."

"I will. Lavellen, you have to go now, and if you so much as breathe a word of this place or what Rowena told you to anyone outside Ash Hollow, I will show you how much like my mother I can be."

"Oh! I promise!" Lavellen sounded desperate.

Desi grabbed Lavellen's hand and yanked her, protesting, up the stairs. Foni followed them.

Desi pushed Lavellen out of the panel. She stumbled, gripping her walking stick so she wouldn't fall. Foni shut the panel tight behind her. They would have to come up with an outer lock now.

"Rowena!" Lavellen gasped.

Rowena stood in the parlor holding a sewing basket, face pale as she took in the three of them.

"Desi, how *dare* you take Lavellen down there!" Rowena accused.

"She didn't," Foni said, her posture defensive. "We found her down there."

"You, ugh, don't talk to me. What does our cousin," Rowena sneered, "mean?"

"I found Lavellen downstairs because *you* told her about it."

"Lavellen, I asked you to keep it a secret!" Rowena cried, hurt prevalent on her features.

"I'm sorry, Rowena, darling. I couldn't help it. I wanted to see the fish."

Lavellen's simpering didn't win over Desi. The longer she was in the other woman's presence, the more Lavellen was like too sweet candy, delicious and sickening. How could Desi have ever enjoyed her company?

Emotions warred over Rowena's features. "Desi, I know this isn't good, but it's not like Lavellen will tell anyone, right dearest?"

"Of course not. I promise."

"How could you do this, Rowena?" Desi barked at her sister. "You know this isn't something we tell people, especially strangers. You put the entire household in danger!"

"Oh please, that's a bit dramatic, isn't it? Lavellen isn't a stranger. We're in love. Right, dearest?" Rowena held her hand out to Lavellen without diverting her attention from Desi—and she didn't see the look of hesitation on Lavellen's face.

But Desi did.

"Of course! I would never put you or your family in danger!" Lavellen limped over to Rowena and took her hand, tucking herself against Rowena's larger frame.

"You're disingenuous," Foni said. "I can smell it on you."

"Excuse me? You can smell what on me?" Lavellen asked, but her indignation felt stale. "Rowena, what in the world is wrong with your cousin?"

"Ignore her, Lavellen. They're just jealous," Rowena said. "Come on. We'll go up to my room."

"Rowena, I will be telling Mother."

"You wouldn't." If possible, more color fled her face.

"I will." Desi was about to add something else when the front door slammed open. Sagging against it was Samael. His eyes were feverish and his face a sickly shade of unnatural orange.

"Samael!" Lavellen screamed. With her injured foot, she couldn't reach him when he crumpled. He hit the ground, twitching violently.

"Foni, get Helen," Desi commanded and called for her other siblings.

Marian and Ambrose came down the hall simultaneously, refusing to look at each other. Upon seeing Samael, Marian cried out and started to rush forward, but Ambrose grabbed her arm.

"How dare you?" Marian yelled.

"He doesn't know who you are, and Lavellen won't appreciate strangers trying to help with her brother," he said, "especially someone they know used magic on them."

"What is going on here?" Avery demanded, coming into the room as well. She looked irritated, a feeling Desi understood all too well.

"Mom, Samael is sick," Desi said. "I've sent Foni for Helen."

"Good." Avery knelt by Samael and placed a hand on his head. "He's burning up. Ambrose, I need a cooling tea, quickly. Rowena, Marian help Lavellen take her brother back to the guest house and get him into bed with a wet rag on his forehead until Helen gets in from the field."

Marian opened her mouth and Avery placed a hand over it.

"You are not to speak. Not once. Get him in bed and come straight back."

Marian lowered her eyes, ashamed, and went to help Samael.

"He didn't look good," Desi said, watching her sisters take Samael from the house with Lavellen.

"He did not. I'm very concerned. Whatever sickens him, it caught fast."

"Do you think Helen can help him?" Desi asked.

"I don't know. She can't heal everything. You know that."

Foni returned and grabbed Desi's arm. "Helen went straight to the guest house."

"Good," Desi said. "Do we have any idea what could have caused this? Have you seen anything like this before?"

"No, never." Foni frowned. "Is anyone else sick? Could it have been the food?"

"Are you accusing me of poisoning him?" Ambrose came from the kitchen, a large mug of tea in his hand.

"Of course not!" Foni exclaimed.

"You better not be, glass houses and all that." Ambrose glared at her.

"I never poisoned anyone," Foni argued.

"That wasn't kind, Ambrose," Desi said.

"I don't care." He walked past them to deliver the tea.

"You take that tea to Helen and come straight back," Avery said.

Ambrose paused mid-step for just a second, straightened his back, and kept going.

"It was a bad idea, coming up here," Foni said softly as she watched him leave. "I should have stayed downstairs."

"Don't think like that," Avery said, getting to her feet. "My sister, your mother, would not have wanted that for you. Now we have work to do."

When her mother motioned to the panel near them, Desi realized she hadn't had a chance to tell her mother about Lavellen's snooping.

Chapter 18
May 1900
Day 18
Ash Hollow

Desi and Foni stood near the tree with the old swing. It was early morning and Desi listened to the animals moving in their pastures. All the animals woke and began moving around with low moos, high-pitched clucks, and throaty huffing.

"Is Helen taking care of the animals or Samael?" Foni asked. Her stark white apron and her ink-colored hair flowed freely in the wind in a striking combination.

"I think Rowena and Lavellen are with Samael this morning," Desi said, biting her bottom lip. Their mother confided in her that morning that Samael was worse than before.

She wouldn't allow herself to reflect on that for long. It was time to do the spell her mother wanted them to perform, a powerful spell. Desi only agreed to do it because she was smart enough to know this was a protection spell. She and Foni had studied it well and Desi was growing more and more confident in her magic. She did wonder why her mother hadn't done it herself.

"She wants us to do this now?" Foni asked.

The sun burned off the darkness overhead, the sky turning blue as they waited.

"Yes, and from what I can see, she's right." Desi pointed to a spot on the horizon where dark storm clouds gathered.

Foni sucked in a breath. "The Nebula?"

Desi shivered. "Yes. I can feel it, lingering. Our wards are strong, but I think Mama's right. An extra layer of protection can't hurt."

Foni closed her eyes. She stood still and silent for a moment before saying, "You're right. It's out there... like it's waiting for something."

Desi's eyes caught movement, and she watched as a pale and tired Helen made her way from the house to the barn. Helen either ignored them or didn't see them. No warm wave or acknowledgment.

"Okay, then let's get this over with," Foni said, straightening her shoulders.

"This will work," Desi said.

"We've prepared all we can. Time to anchor it to this tree and hope for the best."

Foni grinned at her and Desi smiled back, as though they were eight again. They stood on different sides of the tree and placed their hands on its rough bark.

"Remember to focus!" Foni's voice wavered but Desi felt her magic flare. "Here we go!"

Desi closed her eyes. She could smell the bark, dirt, leaves, and grass around her. The wind brushed her cheeks, tugged at her braid and clothes, and wafted in the scents of the animals and cooking.

Digging her fingers into the tree bark, she concentrated on how it felt. Scratchy and spongy simultaneously, bits of the wood tried to burrow under her fingernails. Everything had magic in it, from the soil to the air and light. The black behind her eyelids started to burn with bright pops of color, almost like stars. She no longer felt the ground beneath her feet, as though her body and mind were spinning out of control into a void.

Desi forced her eyes to stay closed. She couldn't break the spell.

Magic lurched within her chest, flooding her body with energy. Her heart pounded just beneath the surface of her skin. Did Foni feel the same way? Was it a heady feeling for her or something else?

"Praesidium," Foni whispered. It was time to start.

Gathering the magic together, Desi knew she must give it purpose with words and ritual. "Clypeus," she murmured.

A jolt of electricity shot through her legs down into her feet. Was that supposed to happen?

"Imperium." Foni's voice sounded so far away. It was an illusion. Desi was certain if her eyes opened, she would see her cousin only a few feet away.

"Auxilium," Desi said. Another burn of power, this time from her shoulders to her fingers. The wood beneath her skin felt like it was on fire. She wanted to pull her hands away but knew it would break the spell. The magic made her feel strong, powerful.

And you are. Desi heard the words clearly in her mind. Who had spoken them? Was she hearing the voice of the Infested? Or was it her own inner monologue?

"Tectumque," Foni said. Desi squeezed her eyes closed tighter. She wanted to open them and find Foni's face. Why did her cousin sound breathless?

As Foni started the spell, Desi would end it.

"Praetexo!" Desi shouted the last word, and it felt like her magic was ripped from her.

Foni cried out and Desi's eyes snapped open. Foni was bent over, gasping for air. Desi rushed over to her, feeling weak and starving.

"Foni, are you okay?"

"Yes... Just... need," she gulped air, "to... breathe."

Desi helped her sit on the grass.

"Wow," Foni gasped and pointed.

"Wow, what?" Desi looked up and her mouth fell open. Above the farm shone a glinting silver dome, a shield to prevent harm from coming to them and the property. Desi blinked and released the last of her magic, and the shield winked out of sight.

"Well, thank the Spirits, it's not visible to the naked eye," she said. She helped Foni to stand and her stomach grumbled as if in protest.

"Food," Foni agreed.

They strolled back to the house. Climbing the few porch stairs winded both girls and Desi knew they needed not only fuel but rest too.

As they entered the kitchen, Desi spotted Ambrose stirring something on the stove and asked, "What smells so good?"

"Vegetable soup with squash pudding," he said. Pausing to look them over, he narrowed his eyes. "Did you just cast a spell?"

"Yes, something Mama wanted," Desi replied, slumping against the counter. "How did you know?"

"I saw a shower of sparks through the window a few minutes ago and here you both are now, looking pale and exhausted." He wiped his hands on his apron before moving to the icebox to pull out eggs, cheese, butter, and thick-sliced cured ham.

"Are you really giving me ham?" Desi asked. They rarely slaughtered their pigs, so she considered ham a luxury.

"Yes. You and... You guys need the protein. Go sit in the living room and I'll fix you up some egg and ham sandwiches."

"Thank you, Ambrose," Foni said. He didn't act like he heard her. She shot Desi a knowing glance and left the room without another word.

"You could be nice to her, you know," Desi said. "She hasn't done anything to you."

"I know…. It's just… I don't trust her. How can I after what she became?" Ambrose pulled out a loaf of bread and began cutting slices.

"She's better. Mama fixed her. And she just helped me cast a protection spell. Try, at least? For me?"

"I promise… to try." He gave her a smile over his shoulder.

"How is Samael?" Desi asked.

His smile died. She'd have given anything for it to come back, but she also knew Ambrose was infatuated with Samael. Even if Samael didn't remember who he was.

"Feverish and delirious. I'm worried. I've never seen an illness Helen couldn't cure, except…."

"Except when Mama died," Desi finished somberly.

He nodded. "I keep waiting for someone to come in and tell me the fever broke, and he's awake."

Ambrose put a skillet on the stove and cracked the eggs into the pan. The smell and sizzle made Desi's stomach growl again.

Ambrose chuckled. "Go sit down before you fall down. This won't take long."

Desi blushed, but she obediently retreated back down the hallway. When she entered the front parlor, she saw her mother sitting next to and speaking to Foni.

"Mama?" Desi asked. She assumed her regular spot, back against the wall, and slid to the floor. The wood paneling behind her was cool and comforting.

"Foni says it went well? From what I can see, she is correct," Avery said proudly.

"Yes, though now I need food and a nap," Desi joked.

"You girls did well. Eat and sleep. I'll take care of your chores. You deserve a day off."

"I have to tell you something," Desi said. Now was as good a time as ever. Foni frowned at her.

"What? Is everything alright?" Her mother asked, concern wrinkling her forehead.

"Rowena told Lavellen about downstairs and how to open the panel. I found Lavellen down there before Samael got sick."

Avery seemed to think on this for quite some time. Desi could tell a wave of quiet anger simmered beneath her eyes but, to Desi's surprise, her mother remained composed when she finally spoke.

"I will speak to Rowena about this and possibly consider a mind-wiping drought for Lavellen. Right now, they're all so focused on poor Samael that I don't have the heart for a lecture or threats." Her mother's mouth was pinched, but she smiled. This didn't sit right with Desi. It was unlike her mother to show compassion to someone who could have endangered them.

"What now, Aunt?" Foni asked. She leaned back against the settee, head lolling as she stared at the ceiling.

"What do you mean?" Avery asked as she stood up and patted Foni's leg.

"I think she means the protection spell worked, but we can't keep it up forever," Desi said. "We need a plan. What are we going to do about the Nebula?"

"The Nebula?" Avery blinked, "Oh yes, I did have a thought about how I might defeat that."

"You don't want us to help you?" Desi asked.

"No, it's too dangerous. There's a possibility I won't make it out, and then you need to take charge."

"Don't talk like that, Aunt," Foni said.

Avery sighed and frowned, rubbing her forehead.

"Are you okay, Mama?" Desi asked.

"What? Oh yes, of course." She sounded distracted.

"You said you had a plan, or the start of one."

"If I drew some of the excess magic from Foni, I might be able to boost my own abilities long enough to get rid of the Nebula," she said in such a way that the words seemed to freeze in the air in front of her.

Desi shook her head, dread tightening in her stomach at the thought. Combining magic for a spell was one thing; siphoning from another Bonum was forbidden *and* illegal. Did their mother really think the Nebula posed that big of a threat?

"Would that even work?" Desi asked. "Wouldn't it put her in danger?"

Avery glared at Desi. "Yes, it would work. It would be the excess magic leftover from her condition. She should come out the same. If my sisters were here, I wouldn't need to take such drastic measures."

Foni and Desi exchanged glances, but their conversation was interrupted when Ambrose appeared with a plate with hot sandwiches and two mugs of tea that smelled like peppermint and lemon.

"I think I'll leave you girls to eat. I told Helen I would check on Samael as she's tending the animals." Avery swept out the front door without a backwards glance.

"You think she'd let me go with her?" Ambrose asked wistfully.

"I doubt it," Desi said, holding out her hands for food. Ambrose huffed, passed over the plate, and disappeared back down the hallway.

"Desi, I'm concerned about your mother," Foni said. "There is something just- When I look at her, it gives me a headache."

Desi looked at Foni. The tone of her voice didn't sound like she was really that worried, but Desi agreed.

"I think... I think it might be a good idea if I leave here," Foni said.

Desi's mouth dropped open. "What?"

"She's not... herself.... She's not thinking, or she'd never have suggested something so...."

"Appalling," Desi finished the sentence, resigned.

Foni was right. Once the West got over their fear of Bonum, they crafted new laws; primarily to protect Bonum, but some were for the protection of everyone. If a Bonum grew too powerful or had too much magic in them, they became one of the monsters, part of the Infested. It had happened to Foni, whether she'd been dangerous to humans or not.

Bonum lived peacefully alongside humans. Bonum were born from humans. They were a gift from the Infested. That's what their father always said.

Among the Bonum, taking another's magic was verboten and only for times of great peril. No family wanted to hunt down and kill a Bonum gone bad, drunk with power. It had only happened twice in their entire history.

"But Foni, where would you go?" Desi asked, even as an idea took form in her mind.

"To Fort Kearney. It's only a month's journey—less if I use magic. You could come with me."

"No, but maybe... maybe Lavellen and Rowena?" Desi's twisting stomach settled now that she had the beginning of a plan. Maybe this could work?

"What about the Nebula? I didn't even think of that. I don't know if I'm strong enough to fight it." The panic in Foni's voice gave Desi pause. Maybe they were overreacting to her mother's words?

"I don't know. It was just a stupid thought... Let's not talk about this anymore." Desi yawned. She really needed a nap and time to think things through before discussing them aloud again. She didn't want Foni scared.

"Later." Foni promised.

They dug into the food Ambrose had left for them. With each bite of salted meat, creamy egg, tangy cheese, and crunch of the bread, Desi felt better. She could tell her cousin did too, as color returned to her cheeks. Desi drank deeply from her cup of herbal tea and felt Ambrose's magic call to her, asking her to wake up, to rejuvenate. Maybe she didn't need that nap after all?

Ambrose came back into the room and silently began to collect the dishes.

"Oh Ambrose, this is so good!" Foni exclaimed.

"You're welcome." The words were slow and short, but Desi appreciated he was trying.

"Yes, thank you." Desi took another drink. "The tea is a bonus, and you know me; I don't normally like tea."

"Heathen." Ambrose laughed, but there was sadness in his eyes.

"Squash pudding, huh?" Desi asked as she finished the sandwich and handed over her plate. If she could get him talking about his cooking, it might help to normalize the situation with Foni, even if she couldn't fully take his mind off Samael.

"Yes, with cream, flour, eggs, and butter. I added some of the spices Papa brought back after the last Caravan before I baked it. The recipe came to me this morning while I was trying to decide what to do with all that squash we harvested."

"Are you going to add it to the family recipe book?" Desi asked.

"Not sure. It depends on if it's any good."

"Well, if it's as good as what I just ate, you must," Foni said.

Desi was happy Foni felt like she could enter the conversation. Maybe things were getting back to normal. However, the cloud of her mother's request still lingered in the back of Desi's mind.

"Do you hear that?" Ambrose asked suddenly, stiffening with alertness.

"No, what?" Desi asked. She couldn't handle another emergency. Her magic was all but tapped.

"Crying." Ambrose was out the door in seconds.

"Oh no." Foni frowned.

They stood and helped each other out the door and onto the front porch. On the path from their house to the guest house, Avery held onto Ambrose, who struggled to get past her.

Foni inhaled deeply through her nose. "I smell death."

"Impossible." Desi shook her head. She refused to believe someone had died on their property, again.

Avery dragged Ambrose away from the guest house as Marian appeared in the open doorway. She was pale and weeping like her heart was broken, and perhaps it was.

"Marian?" Desi called ahead as she and Foni hurried along the path.

Marian sagged in the door frame, a hand clutched at her chest. "He's dead, Desi. How could he be dead?"

Desi looked around. Where was Lavellen? "Mama, what happened?"

"When I got here, he was barely breathing," Avery replied. "I sent Lavellen and Rowena to fetch Helen, but they took too long and he was too sick."

Ambrose collapsed against their mother. Avery made cooing noises and rubbed comforting circles into his back.

"Are you sure he's dead?" Foni asked.

Avery simply nodded.

"Why didn't you have Marian make a wish?" Desi asked.

It was a stupid question, born from shock. Of course, Marian couldn't fix this with a wish. Desi lowered her head, kicking herself for even opening her mouth.

"Desi!" Marian wailed. "I couldn't make another wish. Who knows what would have happened?"

"Zombies," Foni said under her breath, earning a glare from Avery and Marian.

"I wouldn't ask your sister to do that," Avery said sharply, "not even to save a life. She's already made too many wishes recently, and you know that."

"I know, I'm sorry. Foni, help Marian? I'm going to go get Lavellen," Desi said. She broke away from her cousin and jogged towards the barn. Her tired muscles strained, but she needed to intercept Lavellen and Rowena.

The path wound around the guest house and past Rowena's workshop. The air smelled like metal and oil, familiar. Desi moved faster upon the dirt path worn into the grass by thousands of footsteps. She took a sharp right near the stables, listening to the animals' sighs and grunts within, and found herself facing her sisters and Lavellen.

Rowena saw her and stopped dead. Helen mouthed the word 'no.'

Desi halted and waited for them to come to her, grateful they couldn't see the front of the guest house from this turn of the path. Nor could they hear Marian's mournful sobs.

"Desi?" Lavellen asked.

She looked haggard, hair not done, hat and veil missing, dress rumpled. White knuckles clenched around her staff, her bad foot wrapped tightly in muslin.

"Lavellen…" Desi couldn't get the words out, but her expression must have told Lavellen enough because her own fell into despair.

"No…" Lavellen whispered.

"Dearest one." Rowena wrapped an arm around her waist.

"What happened?" Helen asked.

"I don't know. Mama says… She says Samael is dead." Desi didn't want to say it out loud, but there it was, and she couldn't take it back.

Lavellen wailed, an inhuman sound that Desi was sure carried for miles. If not for her staff and Rowena, Lavellen would have crumpled to the ground.

"I have to go see him." Helen rushed off.

"Take her into the house, Rowena," Desi told her sister. "She doesn't need to see him until we've had a chance to clean him up."

Desi watched as Rowena coaxed the girl towards the back of the house, murmuring sweetly into her golden hair. Lavellen's cries, a high-pitched keening, would haunt Desi's nightmares.

Chapter 19

May 1900

The Caravan

After Fort Kearney, we are relieved that the hundred miles to Confluence Point passes without incident. We lose no more people, animals, or supplies.

However, it gives the Caravan a sense of false hope that things are safe and returning to normal. It is *not* safe, and I have half a mind to recommend halting Caravans for the next few years.

It would hurt the West. People love the goods from the East. It is all a luxury. We bring back news, mail, books, tobacco, exotic spices and dried goods, fabric, and all manner of soaps, lotions, and perfumes—just to name a few. Shops from the West pay the Caravan handsomely for goods so they can turn around and re-sell them to a grateful public.

However, the Caravan isn't the only way to get these sorts of items. Once a year, a ship delivers items to California. The vessel normally brings larger items or bulk supplies, like cotton and things harder to grow in our climate. It also takes back goods. Surprisingly, we export more than we import.

I hear my people sing their prayers to the spirits and laugh as they tell the old stories of what the land was like before, when demons and their ilk didn't haunt the plains.

"You look deep in thought, Harrison," Chloe says from where she rides beside my wagon.

She keeps her shotgun in hand and her haunted gaze scours our surroundings—the same look she's had since we fought off the monsters. This will probably be her last time out. She'll go home and marry a lovely young woman, raise horses, and try to burn the nightmares from her mind with laughter. I won't tell her that while it helps, it doesn't keep the memories at bay for long. Given what Avery has seen for the future, I don't want her to keep riding with the Caravan.

"I see the wagon rest ahead," I tell her. "I'll feel safer once we're all within its wards."

For miles, the land is green with short grass and soft hills in the background. The sound of trickling water comes as a relief. For some reason, most creatures in the Infested won't cross running water. Confluence Point is a safe space at the junction of the North and South Platte rivers.

Chloe squints and a smile blossoms on her face. She must see the sign.

A large thick pole sticks up ten feet from the ground. Nailed to it is a wooden plank that reads: "Confluence Point—as safe as it gets."

Those of us who make this journey are a strange bunch.

A whoop goes up from the other wagons as the rivers come into view. Dark, murky water flows freely into the V where the rivers converge, framing a narrow strip of land where we can take our rest. Indeed, I will be able to sleep for the first time in five days since we left the fort.

Half an hour later, we circle our wagons in the lush green. The animals seem happy to graze in the middle, even if it's a bit cramped. Without much room for tents, most of us will sleep in or under the wagons themselves.

Soon fires burn and I smell food, coffee, and booze. I caution them not to overindulge. This place is safe, but as the sign says, "as safe as it gets." There is still danger and precautions must be maintained.

I volunteer for the first patrol.

"You should relax," Marcus says, pipe in hand. The tobacco smells rich and woody.

"I can't. This trip has been difficult. I don't completely trust we've seen the last of the what the Infested is going to throw at us, and they think more people here is a good idea?" A sardonic laugh leaves my mouth.

"We'll fight it. You, Chloe, and I know it's an awful idea. People will die. But we can't do anything about that now, so stop worrying. You'll sleep tonight, yes?"

"Yes."

"I know you're worried about your family."

"We're behind schedule. Avery will worry, and so will the kids. I have no way to reach them."

It has been on my mind the past few days. I should have been home a week ago. What if they think I'm dead? What if Desi tries to come and find me?

"This can't be the first time you've been late?" Marcus asks.

"No," I laugh, "but the scolding I got from Avery was legendary."

"I can only imagine."

He pauses as a call goes up. The sun is setting; last call for anyone who needs anything outside of the Wagon Rest. This includes fetching more firewood or water, and using the bathroom. Several people hesitantly step from the protected area in pairs and rush to finish what needs to be done. I watch a couple of men near us, keeping a hand on my gun in case they need help.

"Does it make you feel as sick as I do?" Marcus whispers. "When they have to leave the rest?"

"Yes, especially this trip."

The two men give me a thumbs-up as they return from collecting wood. Once they step back inside the rest, I breathe again, a deep in and out.

I lean against my wagon. Marcus and I do what we are good at: standing in silence. We watch as night closes in, and we wait. Small magic will happen once night finally falls. It never ceases to amaze me, even after all these years. Avery and her sisters helped create this protection. It makes me feel closer to her.

One moment, the darkness encroaches. Then, with a crack like lightning, torches ignite with a purple glow about ten feet from the edge of the wagon rest. Their semi-circle connects to the rivers on each end, enclosing the wagon rest inside a three-walled barrier of magic and water. Pride fills me.

For a moment, no sound comes from the camp—then there is cheering and laughing.

"Time for some music." Marcus slaps my shoulder and goes to join the rest of the Caravan.

As much as I hate turning my back on the Infested, there is nothing more I can do tonight. If the torches fail to protect us, that will be the end.

Everyone looks tired and frayed around the edges, but they smile at me as I wander through them. I make small talk and enjoy a full plate of bacon and griddle cakes with some superb black coffee, with just a pinch of what Lotte calls "a little love." I found out years ago her special ingredient is cinnamon.

The moon rises high in the sky and the stars twinkle. There's a faint, pleasant breeze in the air, and I grab my bag and blanket from the wagon.

I settle myself against a wheel, my sack behind my back for comfort and a blanket around my legs, and I get to work on my map. I am trying to update the current Caravan map, find a way around the Winter Quarters, and write out some recommendations for Marcus and Chloe to take back with them.

There can be no more Caravans without more than one Bonum on board nor additional wagon Rests or other safe-havens, not after this year. Chloe is good, but protection spells are not her specialty.

We humans have been foolish all these years traveling the Infested. Things between the Infested and the West need to change. Most do not respect it like they used to.

I'm deep in thought when Chloe kneels beside me.

"Harrison." She speaks in a low voice. "There's something you need to see."

Instantly alert, I set aside my materials, get up, and grab my gun. She leads me outside the circle of wagons and towards the torches.

"One of the men saw something on patrol," she says. We approach the semicircle of torches, no heat emanating from their purple flames, and she points through the gap between two of them.

I peer past the light and out into the darkness, and my heart climbs into my throat.

Floating in the darkness is a seafoam green orb. It bobs in a hectic pattern, as though struggling to come closer.

"Harrison, what is it?" Chloe asks.

"A Will-o-Wisp," I say, swallowing.

"What's wrong? Why would a wisp be out here? They aren't normal in this area."

"I have to go out there."

Chloe grabs my arm. "You can't! That's unprotected Infested, at night."

I close my eyes and take a deep breath. "Chloe, the only reason a wisp would be out here is because it's carrying a message."

A few seconds before understanding lights her eyes. "From your family. Something is wrong at home."

Even facing the creatures at Fort Kearney didn't cause fear like this to rip through me, trying to steal my thoughts and forcing the air out of me.

"Then I'll go with you. Give me a second." Chloe rushes back inside the circle of wagons. She leaves me bathed in purple light, feeling like a child too scared to be left alone in the dark. All I can do is stare at the wisp and imagine the horrible things it may have to tell me.

Chloe returns, carrying her rifle and a lit lantern. She hands me a ward bag and I spy another tied to her neck. The lantern glows white with magic. She's trying her best to protect us.

"At least we may have a little luck." She laughs, but it sounds hollow.

"Don't worry. The wisp will protect us until it gives us the message."

"That doesn't make me feel better," Chloe says.

Together we move between the purple torches and out into the darkness.

The difference is immediate. The Infested feels intense, as if it is waiting for the right moment to attack us, like a thousand eyes are on us the moment we step through the torches.

The only consolation is the noise. Like anywhere else, there are night sounds in the Infested. Bugs sing their songs and trees rustle in the wind. I can still hear the music and talking from the camp behind us, though it's faint.

Nothing turns in the dark but the wisp, but it doesn't have to. The darkness all around us feels alive, and for all we know, it might be. I don't know all of what the Infested has to offer, but I know enough to be respectfully afraid.

The Will-o-Wisp stops and then speeds towards me, halting inches from my face.

I hear Desi's voice, saying my name.

I answer, "Yes, I am Harrison."

It flashes forest green.

I hear Desi's voice again. "Things are wrong at home. Please come back soon. It's urgent." A pause. "Ask him when he's going to be home and find out where along the trail he is when he gets the message, including the date."

I feel like I'm going to throw up.

The wisp again glows forest green.

"Tell her I'm coming," I manage to choke out, "that I am at Confluence Point, and it is May thirteenth. We are leaving on May fifteenth. I will be home as soon as I can."

Forest green.

"Did she say anything else?"

Red.

"Thank you!"

Forest green.

Then it zips away.

Chloe and I stand in silence, the darkness oppressive around us. My mind whirls with the implications.

"Harrison, I don't think we can get you home any faster than we have been," Chloe says in a low voice. "This year has been too... weird."

I don't acknowledge her words. She speaks the truth, and I know it. What is there to say? My family is in danger, and I can do nothing about it.

The sound around us stops. Silence creeps in with the darkness, a reminder that we need to head back to safety. I can no longer hear the noise from camp. Something is blocking it. Which also means we can't call for help.

"Chloe—"

She grabs my arm before I can finish my warning. In silent agreement, we both back up towards the torches and warily raise our weapons. Our lanterns only illuminate so far before the light appears to hit an impenetrable wall.

I want to turn and run towards safety, but presenting my back to whatever is out there is a bad idea.

I glance behind me to make sure the path back is safe. We're mere feet beyond the torches.

Sinister laughter rumbles in the dark.

"What is it?" Chloe asks, her voice so low I almost miss it.

I shake my head because I don't know; and if I can't tell, then it is something truly awful. I pray the torches and the water are enough to keep it away from the rest of the Caravan.

I gently nudge Chloe with a soft, "I'll cover you," and she spins, darting toward the torches. I keep backing up, my eyes on the darkness and my finger on the gun's trigger.

As purple light flickers at the edges of my vision, Chloe yanks me the rest of the way between the torches to safety.

We both breathe heavily. I squint past the violet-colored light into the night, still trying to see what is out there.

When it comes into view, I suck in a breath.

Hovering eight feet off the ground is a grin at least two feet wide, all teeth, with no lips. Above the hideous smile hovers four burning yellow eyes. I see no body, nothing but that same deep gloom. I don't know what it is.

The smile and eyes linger for a split second, almost too briefly to scream, and then vanish. I don't know if it left or is still out there, waiting.

Chapter 20
May 1900
Day 22
Ash Hollow

"Lavellen isn't feeling well," Rowena said.

Desi was standing in the cemetery, looking at Samael's grave.

It was a plain grave, a simple wooden cross with his name and birth and death dates. They buried him next to the empty tomb that used to be their mother's.

"Have Helen look at her," Desi suggested.

Lavellen hadn't been well since their trip to the Will-o-Wisp. The loss of her foot had taken much of her spirit with it. The loss of Samael had stolen away the rest. Desi couldn't blame her. It was difficult for anyone to handle, let alone someone like Lavellen, who felt things intensely.

"I have. Helen says she can't tell what's wrong with her, but that—" Rowena paused, a sob in her throat, "that it might be what took Samael."

Desi looked up and focused on her sister's face. Rowena was pale, eyes hollow and haunted. Her dress was torn at the bottom and a button had fallen off.

Desi took a deep breath. She had bad news of her own to share.

"I hear you, Rowena. Have Helen make Lavellen comfortable."

They needed to talk to all of them, but where? This conversation had to be done out of the earshot of their mother.

"Is that all you have to say? Desi, I think someone has made Lavellen and Samael sick on purpose!"

Desi shushed her and glanced up. Their mother stood in her bedroom window, watching them. Desi smiled and waved at her. Avery's face broke into a matching grin. She blew them both a kiss and shut the curtains.

Desi rubbed her nose. The tingling was ever-present now, almost painful, the warning apparent.

"Not here, Rowena. Get the others, including Foni. Meet me behind the barn in ten minutes."

Desi walked off, not answering as Rowena called after her. She still had things to do, after all.

Trying not to look like she was rushing, Desi made her way along the fencing that surrounded the house, towards the front gate, and opened her senses. Her heart rate sped up as she glanced at the fencing. The bubble shield she and Foni created burned intensely above her, but the wards along the property line were dim. They all looked drained and working at one-fourth capacity, which shouldn't have been possible unless something was routinely hitting them, searching for weak spots. Or, something from the inside was feeding off them.

Both thoughts made her cold and her skin crawl. She trailed a hand along a piece of fence. The wood was rough beneath her hand, but it felt wrong, sick. She closed her eyes and pushed magic at it, trying to heal, to strengthen the wards—something she had done a thousand or more times before.

The fence glowed bright silver for a second and then dimmed. This had started after their mother's resurrection; were the two linked? She wasn't sure, but she knew it would be easier to find out with fewer people at the homestead. She was spending too much time wrapped in her siblings' drama and emotions to concentrate on the bigger picture. The Infested was telling her they were in danger.

Making her way to the gate, she was relieved that the wards were still in full force over the entrance and the fencing over by the workshed, barn, and animals. So far, whatever was happening was only in one section of the property.

As she passed in front of the gate, she saw the wisp's green glow on the other side. Sweet, calming relief filled her. It must have news of Father!

Rushing the fence, she ignored the wood's creaking protests as she climbed the rungs, until her head peaked over the top slat. She waved to the wisp, which drifted closer before pausing and glowing bright red.

"Yes, yes, I know." She stuck an arm through the gaps, scanning around her. It should be safe enough. She had to push past the invisible shield, which felt like punching her hand through slime, before it broke free on the other side.

The wisp hovered close enough to touch and pain burned through her palm as it took its payment. She retracted her hand.

Forest green.

"Tell her I'm coming." Hearing her father's voice for the first time in months, Desi felt absolute joy, followed by despair. *"That I am at Confluence Point, and it is May thirteenth. We are leaving on May fifteenth. I will be home as soon as I can."*

"Thank you."

Forest green and the wisp flickered out, back to its home.

He was too far away to be of any help now. But maybe, if Foni could leave, she could meet up with him and have the safety of the Caravan. Desi wondered if she would ever see her father again. Something primal inside of her had been screaming a warning, one it had taken her too long to recognize.

Desi dropped down from the fence. Hopefully, her siblings were waiting for her.

She wandered the flattened path to the barn. The building loomed over her, casting shadows that brought relief from the warmest part of the day. She could smell and hear the animals inside, going about their typical day. She envied them.

Behind the barn was a strip of grass and the cow pasture fence. The grass was yellowed and dying, usual for that time of the year.

The sharp stench of cow manure wrinkled Desi's nose. Aside from Helen, the rest of them never came to this area because of the stench. You couldn't see this hidden alcove from the house, and it was the last place anyone would look for them.

When Desi rounded the corner, Marian said, "Ugh, Desi, this is such a gross meeting place," in lieu of a greeting. She stood, not touching anything, arms wrapped around her middle.

Desi hated that none of them stood together. They used to cling to each other for support. Ambrose leaned against the back of the barn, glaring. Rowena paced with anxious energy. Even Helen perched on the fence like a ghost, giving Foni as much space as she did the others.

"Can we hurry up, whatever this is?" Rowena asked. "I need to get back to Lavellen."

With an uncomfortable expression, Foni shuffled over to stand beside Desi.

"I think there's something wrong with Mom," Desi began.

Marian sniffed disbelievingly. "Please, Desi, that's ridiculous. She's acting just like normal. We should all be thankful she got better."

"What makes you say that, Desi?" Helen asked.

"She wants to siphon magic from Foni."

"But that's illegal!" Ambrose exclaimed.

"Not to mention, one of Mother's unbreakable rules," Helen added.

"Anything else you're not telling us?" Rowena asked.

"No," Desi replied softly. "It's just a feeling really, every fiber of my being says there's something wrong."

"It's just your anxiety, Desi. You liked being in control and now you aren't because Mama's back."

"Rowena!" Ambrose exclaimed. "Look around and start thinking with something other than what's between your legs. Even I've noticed something is off around her."

"That's a sick joke, right? Coming from you, you're the only one who is thinking with that." Marian's mouth spewed hate so quickly Ambrose looked like he'd been smacked.

"Enough!" Desi yelled. "What is wrong with all of you? Look, *something* is feeding off the wards and it started happening after Mama came back and the shadow creature disappeared. I need you to help me!"

Silence fell over the group. Her siblings refused to meet her eyes.

"We never did figure out where that creature went...." Helen ventured.

"Maybe Mother could have helped us if Rowena hadn't lied." Marian sounded like she was about to burst into tears.

"I lied so she wouldn't have the added stress! She didn't need to worry. Why does it matter now? The monster is gone, and our mother is back with us, alive...." Rowena's defense came to a halt as they all heard the correlation in her sentence.

"Exactly," Desi said.

"No," Rowena said. "I refuse to believe that thing could have had anything to do with her."

"And her wanting to draw off Foni's magic?" Helen asked.

"Mother always has a good reason for everything," Marian said.

"You naive little princess." Ambrose sneered.

Before they could start sniping again, Desi held up a hand and spoke. "Even if you don't believe there's something wrong with Mom, we all have to agree that Samael and Lavellen both getting sick is suspicious. While I don't think we're in any danger, I think Lavellen and Foni are."

"Of course. " Rowena rolled her eyes. "That's who you're worried about. *Foni.*"

"Rowena, not now," Helen admonished.

"Helen, tell us about Lavellen," Desi requested.

Helen sighed and hopped off the fence. "She has all the same symptoms as Samael. If I didn't know better, I'd say she'd been poisoned. But I can't tell by what. I'm worried if we can't figure out what's wrong, she'll die too."

When a broken sob escaped Rowena, Marian closed the distance between them and wrapped her arms around her sister. The girls clung together, Marian weeping as well.

"If anyone could poison them, it would be Ambrose," Marian accused.

"What! Why would I do that?" Ambrose demanded, rage filling his features.

"Because you were jealous!" Marian snapped.

"You're the jealous one. You used a wish to get your revenge. Besides, Helen would know more about poisons than me."

"Excuse me?" The hurt in Helen's voice felt like a slap to even Desi herself.

"Helen wouldn't do that," Foni said.

"That's right, because it was *you*, whatever you are." Rowena pointed the finger at Foni, who flinched.

"Enough," Desi said, holding up a hand again. What was happening to them? "Accusations get us nowhere. I have a plan, if you'd all stop bickering."

"Okay, let's hear it," Ambrose said.

"Rowena and Lavellen will leave in Lavellen's wagon, taking Foni with them. I heard from the wisp—"

"You got a message from Father?" Marian interrupted, wiping tears from her cheeks. "Is he okay?"

"Yes, he's trying to get back to us as soon as he can. He was at Confluence Point. You can all meet up with the Caravan and return to Fort Kearney. Someone there may be able to save Lavellen, and Foni will be safe."

"Safe from what, Desi?" Helen asked.

"I think Mom is so preoccupied with making us safe, she may do something drastic. Or maybe her sickness changed her in some way and she's not thinking clearly. With Foni and Lavellen gone, I can talk to her. We can help her."

"It's not a bad plan." Ambrose shrugged.

"I want to go too," Marian pouted.

"No." Desi shook her head. "You, Helen, Ambrose, and I will stay. It will be hard enough to get the three of them out of Ash Hollow."

"I don't like it, but you know she's right," Ambrose conceded.

"Okay, so you each will pack a few bags. Ambrose, they will need food and water. Helen, are Lavellen's horses good for the trip?"

"Yes. They've done well with the rest."

"And the wagon is as repaired as I can manage," Rowena added.

"Tonight then, as soon as Mom's asleep," Desi said.

"Will you be okay without us?" Rowena asked.

"I can take care of Mom, and when Dad gets back, that will help."

"I don't feel like I should leave you," Foni whispered. "You've done so much for me."

The decision made Desi's chest tight and anxiety rippled through her veins, but she knew this was the right course of action. She was getting better at relying on her instincts, something she should have done from the start.

"That's why you have to go, Foni. Aunt will be happy to see you, and you can have a fresh start. I'll be fine here. I was never going to leave to begin with."

It was depressing to admit out loud, but Desi was content with her decision. She had to stay to take care of her family and Ash Hollow.

"Then let's not stand around here any longer," Rowena said.

They all rushed off to implement their part of the plan, and only Helen and Foni remained with Desi.

"Do you think this will work, truly?" Helen asked.

"I don't think Lavellen will make it, but hopefully Rowena getting away will be good," Desi answered.

"You really think Mom might be dangerous?"

"I'm not sure what's going on around here, but I think Mom is serious about doing whatever she can to protect us. I don't think she'd let anyone leave what she views as our safe place."

"Who do you think is hurting Lavellen and Samael?" Foni asked.

"And do you really think that shadow monster and Mom are linked?" Helen asked.

"I have no idea what made them sick," Desi said. "I just know that shadow monster disappeared, but I'm not certain it actually left. We were all so preoccupied with Mom returning, our visitors, and Foni getting better…. We weren't vigilant enough. I should have tried to find it."

"It's not your fault," Helen said. She reached out and gripped her sister's hand. "You can't be everywhere at once."

"Helen, you go," Desi said, ignoring her sister's words. "Make sure the horses are ready and pack up whatever you think they'll need."

With a solemn expression, Helen released Desi's hand. She hesitated for a moment before slipping around the corner of the barn. With a sigh, Desi headed towards the graveyard. Soft footsteps pattered after her as Foni hurried to fall into step at her side.

"I need to say goodbye," Foni said, as though explaining herself.

Their feet left shallow footprints along the dirt path as they walked. The fastest way was through the garden, weaving among the fruits and vegetables. Towering cornstalks hid them from view.

A hush fell when they crossed the border from the fresh green garden to the barren section dotted with headstones. Desi didn't know if the quiet was in their minds or because of the solemn feelings of being among so many of their dead relatives.

They stopped at a small stone toward the back. Chiseled into the stone was the name of Foni's mother, her dates of birth and death, and the words "beloved sister" under her name. Foni reached down and caressed the white, weather-worn stone. Serenity had been dead almost a decade.

"Do you think about that day much?" Desi asked, closing her eyes and tilting her head up.

"I try not to."

"Do you still blame Marian?"

"I try not to."

Desi opened her eyes only to roll them upon seeing her cousin's sarcastic grin.

"She didn't know what she'd done nor how the wish had gone wrong," Foni said. "She and I both learned hard lessons that day."

"I agree, and you have yet to learn the most important lesson."

Both girls jumped as a new voice spoke and they spun around to see Desi's mother.

"Relentless caution is the only way to survive the Infested," Avery finished. She stood tall and formidable with the sun directly behind her, making the girls squint.

"Mom! You scared us." Desi recovered first. "Is everything alright? Do you need help?"

"Yes." Avery's gaze slid to her niece. "Foni, have you thought about what I asked? I hate to push the issue, but the wards you girls set won't hold forever, and I feel something growing along the edges of the property."

Desi wrapped her arms around herself, suddenly cold. Her mother was so severe, so intense. She had never been a carefree woman, but it was a hundred times worse since she returned. Desi was happy their father would be home soon.

Foni frowned at Avery. She rubbed her eyes and squirmed like she was uncomfortable.

"Are you alright?"

"My head just hurts, Aunt Avery. I'll have an answer for you tomorrow morning. But I need to go lie down now." Foni smiled, but it looked far too stiff to be reassuring.

She took one last look at her mother's grave and quickly left, back to the house.

"I worry about that girl."

Desi raised an eyebrow at her mother's words. "Why? She's so much better."

"Is she? I wonder how much we actually helped her. Come. It's almost dinner time, and the smells from the kitchen are delightful." Avery's voice sounded preoccupied. She stared at the fence line behind Desi with a blank expression on her face. Desi looked behind her, but there was nothing there. When she looked back at her mother, her nose tingled so hard that she had to rub it away.

Her mother linked arms with Desi and walked back to the house. Her mother's touch caused chills to run up Desi's arm. But the entire time, her mind was spinning. What had her mother meant? Was there something wrong with Foni? Had Desi made the wrong choice? Was she sending Rowena and Lavellen out with danger or fleeing from it?

Chapter 21

May 1900
Day 22 – Evening
Ash Hollow

Desi, her siblings, and Lavellen quietly made their way to the main gate. Everything was ready. The wagon was packed and the horses hitched.

"Where's Foni?" Desi asked, looking around for their cousin.

"I haven't seen her for hours," Ambrose answered. "She vanishes all the time. Haven't you noticed?"

Desi had noticed that Foni seemed to need much more alone time than she had before her change. Desi thought it was just a side effect of what Foni had been through. Was she wrong?

Looking pale and a little green around the edges, Lavellen lay on a pallet in the back. "I can't leave. We can't leave," she kept saying over and over.

It didn't do any good. Between her foot and her sickness, she was in no position to argue.

"Hush, dear one," Rowena murmured where she crouched at Lavellen's side. She wore traveling clothes, thick trousers, and a wide-brimmed hat under which she had crammed her hair. "We must be quiet and leave now to get you help. Helen can't heal you."

"Rowena, do you have a gun?" Ambrose asked, glancing at the windows of the house.

All was dark and quiet upstairs. They were all nervous, and they each wore it differently.

"You've asked her that three times. Yes, she does!" Marian snapped and was instantly shushed.

"I'm here. Are we ready?" Foni appeared from the shadows wearing a dark green cloak with a hood. Was that excitement or trepidation in her voice? She threw her bag in the back and, with no effort, swung herself into the seat and scooped up the reins. Desi couldn't see her face. "Ambrose, don't worry. I'm here if something goes wrong."

It didn't seem to make him feel better.

The moon was high in the sky and stars twinkled, but Desi wished it was darker. If their mother looked out the bedroom window even in passing, they would be just as visible as if the sun were shining.

Desi took a deep breath, longing in her stomach. She wished she was going.

Helen appeared at her side. "Something about this doesn't feel right."

Desi agreed, but things hadn't felt right in weeks. She glanced at their cousin. Was Foni causing this? Was Desi playing a part in an elaborate game so that Foni could escape Ash Hollow?

Helen's gaze followed Desi's before returning to her. "No, I don't think so."

Desi closed her eyes. She didn't know what to believe or who to trust. She just knew her gut said to get Foni and Lavellen out of Ash Hollow.

Desi pulled out tinkling bags full of charms and hung them all over the wagon. She lifted her hands and closed her eyes, humming deep in her throat. She touched the magic all around them and pulled them closer to the wagon and horses, almost like knitting a silver blanket over it, invisible to everyone but her.

She held it tight and opened her eyes, concentrating on the feel and taste of the magic, holding it together, bound to her chest.

"Hand it off to me," Foni said. "I have to be able to keep it going."

Desi passed the cord and magic to her cousin with a hand gesture. Foni grasped it and, for a second, the silver magic pulsed purple and rippled, then settled again.

Foni let out a breath. "This will take a lot of my energy to keep up."

"What are you doing?" Marian asked.

"The Nebula is still out there," Desi answered. "It's decided Lavellen and Samael are prey and will hunt them until it gets bored or something better comes along. If they leave without protection, they'll die."

"Desi has made us invisible to it," Rowena piped up. She stood, dusted off her clothes, and circled the wagon to join them. "As long as Foni keeps the spell going, we should be able to get away without it noticing. A few miles from this area, and it probably won't come looking for us, right?"

"That's the hope," Foni said.

"You have to go. Now." Desi hugged Rowena tightly. Her sister smelled of oil, fresh laundry, and lavender. Desi tried to memorize every inch of her.

"Ugh, don't hug so tightly." Rowena pulled away. Anticipation glittered in her eyes and a flush colored her cheeks. "We'll see each other again. As soon as Lavellen is well."

Desi couldn't do anything but nod. The burning in her throat made it impossible to speak and she didn't want to cry.

Instead, she left the rest of her siblings to say their goodbyes and went to the gate.

She grabbed the metal latch, feeling the magic that soaked into and around the mechanism. Blinking, she focused on the silver magic, faded more than it should be. With her second sight, she could make out the bubble that surrounded the property.

She would let them pass through the barrier like a knife through soft butter. They might feel uncomfortable for a moment, but it would pass.

Hearing the soft sounds of uneasy horses, Desi glanced behind her to ensure everyone was ready.

Ambrose, Marian, and Helen stood to one side. Their collective anxiety beat at Desi's mind with her magic so wide open. Foni and Rowena sat side by side, tense and ready.

"We only have one shot at this," Desi said as loudly as she dared. "I'll lift the latch, Ambrose and Marian will open the gate, and you go as quickly as you can while I hold back the magic. The wards will push against you. Just breathe, and it will be over in a second."

"Rowena," Lavellen's quiet sob came from the back, "please, I can't leave this place."

"Why would she want to stay?" Ambrose muttered as he and Marian hurried into place.

"I wouldn't want to leave either," Marian said. "Samael is here."

"That's ridiculous. Samael is…." Ambrose swallowed, eyes bright and dry, "dead. His body is in the ground, and he's gone back to the spirits."

"Concentrate," Desi warned, keeping her hands on the lock. "This is dangerous. I have no idea what's outside the wards, but Mom says something is brewing out there. Pray it's nothing more than a Bog Storm, or they won't make it to the Caravan."

Suddenly Desi couldn't see. Everything was black, as though the moon and starlight had been snuffed out like candles. She blinked and shook her head. The gate was barely visible, even though it was right in front of her.

Spinning around, she pressed her back to the gate and squinted. Flickering silhouettes of her siblings and the horses stood out from the shadows. A small shaft of light shone from between the curtains in the living room window in the distance.

Suddenly, Rowena gasped and Ambrose cried out. Marian screamed a split-second later.

Desi froze, her blood turning to ice. A hand came down on her shoulder.

"Are you all going somewhere?"

Moonlight poured across the homestead, revealing their mother beside Desi. Her nightdress was askew, her hair down and her eyes wild.

"Mom…" Desi took a deep breath. "Yes. Rowena is taking Lavellen someplace to get better medical care."

"And why is Foni sitting next to her, under that cloak?"

Desi watched her siblings gather around the wagon. They could all feel that something was wrong, and they watched it like a play unfolding.

"She's going with them."

Their mother stood in silence for what felt like hours. Desi's heartbeat pounded in her ears and her hands were clammy.

Rowena climbed down from the wagon seat and into the back with Lavellen. "Mom, what's wrong? Why not let us go? I promise I'll come back," she pleaded.

"Why did you have to make this so difficult?" Avery asked. Her voice had taken on a gravelly tone. She didn't sound angry, just exhausted.

"What are you talking about?"

Foni gasped. "Desi, you should come over here," she said. Her words were slow and calm, but what little of her expression could be seen under the cloak's hook was not.

Avery turned and looked at Foni, but she wouldn't make eye contact. "Oh well," her mother intoned.

"Mom, please let me open the gate so they can leave," Desi requested.

"I'm afraid that's quite impossible and has been for some time now."

Desi watched, horrified, as her mother brought out the vial of silver potion and drank it. Then she raised her arms and was plunged into shadows. Darkness pulled from every inch of the property, swirling around her in a vortex.

"Mama!" Marian exclaimed. She took a step forward, but Helen grabbed her arm. In the wagon, Rowena struggled to sit Lavellen up.

Tangles of blackness swarmed around their mother. Desi focused on a glow from the inside the shadows, a red glow.

What stepped from the mess of shadows made Desi's heart skip a beat. The shadow creature loomed in front of her, its body like tendrils of ink sweeping from the ground up.

Desi watched those red eyes that burned with amusement and that mouth split into a hideously stretched grin of sharp teeth. Above that smile and glowing eyes, its hair danced like tentacles.

Rowena and Ambrose each grabbed one of Lavellen's arms and dragged her from the wagon. Desi felt Foni release the magic on the wagon when its wave passed over her and slammed into the black mass, freezing it in place. Desi knew it wouldn't hold long.

"Run!" Desi yelled.

She ran faster than she ever had before, not stopping until she felt the porch beneath her feet. She ripped open the door and held it out of the way as her siblings all flew into the house, Lavellen being dragged the last few steps.

Laughter rumbled up the path to the house. Even after Desi slammed the door shut, it seeped into the house.

Throwing her arms wide, Desi cast a warding spell of pulsing silver around the house. The spell wouldn't last long but she didn't have enough magic to reinforce it. To keep out something that had once lived inside, something that powerful, would take more energy than she had been able to recover after performing the spell with Foni. This small barrier would have to be enough.

Out of breath, she sagged against the wall and sucked in air through her teeth.

They all jumped as the front door thudded, bowing in as if pressed by an immense force. She felt the creature already licking at the wards like it was candy, sucking the magic out of the spell.

"What the hell just happened?" Ambrose asked.

"I don't have any idea, and we don't have time to talk about it." Desi pounded on the wall next to the door and the panel slid open.

"Desi, you need to eat," he said. "You won't be able to do any more if you don't fuel yourself."

"There's food downstairs. Everyone in." Desi pointed to the passage.

"Wait, what? We aren't allowed downstairs," Marian said with a shocked expression.

"Marian," Desi grabbed her sister's arms, "my wards won't hold much longer. We need more time."

A hint of confusion disrupted her sister's look of astonishment.

Before Desi could clarify, Helen said quickly, "Marian, she needs you to make a wish."

Marian flinched and averted her eyes.

"We have seconds before that thing is done playing around," Desi implored, "and I don't think it'll be content with haunting us this time."

"What- what should I wish for?" Marian gulped. When she finally met Desi's eyes, her own were wide with dread.

"Wish for that creature not to breach the wards for...." Desi trailed off. How much time would they need? How much could Marian spare?

"Ten minutes should give us enough time," Foni said, pushing the hood back from her face. Desi felt a flash of guilt for even considering her cousin may have been causing the troubles.

"Yes, that works. Marian?" She worried about the repercussions, but they had no other options.

Marian took a deep breath. "I wish that the wards will hold, not allowing the shadow creature in for at least the next ten minutes."

When the last word tumbled out, she began to gag. Helen rushed over to her, laying hands on her forehead as their sister crumpled to the ground with the force of her violent heaves.

"She's feverish," Helen said, glancing up at Desi as she tried to soothe Marian.

"I'm sorry." Desi meant it, but she could do nothing for her sister now and she refused to waste what precious time Marian had bought them. "Grab your healing bag, and let's go."

They all scrambled through the open panel and crowded onto the landing. Desi lit the lantern and shut the door, feeling safer. There were additional wards and charms farther underground— more ways for Desi to protect them.

"Follow me and be quiet. Don't touch anything," Desi warned, leading the way down.

No one spoke, but quiet sobs, sighs, and sniffles accompanied the descent.

She breathed her own sigh of relief when the large iron door came into view. She fished the key out from under her dress and unlocked the door.

Twisting music swirled around them.

"Ah, you're back," a voice said from the darkness.

"Ignore everything and don't respond," Desi ordered as she ushered them all inside. The door shut with a large clang, and Desi locked it and ran to the desk. She grabbed a small penknife and stabbed her finger. It hurt, stinging as it welled with blood.

"What are you doing?" Helen asked.

"Blood magic. It will keep that thing out of this room longer, don't worry." Desi rushed back to the door.

It was hard to find the fingerprint in the door frame in the dim light. Once she saw it, she smeared her blood and felt it in her soul when the emergency protections snapped into place. Guiltily, she thought that if only they had such safeguards installed around the entire house, she could have spared Marian a wish.

"How long?" Helen asked.

"I don't know," Desi admitted. "Longer than Marian's wish, maybe an hour? It's all I can do right now. Ambrose, there's another set of lights attached to the one on the desk. Light it, please?"

"I don't have magic like that," he huffed.

"There are matches."

"Oh."

A few seconds later, the dimly lit room filled with light.

"Wow, I thought this place would be more impressive," Ambrose said with a chuckle.

Rowena stood next to him with an arm around Lavellen, whose head whipped around as if desperately searching for something.

"What do we do now?" Ambrose asked.

"We need a way out," Desi said. "Dad can't come here with that thing loose."

"Can we kill it?" Rowena questioned.

"I don't know. Suggestions?"

"I know a way out, but it may be hazardous," Foni said. "I'm not sure what will happen when we reach the end. This thing has been playing with our minds the entire time."

"Was it ever really Mother?" Marian asked. Her voice was weak, but she had made it down the steps without further upchucking.

"I believe so," Desi answered, "but whatever killed her infected her. I'm not sure it's only Mother, if that makes sense."

She bit her lip. She didn't want to frighten her siblings more, but it was hard to hide her own terror. It was the only explanation that made sense. Her mother got sick, died, and came back—but she came back different, full of dark magic, pure Infested.

Looking at Foni, she whispered, "It had to be the illness, right?"

Foni leaned in close to speak, so the others couldn't hear them. "Desi, I don't think illness took her. I think she embraced the Infested. Like I did."

"You weren't like that," Desi argued.

"Everyone handles it differently. Before she died, I overheard my mom and yours talking. Bonum go wild all the time, but we kill them before anyone hears about it. They aren't always dangerous."

Foni's answer caused chills to run up and down Desi's spine. She knew their mother hadn't always told her everything, but she was getting the impression she hadn't told her anything.

"Desi, what's the plan?" Ambrose sounded impatient and the suspicion in his eyes didn't help.

"We eat, hydrate, and make our way to the back of the cellar—" Desi paused as the whole house shuddered.

"Quickly," Helen advised.

"Yes please," Marian said in a strained voice. "A time wish like that will probably have time-related consequences."

Foni showed them where to find the food stored in their mother's desk while Desi grabbed a few items and shoved them in the pockets of her skirt. She let her siblings' chatter fade into the background as Foni led the way to the prison's back.

They made their way past the inhabitants and, as they got deeper in, her siblings stopped talking. Desi watched their faces contort with horror as they investigated the creatures.

"I can't believe you came down here every day," Marian whispered. I couldn't do it."

As they passed the cage with the sleeping woman, Lavellen broke free and rushed the cage. Hands gripped the bars as her strained cry echoed off the walls.

"Mother!"

Chapter 22

May 1900
The Caravan

I fidget as the Caravan sets up camp. We are a week from Ash Hollow and the knots in my belly intensify with every day. Something is wrong at home. Desdemona wouldn't have risked going outside the fence to send me a message unless it was dire. This entire trip has felt wrong, and I wonder if it's connected to what is happening at home.

We settle in an old, familiar wagon rest. The wards seem intact and protection bags hang from the trees. String ties tiny silver bells to them, tinkling faintly in the wind.

Coming up from behind me, Marcus asks, "Join me for a smoke?"

I don't usually indulge—Avery doesn't like it—but I nod. He rolls two cigarettes quickly. The fruited tobacco scent is a nice contrast to animals and people, all of whom need a bath.

I take the thin cigarette in my fingers, ashamed that they shake. Marcus lights it for me and I take a deep drag, welcoming the vice's calming burn into my lungs.

"We'll get you home, Harrison. Don't worry," Marcus says. "Avery is a tough gal. She'll keep the kids safe until you return."

"I pray to the Spirits you're right." Smoke curls from my lips as I speak. "I just know my Desi."

Marcus grunts but leaves it at that. We've known each other too long for platitudes.

We smoke in silence for a few minutes before Chloe calls me from the other side of the camp. "Harrison?" Even from this distance, I spot her frown. I stomp my smoke out, grinding it under my foot. The last thing this Caravan needs is a fire.

Marcus follows me as I stride across the camp. People greet me as I pass, but weariness harrows the greetings. They try to find some semblance of normalcy in cooking, mending, or drinking; but even these are temporary distractions. It's been a long journey.

I reach Chloe, who runs a hand through her short, green hair. She gazes out past the wagon rest's boundaries towards a small hill that has a creek running parallel to it.

"I need to go out there," she says without preamble. "Will you come with me?"

"What? Why? You know it's not safe."

"I'd like to do it now, before dark. Something is calling me."

"Something calling you, from the Infested?" Marcus snorts. "No, that's not dangerous at all."

"Chloe, talk to me. What's wrong?" I know it must be severe. Chloe, more than anyone, is cautious. She's like me, and she knows this place will kill you before you even know you're dead.

"The ley lines out here are closer than they should be."

I freeze. That's impossible. Wagon rests and safe places were established far away from ley lines on purpose; they attracted the supernatural. While ley line magic was neutral, it could be used for anything.

"Not possible," Marcus's words mirror my thoughts. "The closest ley line should be miles away."

"I know what I'm sensing. The women in my family have been doing this for years," Chloe scolded him. "There's a ley line over there and I need to check it out. Because you're right—it shouldn't be there."

"Okay, Chloe, I'll go with you," I say. "Let me get my gun."

Hurrying back to my wagon, I put on the coat into which Avery sewed charms and grab the gun. I check my stash, grateful we stocked up at the fort, and load up with bullets. The iron and salt doesn't always kill everything, but it will put a dent in it.

When I return to Chloe and Marcus, they're both armed.

"I told the Harmons to keep an eye on things until we get back," Marcus tells me. "The Caravan will be in good hands."

"Marcus, you shouldn't come with us," I say.

"Stubborn fool. Of course I am," is his reply.

We start out across the plains. The grass is almost knee-high and the sky is a deep blue, the sun high overhead. We should have enough time to get back before dark.

We don't talk. The quiet is unnerving but necessary. We don't want to draw attention to ourselves.

The air smells sweet and I take a moment to appreciate the wonder of the Infested. I wish more people could see that it truly is beautiful, even with all the horrors. It will never be possible to live here like we do in the East and West.

Avery is right: things are changing, and we must change with it.

The Infested is a living, breathing entity and humans are an infection. Some talk about eventually finding a cure for what went wrong here many years ago. But after living here for decades, I am not sure what the correct answer is, but it almost certainly isn't that.

"There," Chloe says suddenly. She turns abruptly to the left and hurries over to the small stream. She doesn't touch the water, though it looks clear and lovely. The rushing noise of water over pebbles reminds me of home.

"Think it's drinkable?" Marcus asks.

"Not anymore," Chloe replies. Her face looks like a storm cloud. She kneels above the surface, getting as close as she can without touching it.

"I don't recall this being here the last time we came through." Marcus scratches his chin and glances around.

With a hum of agreement, I withdraw my map, crouch, and spread it open on the ground. "It wasn't. It's not on the map either. That's not good."

Changing landscapes aren't safe. How long have we not noticed? Months? Years?

Chloe looks at me and raises her eyebrows. "That's an understatement. I think I know why the Infested feels so bad."

She sits back on her heels, dusts her hands off, and stands up. She stretches and holds a hand out to me. I hand her the map and then heave myself up.

Something smells off, almost like a sick room. I sniff the air, trying to place the scent.

"Do you smell that?" I ask.

Marcus nods. We both focus on Chloe, who glances back at the stream. Her expression sobers.

"Something goin' on?" Marcus asks.

"The ley lines are corrupted *and* they've moved. This line," she points to the map, "and the stream should be five miles…" her eyes narrow and nods to the west, "that way."

I stay silent, horror washing over me as I recall everything Avery and her sisters said about ley lines.

"What does that even mean, corrupted?" Marcus asks. "How does that happen?"

"Normally, a ley line doesn't feel like much. It's just an invisible line. I see it as pale green that feels like a small tingle across the back of my neck. It's easy to ignore but always there. But this," she glares at the stream, "this line stinks. It's a deep putrid green color that feels inflamed."

"Have any of the other lines felt like this?" I ask.

"I think so. They all connect. Avery or my mom would know more," Chloe shrugs sheepishly, "but my opinion and the best guess is that if this small line has been corrupted enough to move, then they all have, or at least all within a specific area."

"What could do that?" Marcus questions before I can.

Chloe rubs her arms. She looks cold. It's pleasant enough outside, so this is the cold you get when you're afraid. I am familiar with it. "I have no idea. I think... though, don't quote me... that this has happened naturally. Whatever makes the Infested... well, *infested* is at the root of this."

"This is all academic," Marcus says. "We can talk forever about trying to find the starting place or figure out what caused all," he waves his hands around, "this. But at the end of the day, we need to keep the Caravan safe. Let's go back and hope—"

"Stop talking," I say swiftly, my eyes looking over Chloe's shoulder. "We need to leave right now."

I start backing away. The color of pestilence, a deep green mist coalesces from the stream. Half-shapes of women dance within the cloud.

Chloe swivels around and gasps, "Gas Morbo Mulieres."

We bolt back to the Caravan. We have minutes before the gas cloud starts to move. Gas Morbo Mulieres will infect you with fatal disease and it only takes seconds to kill you. I have never seen one before. The last recorded account was ten years ago.

Marcus screams and I whip around. A tendril of mist grips Marcus by the ankle. Blisters bubble near the cuff of his pant leg as the skin burns and sloughs off. His eyes are full of anguish, his mouth set in a grimace.

"*Marcus!*" I change direction with a stumble.

Chloe keeps running. She won't realize I'm not behind her until it's too late.

"No! Harrison, don't!" Tears pool in Marcus's eyes. He sucks in a breath. The green mist has enclosed his leg up to the knee. It looks like a woman's hand caressing him in a sick way.

"Marcus, I can save you," I say.

I take another step toward him and he throws out a hand to stop me.

"No. I won't survive the gas or the disease," he sucks in a pained breath, his pallor greying around the edges, "and you run the risk of coming within its grasp. Go, save them!"

"No! I won't leave you!"

This isn't part of the plan. Marcus can't die. I don't know how to do my job without him. I've known him almost my whole life. The prospect of him being gone is unfathomable.

"Harrison, *go*, now!"

There's no arguing with him. Rationally I know what he's saying is true. I watch as he struggles to unholster his pistol, his eyes harrowed with fear and anguish. Sweat beads and drips down his face.

Then I turn my back on him and run.

I leave my best friend to die and charge back to the Caravan, heart aching with every footstep that takes me farther from him. This isn't how things should have ended. Before I reach the rest, I hear a gunshot and jerk to a stop, heart racing, sweat breaking out all over me.

Then Chloe is there, shaking my arm, "Harrison, what happened? I heard Marcus scream earlier but when I looked behind me, neither of you were there. Where's Marcus?"

Whatever she sees in my eyes is enough. She purses her lips and gives me a nod and my arm a squeeze.

"We have to go," she says quietly.

Once we're inside the wagon rest, people begin to panic. They heard the scream and gunshot too, and they know Marcus left with us but hasn't returned. They're not stupid.

"Harrison, what is it?" asks one of the Harmon boys.

"Everyone, listen up!" I bellow. "A Gas Morbo Mulieres is forming not a quarter-mile from the wagon rest."

Faces of terror stare at me from the crowd. The power of the wagon rest won't protect us from this. Once the cloud of noxious gas reaches us, the creatures that live in it will touch everyone, spreading sickness everywhere.

"The good news? It can't take form for long, so it won't cover a great space. Bad news, we need to pack up and leave *now*. Don't wait for anyone. Just go as fast and as far as you can. Plan to meet at the next rest two days' ride from here, but if you think it's safe, keep going until the border." People scatter before I finish speaking.

I try to take my own advice, but I cannot. I help Chloe load her bags on her horse and don't board my own wagon until she has mounted.

"I'll wait for you," she says. Her horse anxiously nickers and fidgets under her. "We'll go together."

"No," I insist. "You're faster on just your horse. Go and don't look back!"

"Harrison, I won't leave you. Especially not now without Marcus."

"You will go now, so I know you're safe. I'll be right behind you."

I smack her horse's ass. She glares but takes off at full gallop with only a final glance over her shoulder.

One of the Harmon boys drives Marcus's wagon past me with a grim wave to let me know he will see it back to Marcus's family. Grief claws at me, but I can see the green gas now. If I allow myself any more hesitation, it will be upon me. I have to get home. I can't die now.

It's good I didn't unpack anything. I quickly get my oxen in place and leap into my seat. Within moments, the wagon thunders across the earth. I set a brutal pace that I know will wear out the animals too soon, but I have to. I feel each bump and dip of the ground in my lower back and butt as we move. I can pull over in a few hours and allow them to eat and rest, but we must be safe first.

I hear crying and screaming behind me, but I can't look back and see who didn't get out soon enough, who didn't move fast enough. It's unbearable. I have traveled with this Caravan for years, known many of these people, for a decade.

Movement to my right snaps my attention directly to it— Chloe. Her eyes are rigid but one twitches at the sounds behind us. She must have waited behind the trees until she saw me pass. It was a calculated risk.

"I told you to go!" I call over the sounds of a hard ride.

"I stay with you!" she shouts back.

I'm not surprised. It's been her, Marcus, and me for such a long time. She's been like having another daughter or a sister on the trail.

Dust clouds the trail ahead, thick and congested from the wagons and animals. I can't see who made it out.

I close my eyes for a second and pray. There's nothing else I can do. Not for my family, Marcus, or the people of the Caravan. Not anymore.

Chapter 23

May 1900

Day 22 – Evening

Ash Hollow

"Mother?" Rowena asked and watched in horror as Lavellen threw herself at the bars.

Desi barked out a laugh. "Of course, that's why you were down here the other day."

"Desi, what's going on?" Marian asked, staring at the woman within the cell.

"I think I have an idea," Desi said. "Lavellen, would you like to explain yourself?"

Lavellen pulled her arms away from the bars but didn't get up from the floor. Her yellow hair fell in front of her face. Desi didn't think she could get up, even if she wanted to. Whatever that thing had done to her was killing her fast.

"This is my mother," she whispered.

"So you coming here wasn't an accident. You've been lying to me this entire time?" Rowena's heartbreak was written across her face and heard in her words.

"It was Samael's idea, but no…. We came on purpose, to try and save her." She met Rowena's eyes, poison clouding their bright blue hue. "I swear, Rowena, I love you. Please believe me."

She reached out and touched the hem of Rowena's skirt. Rowena hissed and backed away, wrapping her arms around herself.

"Your mother is a Succubus," Foni said. "It's not like she was here doing good deeds."

"A what?" Marian asked.

"Succubus," Foni said. "I spent long enough down here to know. They aren't Bonum. They're natural creatures of the Infested who can pass as human."

"A sex demon," Ambrose groaned, head in his hands.

"No, we're not like that!" Lavellen exclaimed in a trembling voice, grabbing the bars. "My father was human. Samael and I aren't demons!"

"Foni's right." Desi moved to stand by Ambrose, who stared at the floor. "Your mother was here trying to prey on us. It was a hellish week for all involved. Especially," she rested a hand on her brother's shoulder, "for Ambrose."

"What?" Lavellen asked. Her voice was a whisper, weakening by the moment as the poison leached away her life.

"Your mother fed on Ambrose during a really vulnerable moment," Rowena explained in a gentler voice than Desi thought Lavellen deserved. "Our mother wasn't being cruel. It was punishment for a crime."

"Samael," Ambrose whispered.

Desi wrapped an arm around his waist. "It's okay, Ambrose. You're alright," she murmured.

"What about Samael?" Marian asked. She'd dragged her lower lip under her overbite and worried it raw.

"He… he…" Ambrose couldn't finish his sentence.

"Knew their mother was down here and used you and Marian," Helen finished, hands fisting at her sides.

Lavellen lowered her head. Desi didn't know if it was from shame or from being caught.

"No, Samael loved me!" Marian argued. "He wouldn't use me!"

"Marian, don't be a fool!" Rowena sniped.

"So she loves you, but he couldn't love me?"

"Lavellen didn't fuck Ambrose behind my back!"

Ambrose shoved a knuckle between his teeth and bit down. Desi could tell he was fighting not to engage. She patted his waist in encouragement.

"Enough," Helen said. Desi barely heard her.

"Shut up!" Marian yelled.

"Enough!" Helen's voice cut through the room and Marian and Rowena paused, glancing her way. In a voice softer but no less intense, she continued, "We don't have time for this. We have to get out of here."

A loud thud above them drew all eyes to the ceiling.

"Wait, how much time has passed?" Rowena asked. "I thought we were safe for an hour."

"The wish," Marian moaned. "It must have sped up time. They always come with a price."

Desi looked at her siblings—Marian shivering, Helen's hands in tight fists, Ambrose biting his knuckles, Rowena still hugging herself—and again couldn't believe the space between them. To survive this, they needed to depend on each other.

"There's a passage in the back, through the shadows," Foni said. "It's dangerous, but we should all be able to make it out."

"I can't leave my mother," Lavellen said, "and I'm dying."

She struggled to her feet. With a start, Rowena rushed to her side. Her mouth was a harsh line, and she glared at Lavellen, but she steadied her anyway.

"Can you wake her up?" Lavellen asked without taking her eyes on the sleeping woman.

Desi looked at her—blonde hair dulled by sickness, blue eyes cloudy, expression full of longing and desperation—and remembered how glowing and beautiful Lavellen had appeared the first time they'd met. She'd been mysterious with the veil over her face, so cultured with her fine clothes and manners. A brave companion out in the Infested. Had that really only been less than a month ago?

Desi even considered her a possible lover and a friend for a moment. The light was different with her brutalized foot and the reek of illness upon her. Desi felt sorry for her. Desi also couldn't forgive the lie Lavellen and Samael had told to gain entrance to their lives. Love and friendship were too precious to fake.

"No," Desi said. "I don't know how and even if I did, I wouldn't."

"Desi!" Rowena exclaimed.

"I'm sorry, Rowena. We don't have time, and I don't have energy to waste."

A crash thundered down the secret passage.

"Children!" Their mother's voice sounded twisted, sickening, and sharp like glass.

"Desi?" Marian asked, a sob in her voice.

"We go now." Desi held out a hand to her sister and said, "Come on, Rowena."

"No, I'm sorry, Desi." Rowena sighed and closed her eyes. "I love her. I know who she is, that she lied, but I have to stay with her."

She opened her eyes, and there was a fierceness behind them Desi had never seen before.

"But you'll die." Helen walked over to her and gripped Rowena's other hand.

"I know, and maybe it will give you more time. Get away, find Father, burn this place to the ground with the creature inside. Fire kills everything." Rowena hiccuped.

Helen sounded on the verge of panicking. "That's… that's what Mother always said."

"No, Rowena, go," Lavellen begged. "Please don't stay with me."

"Dear one, how could I? I love you." Rowena gave her a smile and kissed Lavellen's pale cheek.

"I love you too," Lavellen said, leaning against her. "It didn't start that way, but I will die here with you, loving you."

Rowena released Helen's hand. "You must go now. You know the door is strong, but it won't hold, not forever."

One by one, Desi watched her siblings say goodbye, knowing they would never all be together again. Pain radiated in her chest and anxiety swarmed up her throat, preventing her from speaking. She had to keep it together, try and save them. She didn't have time to panic or throw up.

You can't do this. You'll fail them.

She pushed the dark thoughts away. She didn't have a choice. She had to try.

Don't listen to your doubts. You CAN do this, another voice seemed to yell at her.

"I can do this," Desi whispered.

Rowena settled Lavellen on the ground, back against her mother's cage, and hugged Desi. When she stepped back and grinned, the gap between her two top teeth made her look like a little girl again.

"Save as many of them as you can," Rowena whispered.

Not save them all; always a realist.

"Here." Desi shoved two bags into Rowena's hands. "They may slow her down, damage her. If you get in one of the cells, it might keep you safe."

Desi opened an empty cage door. Once inside, Rowena could close it, but she couldn't get back out if she did. Desi figured if they defeated the monster, she could come back down and let them out. It didn't seem likely, but she fiercely held onto that hope.

Rowena looked around. "I actually have been down here before. I didn't tell Lavellen all our secrets. How do you think all of this was installed? Now watch."

She walked with them to where the Tene Avum was, eyeing them as they walked by. When she brushed a foot over the ground, Desi noticed a line on the floor for the first time. Rowena swept over to the wall and hit a lever, stepping back quickly. A black iron gate dropped from the ceiling and smashed against the floor, separating them from their sister and all the locked-up inhabitants.

"Rowena, wait!" Ambrose exclaimed.

Staring back out at them through the bars, Rowena looked scared but determined. Desi had never been so proud.

"Touch it," Rowena said.

Desi brushed a finger over the metal and jerked back her hand with a gasp at the sudden pain. It burned more than normal iron.

"Should give you a few more minutes." Rowena shrugged. "Mother prepared for everything."

Glancing at her siblings one last time, Rowena dragged Lavellen into the empty cell. Desi closed her eyes and heard the clang as Rowena shut the door once more with a sense of finality.

Something pounded on the main door. Marian yelped and backed farther into the room, where the torches stopped and the shadows gathered.

"Where are you going?" the creature's voice, almost singing, called through the door. "Please don't hide! Come to me now. You cannot hide, and you must not fight me. You don't need to be afraid!"

"Lies," Helen whispered.

"At least one of you is smart," said the Tene Avum, Medi.

It and the twisted-looking harlequin, the Coryformia, had long stopped making music, merely watching them.

"No one asked for your opinion," Desi retorted.

"Set us free, and we can help you," Medi said.

"So you *do* think we're stupid," Desi said.

"No, I think you're out of time. You don't know what that thing is. We're dead no matter what."

"Why would you help us?" Marian asked.

"Better than dying in this cage."

"There's something else," Foni accused.

The bird didn't speak for a moment until the Coryformia looked up and strummed a sad note from her wrist.

"Alright, fine, because you wish it," Medi said. "If that thing gets off your property, it will destroy more than your insignificant lives. When a Bonum goes bad like that... well, I've only seen it once."

The Coryformia laughed at Medi's words, a depressing musical sound.

"Free them, Desi, and hurry," Foni said. "I can feel it; that door won't hold long."

Desi agreed. Concentrating on the magic that bound both creatures, she felt the bright silver charm that created their prisons was solid and stable. With a twitch, Desi broke it and the magic dissipated.

The door exploded inwards with a shower of splinters. Tendrils of inky shadows filled the front of the room as the creature entered. Its red eyes glowed, though not as brightly as before. It seemed to shrink so it could fit into the chambers. It glanced around and when it found them, the eyes brightened for a second, blazing the surrounding room in a fiery glow.

"Ah, there you are," it said gleefully. "Tsk tsk. Come to Mama."

The bird looked at the harlequin, who shrugged, and they charged for the shadow creature. Their combined song echoed in the chamber like war cries.

"Go!" Desi yelled as its laughter filled the room.

They ran to the back, Foni leading the way. The shadows darkened and thickened as they made their way to the back wall. Desi had never been all the way to the end of the chamber. There was nothing there but empty cages and darkness.

Reaching the wall, Foni began talking. "I'll lead the way. Marian will take my hand, Ambrose takes hers, and so on. Desi will be last. Don't let go, not for anything, do you understand?"

Eyes wide with tears streaming down her cheeks, Marian nodded.

"What happens if we let go?" Ambrose asked.

"Best case scenario?" Foni grimaced. "You're lost in a realm of shadows with no return. You'll eventually starve to death."

"Then, let's do this. I don't want to be that thing's lunch." Ambrose took Marian's hand. Desi realized it was the first time they'd touched since Marian made her wish about Lavellen and Samael.

"Ambrose," Marian started, "just in case...."

"No, it's okay," Ambrose said. "We're okay, especially now that I know what Samael truly was. Let's just get through this."

Helen took Ambrose's other hand and then reached for Desi.

"Are you scared?" Helen whispered.

"Yes." Desi's answer seemed to help, and Helen took a deep breath.

"You will feel like you're drowning for a second as we pass through the barrier," Foni said, "but stay calm. On the other side, you won't be able to see. Just focus on the touch, the feel of the person whose hand you hold."

Desi remembered the first time her mother and Aunt Serenity had taken them through a shadow path. It wasn't safe, so the trip was brief. Aunt Serenity had given the exact same instructions. Desi wondered how often Foni used this path when she'd been wild on the plains.

"Desi, focus," Helen whispered, squeezing her hand hard.

"Sorry, I'm here. Let's do this."

They all flinched at the sound of an eruption, followed by the creature's pained shriek. The first of the weapons Desi had given Rowena: a gassy substance that scented the air with lavender and quartz.

"It will take more than that—but good to see the fight in you!" Another bout of cackling made Desi's skin crawl.

They finished linking hands and Desi glanced over her shoulder just in time to see the monster hurl Medi against the iron gate. It crumpled to the floor, its neck broken, its song silenced.

Trapped in one of the monster's smoky tentacles, Medi's companion still sang a hectic melody. The music stopped as the creature smothered and absorbed the Coryformia.

"Yummy," it purred and locked eyes with Desi. Its mouth curled with a grotesque, sadistic smile. "Desdemona, come to me. You have to see how much we are alike, daughter. With me, you can be free of all these burdens."

"I am not your daughter!" Desi yelled back.

Even if she wanted to run away sometimes and give in to the power under her skin, she could never harm the ones she loved.

"And what's this? It seems you've left someone behind." Its voice was sickeningly sweet, a warped version of their mother's voice. The creature swept over to where Rowena and Lavellen hid.

"Mother, please, come back to us!" Helen cried, trying to distract it from Rowena and Lavellen.

"Ah, sweetling, I am your mother. I always have been. You shouldn't fear me; you should join me. That's all I've ever wanted."

The words chilled Desi to the bone. How could that be true?

"If you all embraced me, came to me now, you could see. Of course, some of you without enough magic wouldn't survive, but the rest of you could be free. Think of the sweet destruction we could cause."

"Don't listen to it," Desi growled. "Foni, *go!* Get us out of here."

With a crack of light and a hiss, Rowena lobbed the second pouch through the gates of the cell. Stars burst from a second explosion and the scent of sulfur burned Desi's nose. Where the magic stars touched the monster, they sizzled on contact, eliciting howls and shrieks as the creature jerked away from the bars.

"I taught you all so well." Desi couldn't deny the approval in the creature's voice. It began to leak a grey, ethereal substance. The smoke caused the little fear-eating rodents in the cage behind it to move frantically with excitement, their breathy squeaks filling the room.

Desi glanced ahead and saw Foni and Marian enter the shadow path.

Lavellen began to cry, and Desi was helpless to do anything but watch as hoary clouds circled the monster. Rowena made no noise. Desi knew her sister would be holding tight to Lavellen, stoic and brave, as always.

The clouds formed a shield in front of the creature as it grew, its lightless wavering body filling every crevice. It snuffed out the light until an otherworldly glow shone from its eyes and sharp teeth. A rotten stench overpowered the lavender and quartz from the explosive and Desi heard Ambrose retch in front of her. She breathed through her mouth, shallow, so she didn't also taste it.

She looked at her hand holding Helen's and watched as slowly Ambrose, breathing heavily, was pulled into the darkness; but she couldn't help but glance back again. The monster advanced on the cell again, and Desi and Helen heard the soft shriek of twisting metal. One of the bars snapped from the gate with a loud clang. As it clattered across the floor, more began to snap.

Desi took a step forward, every instinct in her to save Rowena.

"Don't break the line!" Helen exclaimed. "You move, and we won't all cross through the shadows!"

Desi gripped Helen's hand harder as Helen was pulled into the wall. It moved around her like pudding, sucking her into the darkness. Fear burned through Desi's blood as she followed into the dark. Before the wall took her, she heard Rowena scream.

Chapter 24

May 1900

Day 23

Ash Hollow

"I can't see!" Marian exclaimed.

They were all on the other side of the wall, in a shadow realm where humans, in particular, shouldn't spend any time and Bonum should be careful with how much time.

"Everyone take a deep breath," Desi commanded.

She could see. All around them was a swirling vortex of black, shadows moving here and there, with occasional flashes of fast-moving white. A cold breeze was coming from somewhere and noise rushed in her ears.

"Close your eyes," Desi instructed. "Gather your magic. When you open your eyes, use your magic to see."

As she waited for her siblings to find their balance, Desi examined each of them in the strange light.

Foni and Desi glowed with purple and silver light, like beacons in the dark. Standing by Desi, Helen's softer glow was less noticeable. If Desi was a beacon, then Helen was a lamp.

Marian and Ambrose both shone too; Ambrose like a candle and Marian like a spark off of flint.

"I still can't see," Marian said, sounding panicked.

"Just hold onto our hands," Ambrose said.

"Are we ready to move?" Desi asked. "It can follow us in here once it gets past the gates. We have to get outside of the shield around the homestead, and then maybe Foni and I can stop it from leaving Ash Hollow."

"Yes, I think we're ready," Ambrose answered.

Moving in this place was difficult, like going in slow motion with your body's movements but speeding through time. Desi tried to ignore the disorientation as the line lurched forward.

"We're almost there," Foni told them.

They could see a light far away—another entrance, hopefully, one that put them just outside the barrier.

"We're going to make it," Marian said, breathing a sigh of relief.

"Did you really think so?" A voice filled the void, loud and chilling.

They froze as every speck of light but their own winked out, plunging them in darkness.

"Did you think I would let you go? My own children? Join me. Let me show you what you could be."

Desi spun around and found herself alone. She scrambled, searching for her siblings, panic rushing through her veins. She couldn't feel Helen's hand in her own anymore.

"Ambrose! Helen! Foni! Marian!" She screamed into the darkness but no one answered.

Desi ran as far as she could in each direction, the light of her magic the only way to see. She stumbled over her own feet, constantly slamming into an invisible wall.

Exhausted, body aching, she fell to the ground and curled up. Would she be here forever, stuck in this place? Was Foni afraid? Were her siblings crying out in the dark, praying that Desi would rescue them? Had she failed?

Wrapping arms around herself, Desi rocked back and forth, trying to come up with a plan. She reached out with her magic but found it limited to the small area where she was confined.

Desi didn't know how much time had passed before realizing she wasn't alone. Someone was sitting next to her. She screamed as she recognized her mother, sliding away until she came up against a wall of blackness, like frozen glass against her back. It was her mother, looking like she did before she got sick, before she turned into a shadow monster—grey, healthy, alive, and normal.

"Desdemona," her mother said warmly. She sat crossed-legged, arms out, hands spread wide.

"Who... what are you?"

"I am your mother."

"No, we buried my mother. I don't know what you are."

"If you won't believe I'm your mother, will you believe that right now, I mean you no harm?"

"Why would I believe that?"

"I have something to show you, something all your siblings and Foni are also watching. It's like a test."

"What are you talking about?" Desi asked, certain the creature was insane.

"Do you want to live? You want your siblings to live?"

"Of course!" Desi exclaimed, but she knew a trap was coming.

"Then make the right choices."

Desi blinked and when the world came back into focus, she was in a large city, standing in the middle of a dirty, packed street.

The skyline was dotted by buildings and the sun shone from overhead, but the color was off—a sickly brownish-yellow. The buildings didn't look right. The one time her father had taken her to a large city, everything had been clean and crisp with sharp lines. Nothing about towns in the West were aesthetically pleasing, but they were defendable.

These buildings were dirty and crooked, some smoking and others crumbling.

Desi heard yelling, crying, and the sounds of running and panting all around her.

Swiveling around, she took in the sights. Hundreds of people fought in the streets in all manner of clothing. People in army uniforms, some dressed in all black from head to toe. She saw women in colorful garments with blackened edges and men whose clothes showed their profession—cook, keeper of the peace, and pastor. Mothers and fathers fought side by side. Peeking out from behind curtains, children watched the chaos through the windows.

Songs rose up all around her, the sweet sounds of battle hymns. She opened her mouth and the air tasted like magic. Taking a deep breath of the awful yet intoxicating air, she dragged her magic around her so she could get a good look.

The magic was everywhere. Fear and anxiety seared her stomach. Every person was touched by magic. Silver, black, purple, orange, green—every color until it muddled together, just a shimmering mess covering everything that moved.

Excitement blossomed in Desi's chest. What she could do with all that magic. She could reach out and gather it up for herself. Desi knew that was the wrong course of action. She knew she shouldn't crave the power. It was her base self to want to dive into the power and drown in it, but not the safest of actions.

She felt a scorching heat near her, and a loud boom rattled through her ears and her body. She almost stumbled. A building down the street had exploded. Desi took a few steps towards it as she heard screams of anguish and cries for help. The acrid scents of smoke and gunpowder burned in her nostrils. What was happening?

Then she remembered. She dropped to her knees with head in her hands, and the memories swarmed her mind with excruciating swiftness.

They were at war; Bonum and the other creatures from the Infested against humanity. The West was falling to the Infested. The Bonum had all broken the law simultaneously and declared war by embracing all the magic the Infested had to offer. They drank it like water and they were being led...

"By us," Desi said, and it was as if the world silenced around her.

"Desdemona!" Her name was shouted from behind her.

She turned and saw her siblings—all of them, even Rowena, whose hand was wrapped tightly in Lavellen's—jogging over to her, Samael right behind them.

Wait, weren't Rowena, Lavellen, and Samael dead? That couldn't be right. Here they were, safe and sound.

Her memories fought in her mind.

No, they lived, and Rowena had been the first of her sister to join Desi because... Yes, Desi had helped start this, had recruited her siblings to fight. Now before them was the final battle.

Her siblings wore all black. They looked greyer than usual, their violet freckles almost glowing against their skin. Desi looked down at herself and saw she was dressed the same way. Aside from Ambrose, their hair was severely pulled back into a bun.

"What are you doing?" Rowena yelled. "The rest of the human army is coming!"

Desi stood and rushed to meet them, grateful to be with them, but it felt like two lives warred her in mind. A grin spread over her face, a face that didn't quite feel right.

"This is it, the moment we've been waiting for," Desi told them.

"Are you sure about this?" Foni asked, gliding out from behind the rest. She looked like she had back in the dungeon, behind the iron bars. Frightening and beautiful. Her hair flowed out behind her like ethereal waves and her eyes glowed.

"Of course she is, and if she isn't, too bad. This has been months in the making." Ambrose grinned, but then the grin faded, and he shook his head, muttering, "Has it been months? That can't be right…"

"Yes, months!" Samael cheered.

Lavellen and Samael were in the brightly colored clothing they always wore, Lavellen's face covered by a veil. Their radiance stood out against the gloom, rivaling even the nearby fires.

"They come," Lavellen said, and she pointed.

The people fighting around them all stopped at once and turned to face the soldiers bearing down on them. The sound of the army marching in on foot and horseback was deafening. The rest of their forces were the last effort to force the Infested back and reclaim… everything.

Wait, how do I know that? Desi wondered to herself.

"Desi? Something doesn't feel right," Helen said quietly, standing next to her sister.

"It's fine. We have something important to do now," Desi heard the words come from her mouth but didn't know why she said them.

"Foolish humans, it's time!" Rowena yelled.

Desi noticed that the responding roar wasn't just coming from ahead of them but also from behind. From the creatures whose help they had enlisted and the… the humans they'd enslaved. Desi had to fight off a wave of nausea. There was no time for regrets. This had to be done.

She could see the soldiers and militia better now, heavily armed with anything they could get their hands on; guns with real bullets, magic, knives, and bows. They were desperate.

Right where we want them, Desi thought with glee.

Stepping out in front, she let the rest fall in the line behind her as she spread out her fingers and flung her arms wide open. Her head fell back and her scream thundered across the battlefield. She was like a death goddess of old.

The people who had stopped fighting mimicked the noise and were the first wave as they ran forward to meet the oncoming force. They were a sacrifice, their unarmed bodies laid into by weaponry. Within minutes, the few hundred people would be sliced open, beaten, bruised, and dead.

It worked as a distraction. The soldiers hadn't expected to have to kill unarmed civilians and their hesitation allowed Marian a moment to step up beside Desi, a gleam in her eyes.

"I wish the soldiers would get the consequence for the next wish," Marian said.

"Marian, what are you doing?" Desi asked.

Marian never made wishes... Or did she make them all the time now?

"I wish they would drop their weapons." Marian finished and turned to glare at Desi. She hissed, "What? Desi, focus."

The soldiers all jerked to a stop and dropped their weapons. Some hit the ground, vomiting, while others started to convulse.

"Charge!" Ambrose bellowed from behind her.

Desi stood still while hundreds of magically armed humans and creatures swarmed around them like they were an island in the middle of the river.

"Wait, no, stop!" Ambrose yelled again, but it was too late.

The cacophony of footsteps, gunfire, and clashing weaponry shook the very earth as the swarm descended on the unarmed humans.

"Desi... I... I'm not sure what..." Ambrose trailed off, but then a grin lit his face. "Isn't battle glorious?"

Desi noticed many of the people fighting on their side held food in one hand, faces smeared with jam and chocolate, and a weapon in the other. Each weapon was saturated with tendrils of Rowena's magic.

"This isn't right," Foni said even as, from the dark of her shadows, something began to stir, something she was drawing in.

"This feels wrong," Helen said, but as she spoke, she began to glow a sickly green color.

They all moved into the fray. It was time for them to join in combat.

It was as if Desi was moving in slow motion. Her body and mind were warring. This wasn't real. It couldn't be. At the same time, she remembered how they got here. Bonum and creatures were sick of the humans everywhere. Humans started to move out into the Infested, more homesteads showed up, and more caravans made the crossing. The plains had become a congested road. The East sent in men to build a railroad. Humans weren't respectful. They killed the innocent and fed the malicious, causing imbalance.

Helen seemed to slide between people, leaving her sickly green magic behind as she touched them. The soldiers from the opposing army fell as their skin burst with oozing sores and boils.

Rowena wielded a large sword that burned with flame; Lavellen danced through the fighting horde. Men and women alike paused to watch her before falling on themselves in lustful rage.

Desi laughed while her magic infested people, turning them against loved ones and each other. It was an addicting sensation, but deeper inside, she was screaming.

"No, wait!" Foni cried, even as her shadows swarmed a woman and ate her alive.

"Helen! Foni! Ambrose! Marian! Rowena!" Desi yelled, struggling to even speak those words.

No, this wasn't right. This wasn't *real*. She was missing something.

Foni and Helen rushed to her side. Her other siblings didn't even look back as they delved into the gore and brutality. Ambrose hesitated for a second, but then Samael grabbed his hand and together, they passed out more food, tainted with magic, to their followers.

"Rowena, please!" Desi begged.

Rowena was like a war goddess, slashing and tearing through everyone within reach. Lavellen, a faithful lover, wove around her like an alluring macabre ballerina.

Whipping around, Desi searched the fray for the others. "Ambrose, Marian, listen to me!" she screamed.

Marian paused, but her face hardened when she saw Samael with Ambrose.

Marian approached Samael on swift feet and whispered in his ear. Desi saw her lips move and knew what she was doing. Samael nodded and kissed her, hard and sloppy. Marian led him away towards Rowena and Lavellen, who stood proudly on the battlefield, covered in blood.

Ambrose watched them go, sadness stretching his mouth. Helen ran over to him, her magic still seeping out and sickening people as she passed. None of them had control of their magic.

Helen pulled Ambrose back to their group. Soon Desi lost sight of the others as they massacred their way through the humans.

"This isn't real," Desi yelled over the sounds of battle.

"Why won't the others listen to us?" Helen asked.

"I think… this is a test."

"A test?" Ambrose scoffed. "Sick, twisted test."

"We have to stop this," Foni said.

Desi agreed, even though every inch of her burned to join the fight. She knew what the end would bring—every human dead or enslaved by her kind. She could feel her darkness trying to blossom and bloom from her chest until she unleashed terror on those who would harm her family. Desi clenched her teeth, shoving against it.

Desi heard a wail and plunged through the crowd without hesitation. No one paid her any mind, not when her magic turned them on each other. She stumbled to a stop. The sight before her was heartbreaking. Lavellen lay on the ground, blood pooling out of her, a large sword through her middle. Rowena kneeled in her love's blood, the red soaking the hem of her skirts as she sobbed. She gathered Lavellen's limp body in her arms and Desi felt a rush of magic pulse out from her sister.

"Rowena, don't—!"

Rowena's eyes blackened and focused on the line of armed humans coming quickly towards them.

"You'll burn out!" Foni yelled, stumbling to a halt beside Desi. "If you use up all your magic at once, it'll kill you too!"

Desi and Foni exchanged a desperate glance. Rowena looked back at them once and shrugged. She stood and lashed out at the advancing platoon.

Desi watched as they all stumbled and, one by one, turned their weapons on each other. Rowena laughed and then slumped over. Helen rushed their sister, frantically trying to save her, but she looked back at Desi and Foni with a horrified expression within seconds. She must have been too late.

"I don't know how to stop this!" Helen's voice barely cut through the noise of war around them.

"Desi, I want it," Ambrose whispered. He rubbed his arms and scoured the scene with hungry eyes. "It's like fire under my skin."

"You have to fight the feeling." She grabbed his hands.

Together, the four of them congregated in a circle. Only the wrath of Desi's magic kept attackers at bay as Foni's deflected incoming bullets.

"Can we fix this?" Foni asked.

"Can we fix *that?*" Ambrose asked, pointing at something several yards ahead.

Without Desi and Foni fighting at the front anymore, their side was starting to take harder hits. Death was all around them, everyone and everything was dying—including Marian and Samael.

The humans must have realized what she was doing; they had captured her and gagged her. She was struggling as they tied her up. Samael knelt at the feet of several men.

"Ambrose, don't look." Desi grabbed her brother and twisted him around right as Samael's head snapped back. She couldn't pick out the individual gunshot from the rest, but she swore she felt it.

Ambrose didn't make a sound, but tears glinted in his eyes. His face contorted with grief and fury.

"By the Spirits, Desi, we have to stop them!" Helen exclaimed. "They are going to hang her like she's a wicked witch in a fairy tale."

"To them, she is," Foni said.

Desi looked around at the carnage. She had to stop this. If she didn't, they would either all die or would be the reason everyone else did.

Then it hit her.

"No," Desi said quickly. "It's not real. Tell yourself it isn't real."

"What?" Helen asked.

"It isn't real. Close your eyes and tell yourself it isn't real. It's a test."

As the last word left her mouth, all sound had stopped.

Desi blinked and found herself sitting in pitch blackness. The shadow creature stared back.

"You passed," it said.

Desi took a deep breath as she remembered her real life, pushing back the fake memories until they were no more than dreams, nightmares. Some were harder to shake than others—Rowena's nonchalant shrug before her collapse, Marian bound and gagged, the sword protruding from Lavellen's limp body, Samael's head snapping backward, all those corpses staring lifelessly into a sky wrought with smoke and magic—but she dug her fingernails into her palms.

It had all been a test. None of it was real.

"What now?" she asked, her voice rasping as though hoarse from overuse.

"You know what. I didn't raise any stupid children."

"Humans can't ever live here again, can they?" Desi asked. "That's what this is all about, isn't it?"

"Humans can never live in the Infested. They can come and go as they've always done, but they cannot treat the Infested like they do the East and West. What you just witnessed is the future if they try."

"Why did you do all of this?"

"To protect our home. For years, your father has been fighting against plans to try and put in telephone lines and a railway, but he's failing and the Infested is changing again—and not in a good way. Humans poisoned it. They can only make it worse. But we are Bonum and it's my job to protect the Infested and the creatures who inhabit it, and it is yours as well."

The creature loomed closer to Desi and she resisted the urge to scuttle away from those red eyes and too-bright teeth. She wasn't as confident as before; this thing could be her mother.

"Of course, I'm your mother. I am what I always, *always* should have been but was stuffed into a fragile mortal form: I am a Bonum who has fully embraced the Infested and soon, there will be many like me." The creature's silhouette flickered and when it solidified, it resembled her mother again. "Well, not exactly like me."

"What about the rest of my siblings? If it wasn't real, where are they?"

"Rowena and Marian failed. Their deaths were real enough. Everything that happened to you was a version of reality."

Desi choked back a sob. She thought of her sisters—their strength and personality, their spirits and warmth—snuffed out, senselessly.

"Why did you do this?" she asked, anger filling her stomach. How could their own *mother* do this?

"Your Aunt Serenity had the gift of sight. She saw that I would have five children destined to protect the Infested and restore balance and peace to the land. I thought it would be all five of you; I was mistaken."

"Do you hate humans this much?"

"I don't hate humans. I married one, and I love him, in this form and any other. I want them safe, and they won't be if they try and reclaim the Infested."

"Did you even love us? Or were my siblings and I just a means to an end?"

"I love each of you very much. You will understand soon and you would do what I have. Sacrifices sometimes have to be made, for the greater good." Avery looked confident, but there was sadness in her eyes.

"You didn't have to do it like this…." Desi felt like tearing out her hair and crying. Two of her sisters were dead!

"Of course I did." There was no remorse in the voice. Maybe her mother had always been like this, deep on the inside.

"No! And I would never do what you did. It was the wrong thing for the right reason. There has to be a better way than this. Marian, Rowena, Lavellen and Samael are dead! You can't fix that and this isn't a good enough reason!"

Desi lifted an arm. She'd never thought about attacking her mother before, but she'd do it. Her father couldn't come home to this monster.

"I know it's tempting but don't give in. You are so much more now, Desdemona. You're embracing your full power, everything you've ever wanted, all the Infested has to offer. You are its protector now. I will go home with Ambrose and Helen. I will not harm your father. You and Foni will go out into the wild and be the powerful Bonum you were always meant to be."

Desi clenched her fists but lowered her arm. What good would it do to strike Avery down now?

"I will be watching you," Desi told her mother.

"I know. I'm counting on it. And for what it's worth, I am sorry, Desi. This wasn't... it wasn't how this was supposed to end."

"How *was* it supposed to end?" Desi asked.

"With you all alive. I didn't count on... The ley lines near the house, they're corrupted. It affected things."

Desi rolled her eyes and wrapped her arms around herself. She knew all about ley lines. "Ley lines or not, you are going to remember you got your children killed. I hope you can live with that."

Her mother smiled and, with a wave of power, the large shadow creature loomed over her again, red eyes shining down on her.

"Tell Ambrose and Helen I love them," Desi said.

"Goodbye, Desi," the creature whispered.

It reached out a black tendril and stroked her face.

That was the last time Desi saw the shadow monster that was her mother. She woke next to Foni on a hill far outside Ash Hollow. She could see her home in the distance, the protection bubble glowing over the land.

"Desi?" Foni asked.

They stood together on the hill for a long time, simply watching and processing Avery's test. They weren't sure how much time had passed. They seemed frozen in place, just watching their home, somewhere they could never return.

It didn't bother them that the concept of time seemed gone. The wild freedom that filled Desi was unlike anything she'd ever experienced. She didn't need to sleep nor eat. Timelessness brought with it a distinct sort of immortality.

Desi saw herself reflected in Foni's eyes now. They looked so similar, like some beautiful specter attached to the land and its magic. They were two pale and glowing things who harnessed living shadows. Still too human to embrace everything the Infested had to offer, but too wrapped in magic to live among humans anymore. Desi could feel how powerful and dangerous she was.

They watched as several lone wagons came to Ash Hollow. Each one was greeted by Helen. Desi was awash with happiness at seeing her sister. People were brought in and cared for, then left a day or two later.

Finally, Desi's father came home. Desi's heart ached to embrace him, to speak with him again. She knew she couldn't, but she could do something just as meaningful.

As his wagon came into view, the Nebula swept in over their hill, cold and viscous. It didn't see Foni and Desi at first, not until it was too late. They devoured the Nebula with ease. It made a good meal.

Desi didn't know why this thing hunted Lavellen and Samael or why it stuck around, but it would hurt no one else. The storm monster was no match for them now. They saved her father. Desi moved towards him, longing to hear his voice and feel his arms around her.

"We can't," Foni said, tightening her hand around Desi's.

They never let go of each other, not now. They danced together, forever connected, magically attached—needing, consoling, and protecting each other.

Instead, Desi watched her father go home, never knowing his daughter had saved him. Helen came to the gate to let him inside. Desi imagined his shock at the change in routine. That had once been Desi's job.

Helen lifted her eyes to the hill. Seeing them, she raised a hand in a sad wave. Desi waved back, smiling, and watched as her sister shut the gate and went back to the house.

"It's time to go now, isn't it?" Foni asked.

"Yes."

Desi didn't know what exactly they were going to do, and she didn't know how her father would respond to what he found inside, but they could no longer watch from the hill. She'd done what she needed to there and it was time to explore the rest of her new world.

Chapter 25

June 1900
Ash Hollow
The Caravan

I slow down after the danger is over. Chloe and I stay a few days at the next wagon rest. We need time to mourn Marcus. After we watch what is left of the Caravan pass our temporary home, Chloe and I block the trail as best we can. I leave a message carved into a rock, warning others off the path. No one will come into the Infested after what transpired, at least not for a long while. This will stop the legislators from their plan of railroads, telephones, and more homesteaders in the Infested.

Chloe leaves before me. She can travel faster with just her horse and send me a missive once she makes the boundary of the West. She has much news to bring back to civilization.

Once I return to the trail, I rush home. My knees and back hurt, and I am hungry and exhausted. I don't spare any time to take care of myself like I should and I barely care for my animals.

I feel desperate.

I'm close to home when the storm attacks. The Nebula screams over my wagon. My beasts are too fatigued to outrun it.

The sky above me turns a violent purple and the wind kicks up. There is nowhere for me to go, nowhere I can run or hide. Will I die this close to home?

I jump from my seat and hide in the back. Lightning strikes inches from the wagon. The pungently sweet aroma of electricity and burning grass reaches me. I wait for the final blow to come. Nebulas leave no evidence of their attack. I will be dead, and my family won't know what happened. They may find a bone or a rusted wagon wheel years from now.

I cower under the fabric I purchased for Avery, squeezing myself between the trunks. Terror beats in my chest. Thunder booms overhead. I think I hear laughter in the wind, but that's impossible. Nebulas do not laugh. They shriek and wail with the elements.

I cover my ears with my hands and close my eyes tightly while awaiting my fate. I have been afraid before, but this feels like doom and despair more than fear. This isn't something I can fight. Even my amulet is useless, its protection destroyed back at Fort Kearney. There's nowhere to hide and no one around to help. Maybe if I hadn't pushed the oxen so hard, we could have outrun it. Now, all I can do is wait.

And wait I do.

Suddenly, all is quiet. The wind dies and silence fills the wagon. Taking a deep breath, I gather my courage, crawl from my hiding place, and peek outside. Is it playing with me? Will it strike once I pop my head out? But no, as I look around, miraculously, the Nebula is gone. Sunlight shines down on me and my oxen calmly graze on the thick green grass as though they were never spooked.

Clambering back into my seat, I search the skies. Where is it? What happened? Is it hiding? I see a few white wisps of cloud, but nothing that sets off alarm bells. If I start to travel again, will it pounce?

I don't dwell on my excellent fortune for long. I need to get home. There is no certainty that the Nebula is gone for good. I must take my chances. I take up the reins.

Feelings of relief roll through me as I see the fence line of home and not a storm cloud in sight. I can smell our animals even from here and the familiarity beckons me closer. The house, the barn, the guest house, our fields and pastures—I wouldn't call it safe, but it is home. The colors are muted and warm, wavering as the sun sets.

I can't wait for a hot bath, good food, and the company of my children and wife. I long for the routine of our days and a soft bed at night. I hope everything is alright and I worry things will not be as I left them.

Desi's message was not pleasant. I haven't been able to shake my anxiety since I received it. Please, Spirits, let my family be safe.

I pull up in front of the gates, curious about the magic bubble around the house. Avery must feel there is some danger if she and Desi cast such incredible magic. Perhaps the Nebula attacked the farm. My chest tightens at the thought.

I ring the bell; even I cannot get inside Ash Hollow without assistance. It is the only way to keep the land and the family safe.

Surprise fills me when Helen, not Desi, comes to let me through the gate. She smiles when she sees me and I notice she looks far too thin… again. I must speak to Ambrose.

As she opens the gates, I see tears in her eyes, but first I lead my wagon and animals inside.

"Where is Rowena?" I ask as Helen closes the gate behind me. "She should come for the wagon."

Helen bites her lip. I climb down and she throws herself into my arms. I stroke her head and feel her tears soak my shirt.

"What's wrong? Where is Rowena? Is Desi alright?" I ask. It's not like Helen to cry. Something is wrong.

"You should ask Mom. I'll take them from here."

Helen lifts her head and backs away from me. She grabs the reins, but she smiles at me now. I'm unsure if it's because she is happy or relieved. Maybe both?

"It's good you're home, Papa." She leads the animals and wagon away.

"Helen!" I call after her. "Are you okay? Something about you seems different."

She seems sad but also so much more vibrant than I remember. Her skin shines and her hair looks glossy in the sunlight.

"I'm alright, Papa. Talk to Mom. I have to get these guys taken care of." She pats one of the oxen.

Something awful has happened, I am sure of it. Something didn't go as planned. Trepidation creeps up my spine.

I slowly walk the path to the house and climb the stairs. My hands shake as I open the front door. The warmth and sweet smell of the parlor greet me, easing some of the tension in my body. There isn't any sound and no one is around. It is too quiet for this to really be home. My children, even as adults, make more noise than most.

"Hello!" I call out.

I hear a door slam and then footsteps.

"Harrison!" Avery rushes down the stairs. She embraces me, kissing me soundly before I register her eyes glowing red.

Shocked, I hold her at arm's length. "What's happened?" I haven't seen this side of her for some time.

"Things didn't... go as planned. I tried to fix it, but the kids weren't as we thought. The ley lines near the house are far more corrupt than they should be. "

"The ley lines? Chloe and I saw corrupt ley lines. They looked sick."

"Things got out of hand and I am so sorry, but..."

"Where are the rest of our children?" I know the tone of my voice is harsh; Avery takes a step back, her eyes wide.

"Helen and Ambrose are here. Foni and Desi are out in the Infested, and they've been watching the house."

Her words sink in and the events from earlier start to make sense.

I close my eyes. *That's* what stopped the Nebula from killing me. I feel grief and gratitude, but my eyes tear up. If Desi and Foni are in the Infested, I won't see them again. A knot tightens in my chest.

Realizing she hasn't mentioned two of our daughters, I ask, "Rowena? Marian?"

"They didn't make it," Avery says, tears pooling in her eyes.

Grief swamps me and I fall to my knees. It feels like the tight knot *explodes*—Marcus, Rowena, Marian—and my stomach turns.

"No, they can't be dead… You told me they wouldn't be harmed."

"I know and I'm so sorry, Harrison. I promise nothing like this will ever happen again." She says the words, kneels next to me, and wraps her arms around me, but something about her expression makes me hesitate to embrace her.

I try to focus on the positive. Helen and Ambrose are here and alive. Desi is alive and was always meant to go out into the Infested; she was never meant to stay at Ash Hollow, never meant for the life of a homesteader. But this is all too much. It's too soon.

"Do you forgive me?" Avery whispers.

"There was a Nebula outside, near the house."

I don't know if she will like my answer right now. This is too much, too new. I need time to process what she's told me. I am still reeling over the loss of Marcus and now my children too. I can't think straight.

"Yes. We had guests who brought the damned thing with them."

"Guests?" I ask.

"Succubi, here for their mom. I believe they're part of the reason we lost Rowena and Marian."

I mull over this information. We will need to be more careful of who we let in through the wards in the future. I stand up slowly, knees creaking, and wrap an arm around my wife as she supports me.

"Come, sit down. Tell me everything." I want every detail.

I will grieve my children later. Some things are lost to prevent greater tragedy and catastrophic events, I know that, but I am not sure that is what happened here. Something doesn't feel right and I will not be content until I get the full story. Before I can do anything, I must have all the facts to quiet my racing and confused mind. Tears sting my eyes and the pain in my chest makes it hard to breathe.

I hear a noise and see Ambrose running down the hallway. "Father!"

I move away from Avery to embrace my son. He looks tired. There are deep purple bags under his eyes.

"Are you alright?" I wonder out loud.

He takes a deep breath in, shuddering. "No, but I will be. Has... Mother told you everything?"

"She was about to."

He's almost my height now and stares at me like he never has before. His eyes dart over my shoulder to his mother and he pales. I don't turn to look at Avery—I don't know if I can—but something about her frightens my son.

"I'll let her tell the story, then. I don't... I don't have the strength."

"If you need to talk to me, I'm here," I tell him.

He gives me a small smile and a short laugh slips from his mouth. "I'm going to finish dinner."

"What was that about?" I question my wife, turning back to her.

Avery sits down on the settee. "He had his first heartbreak and his sisters died. Give him time." She pats the seat next to her. "How did things go for the Caravan?"

She is delaying telling me what went on while I was away. I will let her do things her way for a time. There are things I need to tell her.

I sink onto the settee beside her. "Marcus is dead." Saying it makes it too real.

How does one man handle so much death? Will my dreams ever be pleasant again? I think the answer is no.

Avery covers her mouth with a broken noise. "No... That can't be... Harrison, I am so sorry."

She holds my hands tightly. I look at her strangely, at the tears budding in her eyes again. Avery doesn't cry. This is unlike her. She is a passionate woman, but not an affectionate one.

"I can't believe it," I whisper, letting the despair wash over me.

"What else?" she asks.

"Things are worse than we feared. They want settlements, trains, and telephone lines."

Avery's face pales. "They think the Infested is something they can contain and control. They think the Bonum are their tools."

"Avery, the ley lines in all of the Infested are corrupted. I saw... horrors. I know we don't want other humans out here, but this... this is big."

"Yes, I'm not surprised." Avery says, "but my sisters and I believe that's a natural occurrence. Humans destroyed this land, and the more they travel within the boundaries of the Infested, the sicker it becomes. If we want a chance for it to stabilize so that our children and grandchildren can grow up wild and free, things will have to get worse before they get better." Her explanation makes sense, but it's still terrifying.

"I think it will be a long time before they send another Caravan."

"Isn't that what we wanted?" Avery asks.

"We wanted them to know the Infested is something to be respected and feared, but this was a nightmare." I think of poor Marcus—and Chloe, who I hope made it home safely. I will need to visit Marcus's son within the next few months. The plans Marcus and I made fill my head as I realize I won't be taking Marian with me.

"The loss of Marcus will be felt for the rest of our lives. We will never be the same without Rowena and Marian." Avery tells me, but something in her eyes, a glint in the back, makes me uneasy.

"Are Desi and Foni safe out there with everything stirring in the dark?" I ask. I worry for my daughter. I have been dropped into my home, a place that has been overturned and feels foreign.

"They are the things humans should fear now, my love. Don't worry. I *do* have something to tell you that may bring a little joy."

I don't think there is anything that could bring me happiness right now. All I see is death and destruction.

"I could use some joy…." I say, hesitant.

"I'm pregnant. We can start again."

The end

ABOUT THE AUTHOR

Renee Lake is a bisexul, Puerto Rican mother of four from Utah. She loves bats and is passionate about women's reproductive rights. She is the author of *Forgotten Hills, Blood Born*, and *The Infested*

Other books by Renee Lake